HE WAS WANTED BY
THE TIME POLICE . . .

"Stop him! Someone stop him!"

Shouts followed him.

Jackson spun and twisted, and suddenly charged through a glass door and found himself stumbling toward the street. Like a man pursued by demons he churned his legs until he found his balance, turned up the sidewalk, and ran away from the old UN building.

His lungs burned. His side ached. He didn't know where he was going except away—away from the nightmare behind him.

Jackson ran faster. People dodged out of his way.

Behind him came the relentless steps of the woman with two guns.

For Gigi, with love.

Special thanks to Richard Curtis, Michael Fine, Lou Wolfe, Judith Stern, Victoria Lustbader, Ragnhild Hagen, and Mary Higgins.

TIME POLICE
Volume 1: Vanished
ISBN: 1-55802-006-3
First Printing/November 1988

This book is published by Lynx Books, a division of Lynx Communications, Inc., 41 Madison Avenue, New York, New York 10010. The name "Lynx" together with the logotype consisting of a stylized head of a lynx is a trademark of Lynx Communications, Inc. The name Lynx Omeiga w/the logotype consisting of a stylized O is a trademark of Lynx Communications Inc.

Printed in the United States of America

0 9 8 7 6 5 4 3 2 1

Cover painting by Paul and Steve Youll
Cover design by Dean Motter
Edited by David M. Harris

Volume 1
Vanished

By
Warren Norwood

A Byron Preiss Book

LYNX OMEIGA BOOKS

New York

Warren Norwood spent his childhood summers reading *Tarzan* and *Tom Swift* books one right after another, so it's little wonder he grew up to write science fiction and fantasy adventures. His first novel, *The Windover Tapes: An Image of Voices* was published in 1982, and was followed by three more books in that series. He has since published *The Seren Cenacles,* on which he collaborated with Ralph Mylius, *The Double Spiral War* series, *Shudderchild,* and *True Jaguar.*

Norwood and Gigi—his wife, fellow writer, and collaborator—live outside of Weatherford, Texas. In addition to his writing, Warren teaches at Tarrant County Junior College, and is learning to play a growing collection of musical instruments, including a mountain dulcimer.

Chapter One

The bullet smashed through the ambassador's skull. His head snapped back and jerked his body out of the chair.

In the moment of shock that followed, Jackson wished he were back at Wu Wing's eating cashew cat. Then he screamed and dove to the floor.

A roar of machinegun fire ravaged the speaker's platform, clouding the air with splinters of wood and metal and plastic. Shouts of anger and hysteria filled the small gaps between bursts of destruction.

Jackson's mind refused to work. His body curled itself into a tight ball. His eyes pressed themselves closed. His ears cried for relief. One stupid question kept hammering his brain: How are you going to get back to Wu Wing's Cashew Chicken, Cat, and Dog Emporium in Springfield? Even if the question had stopped repeating itself, Jackson wouldn't have had an answer. He was twelve hundred miles and sixty-six years away from home, and he felt for sure that he was going to die in a past he'd never lived.

Slowly the firing faded away. The ringing in Jackson's

ears did not. With great caution he climbed to his knees and looked around. The ambassador's bloody corpse lay sprawled close to several others.

"*Cabrones!*" someone cursed.

"Stop them!"

"There is but one God and Mohammed is his Prophet. God is great. There is but one—"

"Get back!"

"Where's Security?"

People were running everywhere—some scrambling to get out of the old UN hall—some fighting to get in. Jackson blinked, unable to comprehend what had happened.

"Move, you fool!"

"My god! My god!"

Moans and whimpers rose from two tensets of places around the floor. Suddenly Jackson looked around for his Temporal Projects escort—the Time Police who were supposed to protect him.

They were gone. Or dead. He didn't know which. He did know that he had to get out of there.

"Hail Mary, mother of grace, blessed is thy name among—"

"Someone stop the bastards!"

An old man in black with a long gray beard prayed on his knees in front of Jackson. "The Lord is my light and my salvation. Who shall I fear? The Lord is the stronghold of my life. Of whom shall I be terrified? In my very guts—"

Jackson shoved himself to his feet and started picking his way through the rubble toward the side entrance.

A man in mirrorshades by the door pointed at him—

Captain Slye, one of the Time Policemen. "There's one of them!"

"Freeze, perp!" a voice shouted.

In the split second it took Jackson to realize that they were talking about him—that Captain Slye had accused him—five or six people in blue uniforms started running down the aisles. Jackson had been betrayed and he didn't know why. They thought he was one of the assassins.

Instinct in some primitive center of his brain took over. He spun around and ran across the front of the dais.

"Get him!"

A shot sounded. Then another.

Jackson ran for his life. A dark man in Arab dress tried to block the doorway. Jackson shoved him aside.

Wood splintered away from the top of the door frame as he heard another shot.

A woman grabbed his arm. He twisted away and plowed through two more people. When he cleared the doorway he knocked down several more people in a milling crowd.

Shouts followed him. People cursed. A woman screamed. Another wailed.

Jackson fought his way through grabbing hands and startled bodies—clawing, kicking, shoving, fighting desperately to get away. Escape was his only thought, panic, his only emotion. But it was like swimming against a tide of bodies—a tide that flowed against him from every direction.

He fought harder. A man went down under his fist. A blue uniform doubled over from his kick. Hands grabbed at him. A black suit caught a sharp elbow and fell away.

"Stop him! Someone stop him!"

A green dress blocked his path. He lowered his shoulder and bulled past it. A red shirt caught the richochet of his body and tumbled backward.

Jackson spun and twisted, and suddenly charged through a glass door and found himself stumbling toward the street. Like a man pursued by demons he churned his legs until he found his balance, turned up the sidewalk, and ran away from the old UN building.

His lungs burned. His side ached. He didn't know where he was going except away—away from the nightmare behind him. Through a sea of startled pedestrians he ran, through crowds and down empty patches of sidewalk, his mind racing as furiously as his body.

How had it happened? Why had Captain Slye accused him? He was an interpreter, for god's sake.

A quick glance behind revealed the powder-blue uniform of the Federal District Policeman in pursuit. Jackson ran harder. Then he saw an escalator to the skyrail that had brought them downtown. Without thinking he sprinted up the moving stairs, jumped over the turnstile, and across the platform to a skyrail car closing its doors. He barely managed to force himself into the car before it started moving.

Twenty faces looked at him then turned away. New Yorkers were no different in 2183 than they would become in 2249. They didn't want to know anything about him. Fierce pain in his side bent Jackson over, and he clutched a chrome pole for support as he struggled to breathe. The pain twisted like a knife through his muscles. A hoarse groan accompanied every breath. Sweat rolled down his aching legs. His face burned. The rocking of the skyrail made his stomach writhe.

Yet for the moment Jackson was safe. At least he thought he was safe. He hoped he was safe. There was no way to guarantee it. There was no way to guarantee anything.

He had come to New York in 2183 because the Temporal Projects Center had asked him to interpret the Farsi speech of the Persian ambassador at the ceremonies making Bahai the official religion of the Second Republic. He had come because Suzanne Brelmer had recruited him and because her father had made it all sound so exciting and important. He had come because the idea of time travel was too irresistible.

There on the skyrail so far from home and his own time, he wished he'd stayed in Springfield, Missouri, at the New Nineveh Library and minded his own business. But he hadn't. His old college friend Lester Wu had introduced him to Suzanne Brelmer at a party in Kansas City, and she had recruited him for Temporal Projects, and after six weeks of intensive training and briefings, he had swallowed hard, climbed into the time machine for the trip back to 2183, and . . .

Oddly familiar music penetrated his consciousness. He straightened up and looked at a speaker in the ceiling of the skyrail car and recognized the melody being rendered in a dissonant electronic sound. Ponchielli's "Dance of the Hours." The same funny song they had sung around the campfire on youth retreats when he was a boy— "Hello, Mudda, Hello, Fadda." The memory of those wonderful retreats brought a faint smile to his lips.

By the opposite door of the glass and steel skyrail car there was an empty seat next to a man reading a lap screen. Jackson stepped quickly from his pole and sat down beside the man who promptly turned slightly away and ignored him. That was fine with Jackson. The car was slowing and suddenly he wanted to be ignored by everyone.

What if the FD police were waiting for him at the next stop? What would he do? If they caught him, what would he tell them? That he was a time traveler from 2249? Did they know about time travel? Would they believe him?

The skyrail slid to a humming stop. "West Seventy-Second Street Station, Central Park Wildlife Refuge," a rich female voice said from the ceiling speaker.

Jackson jumped to his feet, but forced himself to leave the car as casually as possible. A woman wearing a black uniform and tapping a stun stick against her leg raked her eyes over him for a long second before shifting her gaze. Jackson tried not to look at her as he followed the knots of people out of the station onto a glassed-in platform overlooking Central Park.

The park was grayer than he remembered it being when he visited it on his sixteenth-birthday trip with his parents. The thought of them made him turn away and walk toward the escalators. They had died in Kansas City's Great Plaza Fire a little more than a year before—a week after Jackson's twenty-fifth birthday—and he still couldn't quite believe they were dead.

Then it hit him. They weren't dead. Not now. Not in 2183. His parents hadn't even been born yet. His Gran'pa Jack was only a teenager living in the woods down in Douglas County in southern Missouri. Jackson lost his balance as he stepped onto the escalator, and grabbed both handrails for support.

His parents hadn't even been born yet. He swayed as the escalator clanked down toward the sidewalk. The instructors at Temporal Projects had talked about the unanswerable paradoxes involved with time travel, but until that moment on the escalator it had only been abstract information for Jackson. Now the full weight of the paradox had him leaning weak-kneed against a post in the Federal District of New York in 2183 feeling like he was going to pass out.

His parents weren't born yet. He could go visit his Gran'pa Jack. He could see—

"Hey, youse. Youse awright?"

Jackson opened his eyes to see an FD police officer in a powder-blue fatigue uniform staring at him. Her stun stick was in her hands. On her head she wore a plastic helmet with an antenna sticking out the top and a tiny microphone curving in front of her mouth. From her belt hung two stainless steel automatic pistols, and a variety of black pouches. A woman with two guns—a street cop. Her eyes squinted with suspicion.

A jolt of fear snapped Jackson upright. The policewoman tensed. "S-s-sure," he said, trying vainly to control the tremor in his voice. "I'm okay. Just a little dizzy, that's all." He pointed up the escalator. "D-d-don't like heights."

She shook her head very slowly, her eyes never leaving his, and Jackson couldn't tell if it was because she didn't believe him, or because she disapproved, or what. Her gold badge gleamed on her shirt pocket. Every instinct in his body told him to run, but he felt welded to the post that still supported him.

"Welllll, youse tourists shoun't ride the skies if they make youse sick. Youse been drinking?"

"No, ma'am." The tremor stayed in his voice.

Her eyes bored into his. "Youse sure?"

"Yes, ma'am."

She blinked. "Where youse from?"

"Springfield," he said without thinking, "Springfield, Missouri."

"Show me."

Again Jackson's spine stiffened. Did she want his ID? Would the one Temporal Projects had made for him pass inspection? A ripple of nausea ran through his gut.

She laughed. "It's the show-me state, right?"

"Yeah, I guess it is."

"Welllll, youse be careful, Show-me. And stay off the skies if they make youse sick. Don't want no sick tourists in my precinct." With a nod the policewoman turned away.

Jackson walked slowly, but as naturally as he could, up the sidewalk—north, he thought—wanting nothing more than to separate himself from the policewoman. He dared not look back to see if she was watching him, but somehow he knew she was. Dear god, just let her leave me—

"Hey, youse, Show-me. Come back here."

Jackson kept walking as though he hadn't heard her, as though his heart hadn't doubled its beats, as though fear wasn't boiling through his veins.

"Hey, Show-me," her voice called, louder this time. "Get your tail back here."

Jackson ran.

She shouted again.

Jackson ran faster. People dodged out of his way. Others he bumped aside. His stiff body cried with pain. His lungs burned.

Behind him came the relentless steps of the woman with two guns.

Chapter Two

Jackson's world blurred to the pain of his body pounding the concrete. People became colored lumps to be knocked aside or bounced off. Never in his life could he have imagined being so careless of people. But never in his life could he have imagined what had happened already. It was a nightmare that defied understanding.

The pain in his legs tore staccato whines from his throat with every jarring step. Yet he dared not stop, dared not slow down. A quick look over his shoulder showed the police·voman still running after him—dropping behind, maybe, but hanging in there. Jackson didn't think he could run much farther. He was dying on his feet.

Over his head a skycar hummed past him. Ahead he saw the escalator to another station. Dare he try? What if he missed the train? Then what?

Without really deciding, he ran up the escalator as fast as his protesting legs would let him, jumped the turn-stile, and stumbled across the platform and into the third of three linked skycars. The crowd in the car barely made room for him.

Gasping for breath, he grabbed a strap and stared

back across the platform while he waited for the car to move or the policewoman to appear. If she did, he knew he would surrender to her, because he didn't have the strength for anything else.

The car didn't move. Its doors stayed open.

Wave after wave of fear and nausea swept through Jackson. *Go! Go! Go!* his mind screamed.

Still nothing happened. The skycar sat perfectly still. Twelve-tone oriental music tinkled from the overhead speaker. The platform remained empty of blue uniforms.

Then Jackson saw a flash of blue. The policewoman was moving cautiously through the turnstile, a pistol in her hands, her eyes scanning the platform. She was talking into the little microphone that curved in front of her mouth from her headset.

He let his knees drop and tried to hide behind the other passengers while still keeping an eye on her. Dear Buddha, let me go, he prayed.

The policewoman walked slowly toward the skycars.

Jackson let go of the strap and sank lower. A woman in a dirty gray raincoat backed against his face, but he stayed as still as he could. He felt like a child behind a blanket. If he couldn't see the policewoman, maybe she couldn't see him.

Suddenly the doors hissed shut and the skycar lurched forward. Jackson dropped to one knee. The woman in the gray raincoat started, then turned around and shoved him with the large bag in her hands. With a grunt of disgust she squeezed herself between two other passengers and left Jackson where he was. No one else seemed to notice him.

For the first time since those days when he had been the only child in a room full of adults, Jackson felt invisible and was glad for it. Every breath burned his lungs. Every movement of his body brought him pain. Every thought reminded him how deeply he was lost, misplaced, and in trouble.

What was he going to do? Get back to the time machine? Could he do that? And if so, what good would it do? He had no idea of how it worked—or how to make it work.

But the time machine was his only link with home, his only way back. He couldn't stay in the Federal District of New York forty years before he was born. He just couldn't. It was insane. Somehow he had to get back to the time—

"Eighty-sixth Street," the dulcet female voice said from the overhead speaker as the skycar slowed, "Central Park Museum, crosstown rail service."

Where had he and the Time Police boarded the skyrail when they arrived? Jackson fought to remember. Columbia University Historical Site. One hundred and some-teenth Street station. The time machine was in the ancient subway station at 116th Street. He remembered that. He'd told himself to make note of it when they left the station without dreaming he would have to find it on his own.

The cars stopped and the doors opened. Jackson held his breath, but no uniformed police rushed onto the car to drag him off. Thirty blocks to go, he thought as the cars started moving again. How many stops? How many more chances for the police to find him? Too many, he decided.

When the skycar stopped at Ninety-sixth Street, Jackson got off. He walked casually out of the car, keeping pace with the rest of the crowd. A flash of blue caught his eye—an FD policeman. But the officer looked totally bored, staring right past the people leaving the cars. Still, Jackson couldn't let himself relax until his feet hit the pavement and he started walking north. He had twenty blocks to go on his aching feet and legs, but at least he seemed to have lost his police pursuit.

What he wanted more than anything was something to eat and drink, but no sooner had he thought that than he realized he didn't have a credit to his name—not a fedcredit, not a dollar, nothing. He'd never thought about needing money, and the Temporal Projects people had never mentioned it. Worse, they told him not to eat for twelve hours before making the time trip in order to avoid nausea when he arrived. It had been almost a full day since he'd had a meal.

As though aware there was nothing he could do about its hunger, his stomach growled and rumbled. Suddenly it occurred to him that if he had to stay in 2183 for any length of time he could easily starve to death. It wasn't like he carried much extra fat to live off, either. Since he and Chrys had become regular sex partners, she had burned more than a few extra pounds off him in the extended sexual sessions she always seemed to crave.

Would Chrys miss him if he never got back? What an odd thought. Chrys was a woman in perpetual heat, and if he didn't come back, it wouldn't take her long to find someone else. It wasn't like she loved him—or he, her. They were just good in bed together—even in an antiseptic bed like the one in the Sex Center where they had met.

Chrys Calvino, woman of a thousand talents—nine hundred of them between the sheets. Would he miss her? He didn't know. Jackson had hoped when they first found out how sexually compatible they were that their relationship might develop into something deeper and long-lasting. Chrys seemed to do everything she could to avoid the things that might bind them more permanently together. "No commitments," she said, "just sex."

Yeah, he'd miss the sex, and because of that, he would miss Chrys, but nothing like he missed his parents—or Martin even.

His stomach growled as he marched up the cracked sidewalk, but he tried to ignore it. Martin would have figured a way to get food by now, he thought. Older brothers are supposed to be able to do things like that. But Martin probably just would have let himself be arrested. Good citizen Martin Carter Dubchek would never have run. Wouldn't have taken a time trip, either. Too dangerous, he would have said. Too full of unknowns.

"You should always calculate your risks very carefully, Jackson, before you stick your foot in the water." Jackson couldn't begin to calculate how many times Martin had told him that. Just like their father.

Jackson shook his head and blinked. Only force of will kept him from stopping right where he was. Instead, he slowed his marching pace to a walk. Fifty meters in front of him two police officers were engrossed in a conversation, and one of them kept tilting his head in funny way, as though listening to a voice in his headset.

Now what? Jackson couldn't turn around and walk the other way. That would certainly attract their attention. And he couldn't cross the street in the middle of the block.

Better to keep walking like he was the most carefree soul in 2183. Best to walk like he was engrossed in thoughts of his own and hardly noticed them. Wrinkle the brows. Squint a little. Walk past. Don't rush. Easy. Same pace. Count steps. One, two three, four . . . steady rhythm . . . five, six, seven . . .

When he reached two hundred, he decided to see if they were following him and chanced a look over his shoulder. The two blue uniforms were walking back in the direction he had come from.

Thank god. A long, slow sigh of relief left him, followed by several gulps for air. Only then did he realize that he had been holding his breath.

The next street sign he saw said Cathedral Parkway, 110 St. Not far to go.

Jackson had to retrace his steps several times between 118th Street and 116th Street before he found the old subway entrance. After checking the street and reassuring himself that no one was watching him, he went quickly down the crumbling stairs.

Newspapers, wine cartons, garbage, the stench of urine, and a scurrying rat greeted him at the bottom, along with a locked metal door covered by graffiti scratched in and painted on its once green surface. "Lousatta does Danny." "733-2121-440 for a good time. AC-DC." "W loves G." The smell of ammonia and fresh feces was almost overwhelming, but Jackson forced himself to turn the sticky handle and push hard with the heel of his other hand. The door never budged—not a millimeter.

W might love G, but at that moment Jackson was sure that nobody loved him. How in Buddha's name was he going to get to the time machine? The door looked as solid as doors got, and the lock—well, what did he know about locks?

Unable to stand the stench any longer, he walked quickly back up the stairs and looked around for someplace to sit where he could keep an eye on the stairwell. Halfway up the block on the other side of the street, a sign said Deli'tess Food. His stomach responded to the sign with growls like a hungry lion.

Could he beg for food? How did one do that? He had no idea. The only beggars he knew anything about were in history books. The senate of the Second Republic had outlawed begging decades before Jackson was born, and enforced the law by making sure that everyone was properly fed and clothed—or institutionalized. Eliminating poverty was one of the things the Senate was proudest of. Jackson glanced down the subway stairs at the filth before he crossed the street and started walking toward the Deli'tess Food sign. Obviously poverty was still a problem in 2183.

He had almost reached the entrance to Deli'tess Food when a police vehicle came racing down the street, its turbine whining. Almost simultaneously a dark-skinned man came out of the Deli'tess Food store and waved to him.

"Hi, Jackson, you old time traveler, you. How you doin'?"

It was a double jolt. Jackson froze, then slowly turned to see the police van slide to a stop in front of the subway entrance.

"Better come in here with me, Jackson," the stranger said quietly. "I think they're looking for you."

Jackson swiveled his head back to the stranger and stared at him. How did this man know his name? Was he right? Were the police looking for him? Of course they were. "Who are you?" he asked.

"A friend, sent by a friend," the stranger said, reaching out and shaking Jackson's hand. "Now get in the deli with me before they come over here to question us.''

The stranger draped his arm over Jackson's shoulder and led him into Deli'tess Food. Jackson was too bewildered to resist. If the stranger was a friend, Jackson was certainly a man in need of one. If the stranger wasn't a friend, why was he trying to protect Jackson from the police?

The unfamiliar smells in Deli'tess Food made Jackson's mouth water. A glass case held tensets of meats and other foods that Jackson didn't recognize, but he would have eaten anything in the case.

''We'll eat in back,'' the stranger said to a woman behind the glass case.

She grunted, but said nothing.

The back was a little windowless room with four tables and a door with a bolt lock that shut it off from the front of the store. Jackson would have felt claustrophobic if he hadn't been so hungry.

''Listen to me carefully,'' the stranger said. ''I'm going back out front in case the gendarmes come looking. You bolt this door and stay in here until I tell you to come out, you understand?''

''I'm starving,'' Jackson answered.

''I'll get you something. But you stay in here until I tell you it's safe to come out. Now, bolt the door as soon as I leave.''

''As soon as you get me something to eat,'' Jackson said. His stomach growled so loudly he was sure the man must hear it.

The man frowned. ''All right. But lock yourself in, now.''

Jackson did as he was told and bolted the door as

soon as the stranger left. Only then did he appreciate the fact that the bolt was two or three centimeters in diameter and twenty-five or so long. The bolt hole was solid steel, built into the wall. He didn't know whether to feel safe or stupid for locking himself—

Muffled voices drew his ear to the door and he pressed against it trying to make out what was being said. He couldn't make out the words, but something in his gut told him the police were just on the other side of his door.

Chapter Three

Suzanne fought to control her anger. "I'm sure, Captain Slye, that you think you had good reasons for what you did, but they're not going—"

"Look, Ms. Brelmer, like I told you already—just like I put in my oral. We did what had to be done under the contingency rules. Dubchek participated in the assassination of the Persian ambassador. We had no choice but to let the local feds have him. It's as simple as that."

"Not quite." She took a deep breath and kept her eyes on his crystal ones. This interview wasn't going anything like she had hoped it would, and it was complicated by the fact that she never felt quite comfortable with the Time Police officers whose genetic alterations were so obvious. Slye's enlarged ears and nose and his crystal eyes always made her uncomfortable.

She cleared her throat. "First, Jackson Dubchek wasn't—isn't an assassin. He's an interpreter, and a fairly passive person from what I can tell." She paused and remembered the party where she'd met him. Not totally passive, she had to admit to herself.

"Anyway," she continued, "I just can't believe he

had anything to do with an assassination attempt. Second, and perhaps more to the point, I checked the computer records, and according to *Gunter's Encyclopedia of History,* the Persian ambassador, Mr. Ahmed Rafsani, wasn't assassinated—he died of natural causes seven years later." She locked her eyes on his. "No assassination took place. Third, one of your own people, a Sergeant Coulter, contradicted your oral report in her oral."

"Sergeant Coulter's dead."

"What? When? How did she die?"

"Doc said it was return-effect shock. Six hours after we got back she just dropped dead. Happens sometimes, you know?" The corners of his mouth edged toward a smile.

Suzanne despised Slye, and she had to look away from him. On the wall behind him hung her favorite painting by Dell Harris III, a picture of an alien creature more human than Laszlo Slye looked to her at the moment. His obvious lack of empathy for one of his colleagues disgusted her, and made her wonder why and how her father could trust Slye.

Then, all at once, she realized that Slye had betrayed her father's trust by acting on his own and, consequently, could—

He stood as though ready to leave her office. "Anything else you need me for, ma'am?"

Her eyes snapped back to his. "Yes, Captain Slye. I need the truth—and I'll have it from you now. Sit down . . . please. As reports officer, I have the right to know the real reason you left Jackson Dubchek back in 2183."

"I told you the truth," he said, sitting in the chair with his feet flat on the floor and his back straight. His ears lay back flat against his head, and his wide nostrils flared with every breath. "We didn't have a choice, so we did what we had to do under the circumstances. It's not like we had a long time to think about it, you know."

"The story in your oral and in what you've repeated to me is one the history books say nothing about. Something that important would have been mentioned in the encyclopedia, don't you think, Captain?"

His crystal eyes seemed to stare right past her, and he didn't respond.

"But I'm sure you understand that if your story is true, you will have to testify to that effect—probably before the Senate Committee on Temporal Projects—the committee headed by Senator Ronald Reuel Voxner, Assistant Secretary of History, if I need to remind you of that. And correct me if I'm wrong—but you are not exactly Senator Voxner's favorite employee of Temporal Projects, are you."

Slye shifted uncomfortably and looked down at his thick, rough hands in his lap before lifting his unnatural eyes to meet her gaze. "That was an accident. I was cleared."

"Yes, you were," Suzanne said, hoping to weaken the defiance she heard in him, and wishing at the same time that he would put his brightshades back on so she didn't have to look at his eyes. His face was repulsive enough without the crystal eyes.

"But, Captain, my judgment is that Senator Voxner still holds a grudge against you because of that little accident your team had in Dallas in 2202. It cost him several million credits of inheritance—or more, I don't remember—all because his grandfather died prematurely when you imploded the assignment."

Slye shook his head. "It wasn't my fault."

"But you did in fact kill Senior Senator David Ronald Reuel, didn't you?"

"It was an accident. He stepped in the way."

"While you were attempting to kill someone else—isn't that correct?"

"Bixby—the man who murdered Judge Kobler."

"But you missed Bixby and killed Senator Voxner's grandfather, isn't that correct?"

"That's what we were sent to do—stop Bixby." Slye's enlarged ears twitched.

"But you failed." Suzanne wasn't sure how hard she could press Slye, but she wanted the truth out of him, and she was going to get it if she could. "And Bixby murdered Judge Kobler anyway. And two of your people got arrested. And we had to send another team back to fix what—"

"It was our first action like that, for Shiva's sake!" For the first time, Slye sounded distressed. "What did we know about doing something like that?"

Suzanne let his question hang for a long moment. "Why did you leave Jackson Dubchek back in 2183?"

Light flickered through crystal eyes. "You're a bitch, Ms. Brelmer. Does your father know you're a bitch?"

"Either you give me the truth, Captain, or we'll find out exactly what my father knows—and what he feels—about each of us, and I'll be certain to tell him your assessment of his only daughter's character."

Slye closed his eyes and let out a deep sigh.

When he opened them and stared at her, Suzanne recognized the hatred on his face—and something else too that she couldn't classify. But she really didn't care what he felt about her. She did care about Jackson—for a whole list of reasons, mostly professional, but some personal. If he had done something wrong, he should have been brought back and tried according to the Code of Temporal Justice her father and Senator Voxner had worked so hard to put together.

She decided to try another tack. "Look, Captain, it's obvious that you and I are never going to be friends, but we are in this together, working toward the same goals. I have to trust you, and you have to trust me, or neither one of us is going to be able to do the job. Tell me about Jackson Dubchek. What's the real problem you have with him?"

"He's a threat," Slye said flatly. "Or he will be. Or he would have been. Hard to know how to say it."

"What do you mean, a threat? What kind of threat?"

"The time scouts have reported Dubchek's been messing with history, and—"

"When? How? Where are those reports?" She leaned forward.

"A lot of times, and a lot of ways—dropping in from the future. And the reports are ultrasecret—so I'm putting myself on the line telling you this. But anyway, it was decided that maybe Jackson Dubchek should just get lost in a past where he couldn't do much harm."

"What do you mean, *maybe he should get lost?* And who decided? Under what regulations?"

"I can't tell you that. I've already told you too much. But you said you wanted trust, so I trusted you." Slye sat straighter in his chair and crossed his arms over his chest.

Suzanne leaned back and mimicked his pose—not believing him, but not knowing an alternative. "What you mean, don't you, Captain, is that you decided it on your own."

"It was officially decided." His face hardened. "That's all you need to know for your action report, Ms. Brelmer."

She let the silence hang between them, hoping it would help put a strain on his unwillingness to cooperate. Finally, when she saw a little twitch of his jaw muscle and several flicks of his left ear, she asked, "What will Senator Voxner say about all this? And what will he ask you when you're called to testify before his committee? Or if he brings you into the Secretariat and grills you? Better to tell me now than—"

"Ask your father."

"He knows?" She couldn't read the look on Slye's face, but she couldn't believe her father would be party to such an action. He wasn't that—

"He's your father, and my commanding officer. He should know what's going on. Ask him."

"You're dismissed, Captain."

He stood.

"But before you go, I should tell you that I'm taking you off temporal duties until this operation has been thoroughly reviewed. I'm sure you can find something to do at your desk for the next few weeks."

He glared at her, then slipped his brightshades on and left without a word, without another look in her direction.

Suzanne tasted a peculiar bitterness in her mouth. Never in her life had she been forced to deal with creatures the likes of Laszlo Slye, and as much as she loved working at Temporal Projects, she was beginning to hate working with the genetically altered Time Police—especially the ones like Slye.

The interview had been automatically recorded, so

she called for a printout of it from her desk terminal, then immediately canceled the order, and sat back with a growl of frustration. What was she going to do? Her father was already working to the point of exhaustion. He certainly didn't need the added burden of this problem. Yet, she couldn't just ignore it or hide it from him. A man's life was on the line—Jackson Dubchek's life—and Temporal Projects had put it there.

She punched up the code for her father's secretary. A second later Tech Sergeant Johann Mildritta's face filled the desk terminal screen. "This is Operations and Reports Officer, Suzanne Brelmer. Is Praetor Centurion Brelmer available anytime today?" She felt silly using her father's formal title, but Mildritta always insisted on formality.

"Praetor Centurion Lieutenant Colonel Brelmer's schedule is completely full for the next week, Ms. Brelmer. Might I be of some assistance to you?" His voice was as warm as the liquid nitrogen they used in the time machines.

"I need to talk to my father," she said, intentionally breaking the formality.

"Personal business will have to be taken care of on personal time," Mildritta replied.

"This isn't personal. It has to do with the last action, the one back in 2183 where—"

"Ms. Brelmer! You forget security." The man looked livid. "We have not established and verified a secure connection and *may not* discuss such information until we do so. Furthermore, unless you can prove that I have a need to know such highly classified information, you and I may not discuss it at all."

"But you already know about every Temporal Project operation we undertake."

"That is quite beside the point, Ms. Brelmer. That of which I have knowledge is of no concern to you. Section fifty-three of the operations—"

"I need to speak to my father today, if possible."

"Section fifty-three of the operations code clearly outlines the specific instances—"

"All right. All right, Sergeant Mildritta. Forget it. I'm sorry I said anything. Can you squeeze me into Praetor Centurion Lieutenant Colonel Brelmer's schedule today or tomorrow or not?"

"Most certainly not, Ms. Brelmer. Perhaps next week."

"That's too late."

"Then I suggest you talk to him in private when he returns from Moscow on Thursday."

"Moscow? You didn't tell me he was out of town."

"You did not ask."

"Thanks, Sergeant Mildritta. Thanks a lot." Suzanne broke the connection before Mildritta could answer.

Now what? Her father was in Moscow. Jackson was in the Federal District of New York—in 2183—and she was sitting in Kansas City with a problem that needed action. Slye had acted on his own. She was sure of that now, for reasons she couldn't explain. But she was also sure that her father would get the blame from the Secretary of History—even with Senator Voxner trying to protect him. Worse, if Jackson really had . . .

For a long time she sat and stared at the Dell Harris III painting on her wall. Then suddenly she blinked several times and knew what she had to do. She'd get a costume from Paress Linnet and go back to 2183 and get Jackson herself.

The very idea sent a chill of fear and excitement down her spine. The farthest back she'd ever traveled had been a couple of weeks during some test runs. Now she was going to go back sixty-six years to rescue a man who just might be an assassin.

Chapter Four

The conversation on the other side of the door went on much too long as far as Jackson was concerned. Cold sweat ran down his spine and made him shiver. The cops had seen him. He knew it. They'd seen him come into the Deli'tess Food store with the stranger, and it was only a matter of time before they would demand that he open the door.

He pressed his ear harder against the door's chipped paint, but he still couldn't make out what was being said. Then a burst of music backed by a heavy bass beat cut him off from the sound of voices. His hand rested on the heavy bolt, and he had to resist the impulse to shove it back and fling the door open to reveal himself.

Only then did he realize that something in him had given up—turned quitter—just because he was exhausted and hungry and misplaced in time and space. His lip curled. With a deep breath he straightened his back and stepped softly away from the door. If they wanted him, they'd have to break the door down. No way was he going to give up or give in. No way he was going to quit on himself. And if the stranger who put him in there turned out not to be a friend after all . . . well, Jackson would do whatever he had to do to get away from him.

Jackson sat in one of the chairs facing the door, crossed his arms over his chest, and prepared himself to wait it out. His gut rumbled up and down through the bass clef—out of time with the music from the store—to keep him constantly aware of his hunger. Slowly, his sore, tired body slouched into a more comfortable position. His eyelids drooped and he let his chin drop to his chest. Need to stay awake, he thought. But he drifted away from thought.

Soft lights. Backbeat music. Wine.

Lester introduced the woman as Suzanne Brelmer, then wandered away to talk to someone else.

She smiled.

Jackson warmed to her.

Her eyes held his with a pale blue light of their own. Her red hair swirled around her head, lit from behind like a frothy aura. Her nose was just a little too big for her face, but he liked it. Character—it gave her character. He said something stupid.

She laughed and made a pun. The corners of her eyes crinkled.

He laughed with her, then touched her hand lightly and said, "That's bad, really bad. I love it." They laughed a lot. People started leaving. Jackson didn't want to go. Neither did she.

Lunch tomorrow? Sure. His stomach growled. Great. Yeah, I can find the place. Standing there by her sleek, tiger-striped Singapore Slingshot, he wanted to kiss her. The spring air and her soft perfume made him bold. More than anything else in the world he wanted to kiss her. He leaned closer.

"Jackson?"

His body jerked upright. Where was Suzanne?

"Jackson?"

Pain shot through him in twenty places. He mouthed a soundless curse and forced himself to sit perfectly still.

"Jackson, they're gone," a voice said from a speaker up near the ceiling. "You can open up, now." The voice had a distinctive inflection he recognized. The stranger.

But was it a trick? Dare he move? Indecision kept him glued to the chair.

"Can you hear me, Jackson? It's all kosher. The police have left. Miriam is making sandwiches for us."

"Food," he whispered as he stood up and stepped stiffly to the door. He hesitated a second before throwing back the bolt. What if . . .?

A grin split the stranger's dark face when the door opened. "What do you want to drink? Beer? Wine? Vodka? Seltzer?"

Jackson looked over the stranger's shoulder, but saw no one except the bony old woman, Miriam, walking toward them from behind the glass case. In her hands were two plates heaped with food. Jackson's mouth watered. "What's seltzer?"

"Seltzer water—you know, carbonated water."

"Sounds awful. Any coffee?"

"Rationed," Miriam said. "Got tea."

"What's rationed coffee?" Jackson asked. "Is that a brand, or what?"

She laughed. "Means you can't get it without stamps—or without someone bringing it down the line for you."

The stranger grinned. "You know the rules. No bootlegging. Tea for me, Miriam."

Jackson shook his head, not understanding, but not caring enough to ask further. "Beer, please," he said, accepting the plates from her. "We eating in here?"

"Yes."

Stepping back into the little room, Jackson set the plates on the table. His hand took a sandwich off one of them and brought it to his mouth before he even sat down. Some kind of meat. And pickles. And other stuff. Wonderful. He swallowed and took another huge bite.

"Don't make yourself sick," the stranger said, sitting across from him.

"Who are you?" Jackson asked as soon as he could swallow.

"A friend. You can call me Rankin."

"But that's not your name."

"It's part of my name—part that won't give me away."

For the first time Jackson connected the odd inflection in Rankin's voice with something else and thought he understood. "You're from the future, aren't you?"

Rankin pointed to his mouth full of food and shook his head yes.

"How did you know my name?" Jackson took another bite and nodded to Miriam when she walked in with two large, steaming mugs of tea. He'd asked for beer, but the tea smelled delicious, and he was too hungry to care.

"A friend sent me," Rankin said. He followed Miriam to the door, shut it, and bolted it behind her before returning to his seat.

A slight chill ran down Jackson's spine. Then he took a deep breath and let it out slowly. Better to be locked in safe than caught outside. "Who? What friend?"

"Someone who cares about you. I can't tell you any more than that."

"Suzanne? Lester? Who? Why can't you tell me?"

"Rules. Look, as soon as it's dark I'm going to take you to see someone who can help you. That's the best I can do. Maybe he can tell you what you want to know."

"Does he have a name?"

"He'll tell you."

"Damn!" Jackson belched immediately after the curse.

"You're eating too fast. Slow down. It won't be dark for another couple of hours."

Jackson took a sip of the tea and almost scalded his mouth. "Do you know what happened to me today?"

"The Time Police displaced you," Rankin said without hesitation.

"What?"

"That's what they do sometimes. They displace people out of their own time. Most people they displace die because they don't know how to cope, and consequently they . . ." His voice trailed off as he looked down into his mug.

Jackson was puzzled. "But why me? And how come you can tell me that and not the other stuff?"

"Eat. Chew. Enjoy. Relax. And stop asking so many questions. I shouldn't have told you about displacement. It's not my job."

"What is your job?"

Rankin looked up and his black eyes met Jackson's eyes across the table. "Traffic . . . That's what you are, traffic." He grinned ever so slightly. Then the grin disappeared. "Now, that's it. No more questions and answers for me."

"You a Time Policeman?"

"No more. I've told you what I can."

Jackson worked on finishing the food on his plate,

trying at the same time to digest the little information Rankin had given him. Several things Jackson felt sure about. Rankin was from the future—another time traveler—or another Time Policeman from a different time. Furthermore, despite Rankin's unwillingness to explain what was going on, Jackson trusted him. For the first time since the assassination at the UN, Jackson felt safe—at least as safe as he could feel under the circumstances.

"Rankin, can you—or your mysterious nameless—friend help me get home?"

"You'll have to ask him . . . I'm sorry, Jackson. I really am. But my job is handle traffic—to keep it moving. That's all. I don't have the big answers or the big picture or anything else like that."

"Okay." Jackson heard the weariness in his voice and finished off his mug of tea. "Anyplace I can take a nap while we wait?"

"Only here. We can push some chairs together—or tables."

"Anything. I'm too tired to care."

Within moments after stretching out on four chairs, Jackson fell asleep.

Jackson awoke in total darkness. He couldn't see anything. Then he smelled food and heard music. Still it took him anothermoment to remember where he was—and why he was there. "Buddha," he whispered, "what bad karma put me here?"

The door opened and a wash of yellow light filled the room, backlighting the figure of a man. Rankin?

"Ah, you're awake. Good. It's time to go. Vaughan's waiting."

"Who?"

"The man who's going to help you, Vaughan Tysonyllyn. I talked to him and he said I could tell you his name. Mean anything to you?''

Jackson sat up slowly and shook his head, still groggy from sleep. "I don't know. It rings some kind of distant bell in my head, but . . ."

"He was—is—one of the founders of the Mnemosyne Historians."

"They're illegal," Jackson said. A ripple of fear shivered through him. "Outlawed. Banned. Criminals, I guess. How are criminals going to help me?"

Rankin leaned against the door frame. "The only reason the Mnemosyne were outlawed was because they objected to the government's revisionist history. All they care about is the truth. What's criminal about that?"

"I don't know. But they're still criminals where I come from."

"Well, they're not criminals here—not yet. So let's get going. Okay?"

"I'm hungry again."

"Of course you are." He held up a cloth bag. "Miriam packed you a few sandwiches . . .There's a bathroom through there. Use it if you have to, and we'll be on our way."

Five minutes later they were walking along mostly dark streets. What few other pedestrians there were stepped wide of them, and Jackson wondered why only every fourth or fifth streetlight was working. The government never would have permitted such a thing in 2249.

"Hey," he said when they turned a second corner, "we're going back the way we came from."

"That's right. We have to take the circular route."

They entered the basement of a building half a block after the turn, climbed two flights of dark, narrow stairs by the light of Rankin's flashlight, passed through a locked door for which Rankin had a key, walked down a flight of worn wooden stairs, then went through another locked door into a two-meter-square room with some kind of exercise bicycle, machine on one side of it.

"Elevator," Rankin said with a grin. He shut the door, locked it, climbed on the bicycle and started peddling. The room began to rise ever so slowly.

"If this Vaughan guy isn't a criminal, why all the locked doors and secret passages?"

"Security. Keeps out the curious."

Jackson sighed. Rankin pedaled. The elevator rose through a bare brick shaft for what seemed like ten minutes to Jackson before the base of a door finally appeared below the ceiling. Rankin stopped pedaling when they were level with the door.

"Pull that brake lever over there."

As soon as the brake was set, Rankin unlocked the door and led Jackson down another long, dark hall, through an empty apartment, and knocked on another door. The sound of the knock told Jackson that the door was heavy and solid. Very solid.

A spotlight came on over their heads. Jackson started.

After a long pause, the light went out and the door opened.

Standing there with a malicious grin on his face was a man who looked exactly like a bad horror holo's image of Satan.

Chapter Five

The man who looked like Satan held his hand out to Jackson. "Welcome to our modest retreat, Mr. Dubchek. I am Vaughan Tysonyllyn, your temporal guide, guardian, and friend."

Jackson accepted the handshake with little enthusiasm and allowed himself to be drawn into the room. The door closed behind them, and to his dismay, Rankin stayed outside. Jackson didn't relish being alone with yet another stranger—especially one who looked like Satan. "Who are you?"

Satan smiled. "I just told you, young man. I am Vaughan Tysonyllyn."

"That's not what I mean. Who are you? What do you have to do with time travel? Rankin said you might be able to help me get home . . . get me back to—"

"Slow down, my young friend. Slow down. All in due time we will concern ourselves with your, uh, temporal location problems." Tysonyllyn gestured to a chair. "Have a seat. Relax. Might you perhaps have something to eat in that bag?"

Jackson was suddenly aware of the bag in his hands

as he sat in the overstuffed chair. "Sandwiches from the Deli'tess Food store. Miriam made them for me."

"Mind if I have one? Haven't eaten all day."

"Eat them all," Jackson said, handing him the bag. As soon as he said that, his stomach growled.

Tysonyllyn smiled more broadly than before and revealed long incisors that gleamed in the room's pale yellow light. "No, you sound too hungry. I shall just have one." He removed a sandwich and handed the bag back to Jackson. "But wait, let me prepare us something to drink. Would you like coffee?"

"Yes . . . but don't—I mean, Miriam said it was rationed."

"It is, Mr. Dubchek, but I have some for special occasions—and you are certainly my special occasion of the week," Tysonyllyn said as he walked into the next room and turned on the light.

For the first time since he had entered the apartment, Jackson took a slow look around. Worn chairs, a scarred wooden table, and two tall bookcases stuffed full of books and papers revealed a man who didn't worry much about appearances. But for all its clutter, the room had the look of temporary occupancy—no pictures on the walls, windows covered with black plastic tacked over them, and a total lack of personal items except for a hourglass-shaped dulcimer hanging by its strap from a nail. A dulcimer? For a moment Jackson wondered if—

"Will you have sugar in your coffee, Mr. Dubchek?"

"Sustene, if you have it," Jackson called back.

"None of that in 2183, I'm afraid. It's sugar or nothing."

"Sugar then. Uh, Mr. Tysonyllyn, is that your dulcimer?"

"Why, yes," he said as he re-entered the room carrying two oversized mugs. "I'm surprised you recognize it. Few people do. Come, we'll eat at the table and pretend we live here."

"Lot of dulcimers where I come from. My dad was in Auntie Suzette's Marching Dulcimer Band . . . until he died last year—or in my last year." As he stood up and walked over to the table, Jackson shook his head. "It's confusing—time, I mean—to know when and where I am."

"Understandable," Tysonyllyn said, "but it may comfort you to know that you are doing quite well, actually. . . . A marching dulcimer band? I never heard of such a thing. Your Aunt Suzette started it?"

Jackson took a bite of his sandwich and chewed it thoroughly before answering. "No. It's been around for a long time. Some guy from Texas started it, I think, a long time ago—before my time, I mean."

"I just came back from Texas. Had quite a terrible time with their customs officers."

"Customs? You mean coming back from Mexico? Or what?"

"From Texas," Tysonyllyn said around a mouthful of food. "They are not too fond of American tourists—or any tourists from the Republic, I suspect—especially ones like me, aging historians who like to curious around."

"What *are* you talking about?" Jackson lifted the mug, but the coffee was too hot to drink.

"Ah, but of course, you do not know." Tysonyllyn shook his head. "I forget, sometimes, what you travelers do and do not know. Texas is a separate country—at the moment—what annoying version of history. It refused to join the Second Republic. Remained independent instead of joining the United States the way we learned it in the proper history books. Has been since 1836—your Time Police were most certainly in on that bit of chicanery, we honestly believe—when Bernardo O'Higgins and that French scoundrel, Leclerc, led the movement for Texas to remain independent."

Jackson's defenses rose around his confusion. "They're not my Time Police. I just came with—"

"They are yours, Mr. Dubchek. They started in your time. And that is exactly where they come from when they drop back and tamper with history."

"I don't believe you," Jackson said, wondering if he could get out of this place and where he could go. The subway station—he had to get back to the subway station. "What do you mean, tamper with history?"

"You are here, are you not? Did you end up with me in the Federal District of New York in 2183 by accident? Did you volunteer to stay here? Or did your Time Police abandon you? That in and of itself is a tampering with history. Furthermore, they were probably instrumental in the assassination of—"

"Who are you, really?" Jackson's every instinct told him it was time to run again—but he had nowhere to go, and he knew it. "And are you going to help me or not?"

"Calm down, Mr. Dubchek. You will be helped. In fact, help is on its way. With any luck you will be returned to your own time before this night is over. And I personally shall be glad to see you go. You are rude, untrusting, obnoxious, ignorant—"

"Hey, wait. I don't mean to be rude. I'm scared, maybe, and worried, and certainly confused, but I don't mean—"

"—lacking in manners and social graces too, I might add."

"I'm sorry, already."

Satan grinned through Tysonyllyn's pointed teeth, and a shudder raced down Jackson's spine. "Give me a break, Mr. Tysonyllyn. I don't mean to . . .Uh, well, look, I'm just an interpreter, and what I know about all this time travel is next to nothing. Furthermore, something really nasty happened to me today, and then I got dumped by the people who were supposed—"

"Displaced. That is what your Time Police call it. You havebeen displaced in time."

"Whatever. Then Rankin pulls me off the street, locks me in a back room, then finally brings me here, and you . . . you tell me some rubbish about Texas not being part of the Second Republic, and you get mad when I'm upset because—"

"Do you know anything about the Mnemosyne Historians, Mr. Dubchek?" Tysonyllyn asked, a frown darkening his face.

"They're criminals."

"We are historians, not criminals."

Jackson heard all too clearly the anger in Tysonyllyn's voice.

"We are dedicated to preserving history accurately— history the way it was before *your* Time Police started tampering with it." His voice climbed the scale, word by word.

Jackson pressed his back against the chair, half his sandwich still uneaten, his coffee untouched.

"*Your* Time Police—not ours." Tysonyllyn took a deep breath and let it out slowly. When he started speaking again, his voice was lower, calmer. "We do not have any, not here in 2183. All we have is ourselves and our collective memories and our books to tell us what is right and wrong." Again his voice rose. "We do not need you and your kind here. But we have to deal with you, or history will become chaos and the world will fall apart at the seams. But I should not suppose the likes of you—"

A knock on the door stopped him. "Ah, perhaps that is Halona, your guide back to the netherworld of 2249," Tysonyllyn said as he walked toward the door. "Finish your sandwich, Mr. Dubchek. You may not have time, later."

Despite his hunger, Jackson didn't feel like eating. He took a big bite anyway and forced himself to chew, without taking his eyes off the door. Moments later Tysonyllyn admitted a woman wearing denims, a black leather jacket, and a red beret. A bush of bright hair stuck out from under the beret.

"Halona, this is Mr. Dubchek, your charge. Mr. Dubchek, this is Halona. She is a Guardian."

Jackson stood and, after hesitating, stuck out his hand. Halona walked to within a meter of him with no indication of accepting his handshake. She reminded him of someone, but he couldn't figure who.

"Where'd ya get those clothes?" she asked.

He lowered his hand and glanced down at the gray suit Temporal Projects had given him. "They were issued to me."

"By the welfare department?" She laughed and held out her hand. "I'm sorry, but it looks just awful on you."

He shook her hand and was surprised by the strength of grip. "I thought it looked okay."

"Wear it when you go to Wheeling."

"Pardon?"

"Never mind that, Mr. Dubchek. Halona, would you care for some coffee? I have just brewed a pot."

"Ugh. Not me. If he's ready, I think we oughtta scat."

"Very well. Mr. Dubchek . . . are you ready?"

"Sure. I guess. Where are we going?"

"Back to your time machine."

"Home?" Jackson was suddenly excited and afraid.

"That's right. We're gonna put ya in that old Buick and send ya home."

"Buick?"

She laughed, revealing straight white teeth. "That's what it looks like, an antique Buick automobile. Haven't ya ever seen one?"

"No." He had no idea what she was talking about, but he finally realized who she reminded him of—Paress Linnet, the costumer at Temporal Projects. She had the same color hair, the same slangy way of talking.

"There's one in the Museum of Antiques, a 1953 Buick Deluxe, green and black and white—ugly as a Wall Street whore. Ya haveta pee or anything before we go?"

"Uh, no. I'm fine." Jackson picked up his mug and drank all the warm coffee. "Thank you, Mr. Tysonyllyn."

"You are welcome, young man. Just don't come back. Stay in your own time."

"I will." He turned to Halona. "I'm ready."

"We'll go out the back, Mr. T.," Halona said, heading through the kitchen.

Jackson followed her, and as soon as they were out, Tysonyllyn locked the door behind them. Halona led him zigzagging through the building up and down stairs until she stopped at a low iron door in a damp basement room that smelled heavily of mildew and rotting wood.

"From here on we haveta be careful and quiet. There's a tunnel that will take us to the old subway station, but we can't come back this way if we're caught, so don't do anything stupid."

"Like what?"

"Like don't say anything or make any noise or take a step unless I tell ya to, okay." It was a command, not a question.

"Okay." A bead of sweat rolled down his neck.

She handed him a small flashlight, and unlocked the door with a six-centimeter-long key, and pulled it open. A wave of cold, damp air rolled into the basement. Reluctantly, he followed her into the dark tunnel, then held the flashlight while she locked the door. Despite the cool air, Jackson felt the sweat in his armpits and down his back. There he was in a two-meter-high tunnel under the Federal District of New York City in 2183 with a woman he didn't even know and—

"Let's go. Watch me closely."

Every step they took down the tunnel echoed with a grating sound, and Jackson was sure that if the tunnel brought them anywhere near the station, the Time Police would hear them coming. Then what would happen? Would they kill him? Or just laugh and leave him? And what if the machine was gone? Or if it was there, what if Halona didn't know how to work it? Jackson surely didn't know how to run a time machine. He had been in the back seat and hadn't been able to see much of anything.

Suddenly Halona switched out the light and put out her hand to stop him. A second later his eyes adjusted enough to see a light in front of them, a pulsating, glowing light. A crackle of static followed, and his heart sank. That was the sound the time machine had made when it left 2249.

Chapter Six

"Praetor Centurion Lieutenant Colonel Friz Brelmer to see Senator Voxner," Brelmer said as he handed his credentials to the guard. The chill in Moscow's spring wind was reflected in the guard's face.

Others might have resented the formal requirement of having to present credentials, but Brelmer found it reassuring. Too many of his contemporaries lobbied for greater informality without understanding that the rules of social interchange were the lubricants of social harmony. Rules and regulations made life easier for everyone to understand, and smoothed interaction between persons of unequal rank—especially under difficult circumstances such as Brelmer faced with Senator Voxner.

The guard looked from the holo in Brelmer's passbook to his face and back several times before she said, "You should really have another pic made, sir. This one makes you look much older than you are." Her accent was as thick as her face.

"I'll take that as a compliment, Corporal," he said absently. "May I enter now?"

"Oh, yes, certainly, sir. Secretary Voxner is expecting you. I believe you will find him in the viewing room in the rear of the dacha—down the main hall to the left.''

"Thank you. I know the way.'' Brelmer walked to the viewing room almost without noticing the marble halls and art-covered walls on the way. He had been in Senator Voxner's Russian home so many times for both official and personal reasons that he no longer took notice of the luxurious dacha that had amazed him the first time he had seen it. However, even if he had never seen the house before, he was too distracted by the problem that had brought him there to appreciate his surroundings.

"Senator?'' he said, knocking on the carved walnut door to the viewing room. "It's Colonel Brelmer.''

"Come in, Friz. Come in,'' the senator's muffled voice called back.

Brelmer entered and was disappointed to find eight or ten people sitting around the holo stage watching a corpulent woman lecturing an even more corpulent man.

"Twentieth-century movie, *My Little Chickadee,* Mae West,'' Senator Voxner said, "and W. C. Fields— fresh out of the Holo Restoration Project. We were told it was a comedy, but we have yet to find anything more than vulgar humor in it. Sit down, Friz. It is almost over, I believe.''

After taking a seat at the edge of the circle, Brelmer glanced around the room and tried to identify people, resolved to make the best of the situation until he could be alone with the senator. Mrs. Voxner sat, as usual, at the senator's left. Assistant Undersecretary of Culture Sarah Hadenforth Elgin, wearing a partially transparent dress, sat with her ever-present guitar case by her chair next to Mrs. Voxner. Beside Secretary Elgin sat a handsome young man, in a muted blue one-piece dress uniform, whose attentions were entirely on her.

Brelmer didn't blame the young officer. He would much rather have listened to Secretary Elgin play her guitar than watch some stupid holo of an antique movie—although Brelmer felt sure the young man was more interested in Secretary Elgin's physical attributes than her musical talents. He was probably too young to realize she was one of the best musicians anyone had ever met, and that she was also a moving force in the worldwide movement back to natural instruments. For all that Brelmer loved rock 'n' jazz, he had discovered through Secretary Elgin a growing attraction to the natural music, played as it was on instruments of wood and brass.

Next to Secretary Elgin's admiring young officer sat the brilliant Senator Laronica and his wife, Spektre, two people Brelmer hoped to know better in the future. Behind them sat the woman he recognized as Madame DeShizzo whose world famous Casa d'Agape l'Animal was at once the scandal and pride of Moscow. Brelmer had heard scurrilous stories about what happened between people and animals at d'Agape—stories that were simply too shocking to be believed. Her presence there at Senator Voxner's home only confirmed for him that the rumors about her must be untrue.

The remainder of the people were unfamiliar to him, but he studied each face he could see and out of habit memorized each as best he could by the light of the holo—which he ignored. Yet even as he recorded each face, his greater concerns made him wonder how long it would be before he could speak to Senator Voxner alone.

The business in 2183 had gone badly, and when the Licinians found out, there would be face to pay for someone—Senator Voxner, if he wasn't careful, or even Brelmer himself. Fortunately, the senator had controlled the Licinian-inspired protests over the first Wheeling incident with great finesse, and Brelmer hoped for no less in this situation.

What ate at Brelmer deeper down was something he couldn't discuss with the senator, something Senator Voxner had declared off limits. What Brelmer feared more than anything, more than he was fully willing to admit even to himself, was that the adjustments Temporal Projects made to history—both intentional and accidental— would one day destroy the very things they were trying to protect. Brelmer would never be convinced that—

Applause startled him.

He looked up just as the lights came on in the room and realized that the holo had ended. The other guests were rising from their chairs and chatting with each other in a way that immediately suggested they anticipated something else. A man placed a chair on the holo stage. Secretary Elgin opened her guitar case. Brelmer sighed. At any other time he would have delighted in the opportunity to hear her play, but at that moment he needed to talk to the senator.

"At Senator Voxner's request," Secretary Elgin said, "I am going to play 'Where the Emerald Kudzu Twines' a traditional Ozark folk song written by one of my ancestors about two hundred years ago. Then I shall be pleased to entertain other requests."

Brelmer sat patiently through her presentation of the unfamiliar song, more than a little amused to learn that the eradicable kudzu vines that once plagued half of North America had been a problem for so long a time. However, he was relieved when the senator signaled him with a tilt of his head toward the door as Elgin began her second song.

Leading the way from the room, Voxner said, "She is quite good, and I hate for either of us to miss hearing her perform, but you and I have urgent business, Praetor Centurion. Your Captain Slye is waiting in my office."

The way Voxner said Slye's name put Brelmer in his formal place as Voxner's subordinate. "Slye, sir? He's here?"

"I sent for him. You know what happened in 2183, I assume?"

"Yes, sir. I just learned of it several hours ago. That's why I requested to see you."

"That man will be the death of us, Colonel," Voxner said.

"He's a good man, sir. Tough. Reliable."

"Dangerous. This is the second time he's eliminated one of the wrong people."

Brelmer winced. The first wrong person Slye had accidentally eliminated had been Voxner's grandfather. "I'm sorry, sir, but my reports didn't indicate an inappropriate elimination."

Voxner stopped in the middle of the hall and stared at Brelmer. "Then what was your concern?"

"The interpreter, sir. The one we sent back. He got stranded in 2183, and there were some indications—"

"Slye dumped him there, you mean."

"No, sir, I don't believe that was the case."

"I do—most firmly. I have my sources too, Colonel. But do not worry about your interpreter. The bigger problem is undoing the assassination of the Russian premier."

"Holy Gautama—uh, I'm sorry, sir." Brelmer felt

his face flush. "You caught me totally by surprise." How in the great Buddha's name had—

"Then you did not know? I take that as a bad sign, Colonel." Voxner turned and continued walking.

"Sometimes we don't know right away, Senator. Was your information . . . uh, concurrent with the incident?"

"No, dammit, it was not. It was worse. Historical. The premier was an accidental victim of the attack. Gerishnikov's death changed the alliance of Russia with the Republic, and we are going to have a real fight on our hands unless we send someone back to fix it," he said, letting Brelmer hold the door of the senator's office open for him.

Slye was not in the office, much to Brelmer's relief. He needed time alone with the senator. "Uh, sir, we can undo the damage. We've done it before." As soon as he said that, he wished he hadn't.

Senator Voxner sat behind the broad, leather-covered desk. His eyes narrowed.

Brelmer's spine straightened, and he squared his shoulders, ready to take the reprimand.

"Yes, I know you have corrected mistakes before. The problem is, Colonel Brelmer, that we should not have to undo the damage. We should be able to accomplish these missions correctly the first time. This was not like the first Wheeling incident where the machinery was at fault."

Good instincts made Brelmer keep his mouth shut and his eyes locked on the senator's.

"Furthermore, I am beginning to wonder if the personnel we have in place are suitable for the assignments we give them . . . not you, of course. I have the utmost confidence in you."

Several times in Brelmer's presence, Voxner had given Brelmer's predecessor, Dr. L. Z. Minor, an identical vote of confidence—twice on the day before Dr. Minor got promoted to some meaningless bureaucratic job shuffling papers for the Junior Assistant Undersecretary for Waste Disposal. Brelmer swallowed hard.

"Project Clio is too important to be allowed to suffer at the hands of incompetents, Colonel. I am sure you, better than anyone, can understand that. Our opportunity to perfect society is precious and must not be mishandled. Do you agree?"

"Most certainly, sir."

"Sit down, Colonel, and after we decide on a course of action, I will have Captain Slye brought to us."

For thirty minutes Senator Voxner lectured Brelmer on the failures of Temporal Projects and the absolute necessity of improving every aspect of their operations. It was a lecture Brelmer had to endure at least once a month, a lecture Brelmer tolerated, but could not accept. What Senator Voxner never seemed to grasp was that time travel and temporal interdictions were far more complicated than the senator wanted to understand. However, Brelmer had learned that there was nothing to be gained by trying to explain those things to the senator. Yet when it—

"Does that seem reasonable to you, Friz?"

"Uh, I'm not sure, sir. My mind hit a tangent there for a second."

Senator Voxner's eyes narrowed. "I suggested," he said slowly, "that we send your Captain Slye back one more time and that if he fails, we remove him from temporal responsibilities—permanently."

Brelmer blinked. "Permanently, sir. You mean . . ."

"I mean, Praetor Centurion Brelmer, that the Second Republic should not be constantly endangered by incompetents."

"Senator . . . I don't think"—Brelmer's mind scrambled for words—"I don't believe Captain Slye is incompetent. He has commanded a whole series of actions in which he was quite successful. Two unfortunate accidents are hardly reason to—"

"Be that as it may, we can endure no more *unfortunate accidents*. Is that understood? Captain Slye must prove himself competent or suffer the appropriate consequences."

Brelmer nodded. What choice did he have? "Yes, sir, I understand."

The lights dimmed. A door slid open to reveal a window into another room. There sat Laszlo Slye on a stone bench looking for all the world as though he owned the tiny room where he sat.

"He's a confident mutant," Senator Voxner said.

"Altered, sir, not mutant. We've all had surgery to—"

"Mutated, altered, what difference does it make, Friz? You and he both are extremely valuable to the Republic—but totally expendable. Never forget that. You can come in now, Captain." The mirrored door slid open as the lights came up.

"Thank you, Senator," Captain Slye said as he marched into the room. "Good evening, Colonel."

"This is not a social visit, Slye."

"No, sir. I understand that." His ears twitched and his large nostrils flared over a slice of a smile that revealed yellowed teeth. "Can I assume we are going back to kill that stinking little interpreter who assassinated Gerish-nikov?''

Slye's remark was so arrogant that Brelmer was almost amused. The cold expression on Senator Voxner's face stilled his own, and for the first time he realized that Slye was more dangerous than Brelmer had ever given him credit for. Consequently, for the first time in a long time, Friz Brelmer questioned his own judgment.

Chapter Seven

The whine of machinery climbed up out of the audible range. Dust swirled. Lights pulsed in brilliant flashes— two, three, four times—orange flashes that smelled like mounds of dirty cat litter in an orchard of blossoms.

Darkness closed its doors. Total darkness. Blind darkness. Silent. Dead. Empty. Eternal.

Time stopped with a painful, choking wrench. Nothing lived. Nothing moved. Nothing *was*. Nothing ever had been. Nothing would ever be. The universe was blank and void and forever without life.

Then a fat man snored.

Sudden sparks bore halos into the empty universe, then whirled away and disappeared. The snores vibrated walls. Basso profundo groans echoed inside Suzanne's skull. Demons roared her name. Snores rolled over her like heavy surf, pounding her against the gritty beach of her consciousness. She giggled in hysteria.

The world vibrated with a fierce determination to shake itself apart. Life hung in the balance between present and past—hung on a shaking thread as thin as memory,

a silver thread that slowly unraveled, twisting itself undone with a quiet whine in the dark pit of forgetting.

Oranges turned to ammonia.

Suzanne wept.

With a grinding jolt, lights shattered the darkness,
pulsing and screaming, spinning through her gut in a mad
whirlwind like a dragon chasing its tail through the universe around the silver thread of memory.

The thread of memory snapped.

Fear jolted her nerves. Pain burned her gut. Suzanne
doubled over. Tears washed her face. She clutched at the
plastic bag attached to her facemask as her stomach emptied itself over and over in great retching spasms.

Travel shock. Worse than she had expected. Much
worse.

Switches clicked. Whines descended their scales. In
the midst of her misery she remembered all too clearly
that she had eaten dinner only a few hours before leaving
2249. That was the problem. Rule number five: Always
travel on an empty stomach. She would never forget that
rule again. Never.

Slowly her nausea eased, and she stopped trying to
heave up the lining of her finally empty stomach. Only
then did she detach the bag and wipe off her face on the
bag's removable wettowel. When she looked out of the
time machine, her whole body jerked upright.

Through the forward window of the machine, in the
glare of its spotlights, Suzanne saw a mirror image of her
own machine. No, not a mirror image, it was another time
machine. But whose? Why? How? She held her dizzy
head in trembling hands. Was it the machine Slye's team
had left behind? Of course. Yes, of course, that had to
be it.

The more traveling Temporal Projects did, the more they were going to litter time with their machines. Suzanne chuckled to herself, but the chuckle was stilled by one last sour burp from her unhappy stomach. The amusement she felt was sour, also. The machines would keep duplicating themselves everywhere they sent someone if they had the power, and the machines could cause as much harm as good—probably more.

As she climbed out of her own time machine, she saw the layer of dust on the other one and finally wondered *when* she was. The 116th St. markings on the walls were correct for the subway station in the Federal District of New York, but *when* had she arrived? What year? What day? *When* was she in New York? From the looks of the other machine, she had arrived long after its last use.

Her empty stomach did a slow, painful roll. Her heart sank. What about Jackson? What had happened to him? Was she too late? How would she know? Realizing how ill-prepared she truly was to accomplish his rescue, she felt very stupid.

There she stood—in she knew not what year—looking for someone who might already be dead or have returned to the future or have gotten himself lost or killed or saints-only-knew-what. Yet in her aching gut she had a feeling that she should at least find out *when* she had arrived and if there was any chance of locating Jackson.

Following the TP instructions for this station, she unreeled a power cord and plugged it into the red box on the wall. The blue light on her plug indicated a proper connection, and a brief wave of relief washed through her. With standard 120 volt 60 cycle power, her machine would be ready for the return in less than five local hours.

Using her hand torch, she found the way toward the

exit, knowing that she had at least those five hours to investigate.

And to get in trouble, a voice added in the back of her mind. And get lost. Or get trapped here. Or . . .

Suzanne refused to accept any of those possibilities. If she were cautious and careful, if she took no unnecessary risks, if she paid close attention to—

A grating sound froze her in place. Footsteps. Outside the exit door. She reached for the monitor switch beside the door and, even as she found it and turned it on, was surprised that it was there. A gray spot on the wall above the switch flickered to life and showed a shadowy figure standing on the other side of the door.

"Jackson?" she said softly, her nose almost pressed against the flat screen, her sour breath heavy in her mouth. "Is that you?"

The figure leaned forward and grabbed the door handle.

"Jackson? Is that you?"

With a shake of its head, the figure turned and walked away from the door.

Suzanne panicked. "Jackson? Jackson?" she shouted.

The figure paused and turned around.

Frantically Suzanne unlocked the door. As she dragged it open, the figure stepped toward her. It wasn't Jackson. It was a woman, a tall, thin woman wearing a heavy coat and a dirty face.

"Whatcha doin' in there, dearie?" the woman asked in a hoarse voice.

"Nothing," Suzanne said, trying to push the heavy metal door shut again.

"Must've somethin'. Let us see, now."

The *us* frightened Suzanne as nothing else could have.

If the woman had company out there, Suzanne was in big trouble. Her heart pounded against her ribs. Sweat broke out on her face. But push as she might, the door wouldn't close. The woman had a foot and one arm in the opening. The arm stank of decay and filth and wet wool and ammonia and oranges.

"Come on, now, dairy dearie. Let us see whatcha got."

"Go away! Leave me alone," Suzanne shouted, bracing all her weight against the door.

"Gotcha some food in there? Vittles for two? Better let us in, dearie. Share and share the guh'ment says."

"Get out of the way, woman," a heavy male voice said. The woman's arm and foot disappeared from the door.

Suzanne slammed the door shut and bolted it. She gulped for air. All her energy seemed to drain from her as she slumped against the door.

"Suzanne?"

She gasped and spun around. Two people were approaching her. One of them was—"Jackson! How did you . . . ? Where did you . . . ?" There was a woman with Jackson, an oddly dressed woman who stood sniffing the air like an animal, at once curious, powerful, and suspicious.

Someone pounded on the door to the outside.

"You two better scat," the woman said.

Suzanne ignored her for the moment. "Jackson, you can't know how relieved I am to see you."

"Yes I can." A small smile played on his face.

"There's another timer coming down the line," Halona said, "and I s'pect that's the local cops bangin' on the door. Time for you two to get out of here."

"We can't. My machine just started recharging." Try

as she might, Suzanne couldn't read the expression on the woman's face. Jackson's expression, however, was easy—pure relief. She held out her hands as they neared each other.

"Use the other one. It's charged and ready."

Heavy banging shook the door. A male voice demanded entry.

"How would you know?" Suspicion and fear gripped Suzanne. "Who are you?"

"Her name's Halona. She's a Guardian, or a future Time Cop, or something," Jackson said, taking Suzanne's hands in his. What he really wanted to do was hug her and kiss her and never let her go, but he wasn't sure she would let him.

Suzanne shook her head, unsure of what to make of Halona or—

"They sound like they're gonna break in. You better hurry." Halona opened the controller's door to the dusty time machine. "Yep, ready light says she's charged and set. I was gonna send Jackson by hisself, but it don't matter, now." She sniffed again. "You only got a couple of minutes—even if the door holds the locals out." She sniffed again. "There's another one close."

"You mean you can smell time machines coming?" Jackson asked.

"Of course you can, stupid. You only have to smell one once to catch the perf again. If you've traveled, you've smelled it. It's that fresh-orange-juice-mixed-with-ammonia smell."

Jackson took a sniff. He could smell it.

"I smell it, too," Suzanne said. "If you trust her, maybe we should go."

"Why wouldn't he trust me?" Halona stood staring at them with her hands on her hips.

"Why would I?" Jackson felt suddenly defensive, angry, and exhausted. Worse, his whole body trembled.

The orange-juice-and-ammonia smell grew heavier, stronger, more acidic. Suzanne felt Jackson shudder and looked from his worn face to the woman, Halona, standing arrogantly beside the other time machine. On the other side of the exit door the man's voice grew more insistent. "Well?"

"I'm telling ya, you two better just scat. You can gab about me later."

"I'm ready if you are," Jackson said.

"Then let's go home."

It took them less than two minutes to strap themselves into the seats of the time machine and put their face masks on. Halona double-checked the settings with Suzanne, then grinned and said, "Better hang on to that bag on your face, Jackm'boy. You just ate—and you're about to lose it all." She slammed the door before he could answer.

"You're going to be sick," Suzanne said, "but there's nothing we can do about that. Just hang on as best you can. Here we go." She flipped the safety cover off the activator switch, held the release button down with her left hand and pushed the switch with her right thumb.

The time machine whined.

Jackson grabbed her right hand with his left.

Dust swirled and danced around the time machine. A second, discordant whine pierced the first one. Lights flashed. The machine vibrated.

Jackson's stomach flipped. His head spun. He didn't remember vibrations. Knives cut through his gut, dull knives with jagged edges.

Suzanne clenched her teeth and scrunched her eyes closed.

Through the dusty window Jackson saw a third time machine wavering in and out of focus like a mirage in the crowded subway station. His stomach turned again. And again. His head swam. Suzanne squeezed the blood out of his hand.

Darkness rolled over them pierced by starbursts of green light that spread like giant blossoms, crying as they faded back into the emptiness where they had been born. Then yellow light blossomed. Then blue. Then . . .nothing.

Moldy death kissed them. Blind death wrapped its cold arms around them. Black, silent death pulled them down to . . . nothingness . . . nothingness . . . nothingnessnothingnessssss—

Suddenly everything Jackson had swallowed in the last hundred years all tried to come back up his throat at once.

Time teetered on the horizon of extinction like a child on the edge of a roof, loosing its balance, ready to fall.

Suzanne's empty stomach turned itself inside out.

Gongs rang.

Jackson wept in hysteria.

The universe smelled like orange juice and ammonia—fresh orange juice, hot ammonia.

Then it exploded.

Chapter Eight

Lights. Satan. Oranges. Nausea. Time machines. Nothing made sense to Jackson. Ammonia. Nausea. Suzanne. Rankin. The ambassador. Captain Slye. Pain. Shots. The woman with two guns. Running. Lights. Trains. Satan. Doors. Locks. Subway. Time machines. Suzanne, Halona, Chrys, Suzanne. Oranges and ammonia. Darkness. Lights. Ammonia and oranges. Nausea. Nausea. Nausea.

Images and objects tumbled through his mind as someone led him, carried him, dragged his leaden body down echoing halls through light and shadows into a dim sanctuary. There he let go and lost track of everything.

Suzanne made him as comfortable as she could on the daybed. After washing his face and hands, she filled a cup with cold water and began wiping his face. He felt feverish, and it was the only thing she could think of to do until he regained consciousness. Then, as soon as he was steady on his feet, she planned to put him on a train and ship him back to Springfield where he belonged. He was a nice man, and she liked him more than she thought she should, and she didn't want anything else to happen to him.

Jackson rose through a dark sea of images toward the light. He felt dizzy and angry and confused and afraid all at the same time, but no matter how hard he tried to hold on to some reality—any reality—each old reality twisted through new ones and slipped away from him in whirling currents of mist and confusion. Nothing would stay in focus. No thought would stay still.

The harder he swam through the dark sea, the colder and rougher it got until finally, finally, his head broke the surface and he opened his eyes. Suzanne wiped his face with the cold wet cloth until it felt like sandpaper.

"Okay," he said. "Okay. I'm all right now." He was a far cry from being all right, but he couldn't stand the cloth for another second. It distracted him from everything else, everything that seemed important, every memory that shifted through his mind like ghosts in the twilight. He wanted to remember, but he couldn't remember what he wanted to remember—or what he had to remember, or why, or if he had anything at all *to* remember.

"You look like warmed-over death."

The look of concern on her face gave him some small comfort. "I feel like warmed-over death—warmed-over leftover death—but at least I stopped throwing up."

"You stopped that quite a while ago."

He looked around. "Where are we?"

"My office restroom. It was the only safe place I could think to bring you."

"What do you mean, safe place? Am I in danger? I thought I was going back to interpret for the Persian ambassador . . ." His mind froze. The Persian ambassador was dead.

"You don't remember?" she asked.

Jackson shook his head, then nodded. Both movements made him dizzy. He closed his eyes, but that only made it worse, so he opened them again. "I do remember, I think, but then I don't. Did I really go back in time?"

"Yes."

"Then all that really happened? Was I really there when the ambassador was assassinated?" He let his spinning head sink deeper into the pillow and risked closing his eyes again. "Dear Buddha," he whispered, "it's so confusing, it's frightening."

Suzanne brushed his hair from his eyes. "You went back, Jackson. You left here about three hours ago, local time, and you and I just got back, thirty minutes ago—local time, again."

"But . . ." He opened his eyes and looked to her for some kind of reassurance. "But I spent the better part of a day back in 2183, didn't I?"

"It's part of the paradox. Don't you remember? You can stay for a long time in the past, but you can only come back inside a nine-point-six-hour window following when you left. So, however much time you spent back there is going to be compressed into your real-time memory of nine-point-six hours or less."

"That didn't make any sense before, and it makes less now." Jackson closed his eyes. He saw the ambassador's bloody body dancing in the air, heard the automatic weapons fire, felt the shower of debris. Quickly he opened his eyes again. "There's more to it than that, isn't there?"

Suzanne hesitated. "Yes, but it gets pretty technical, and I barely understand it myself—certainly not well enough to explain it to you."

Through all his confusion, Jackson sensed that she wasn't telling him the truth, that there was more that she could explain, but that she wouldn't. "You said something about being safe?"

"I said this was the safest place I could think to bring you until we can get you home."

"Why? I mean, what's the danger?" Then he remembered part of something else—a man by a door pointing at him through the heart of the confusion. "Captain Slye?"

"No, not exactly. It's just that my trip back for you wasn't exactly authorized, Jackson, so there was no sense in drawing any more attention to it than necessary."

"I don't understand."

"Don't worry about it."

"Don't do that." Jackson pushed himself up on his elbows. "Don't dismiss me like that. It's not fair."

"I'm sorry. You're right. It's not fair." She hesitated, resisting the urge to pull him into her arms. "But there's a lot about this world that isn't fair. When you get back to New Nineveh, you can reevaluate fairness there."

"Why are you sending me back to the library? Shouldn't I stay here for some kind of investigation, or something? I mean, do you *know* what happened back there?"

She nodded slowly. "Jackson, I know what you experienced, and you should understand that in some very real sense it actually did happen, and you were there. But in another real sense, it unhappened. It was fixed. Undone. According to Gunter's there was no assassination."

"But I was there. I saw it."

"Yes, but someone undid it."

"You mean . . ." Jackson shook his head. "You mean that someone else went back and arranged for the assassins not to be there or something, and for the ambassador to live? . . . Was I there for that, too? . . . No, I couldn't; I mean, unless I haven't gone back for the rerun yet." He took a deep breath and let out a long, hard sigh. "By the Sakyamuni, this is worse than confusing. This is impossible."

"You're a Buddhist, aren't you?"

"No," he said, "I'll never . . . Well, let's just say that I try to practice the teachings of Buddha and the masters who followed him, but that I am a poor student, at best."

"That's good enough, Jackson. My mother's a Buddhist, and she says that's all you can do. So that's all I'm asking you to do here. Accept what has happened and go on."

"I don't know if I can."

"Mother used to tell us a story about an old Zen monk who was accused of fathering a child. He said, 'Is that so?' When the child was given to him after its birth, he said, 'Is that so?' And when the mother of the child finally admitted that someone else was the father of her baby, and she and her parents went to claim the baby from the old monk and make apologies, he—"

"When they brought the baby to him, the old monk said, 'Is that so?' I know the story." The slightest of grins curled the corners of Jackson's mouth. "Is that what you think I should say?"

"I don't think either of us—any of us involved in Temporal Projects—is going to have much of a choice after a while. I think we're going to be faced with too many things where we have nothing else we can say."

He reached up and she took his hand. "You're worried, aren't you, about this whole project?"

She squeezed his hand, then laid it back on his chest.

"The more I learn, the more I have cause for concern. But that's not your problem. I'll get you back on the train to Springfield and you'll be out of the project and you won't have to worry about it anymore."

Jackson knew that wasn't true. He would worry about the project and what it meant—especially what it would mean to her. "I might, though—worry about it, I mean . . . and about you."

"Don't. You can't afford it, and neither can I."

The harshness with which she spoke surprised them both.

"Well, excuse me, lady."

"I didn't mean it like that."

"You most certainly did."

"All right, I did," she said, knowing that it would be better to cut off the growing affection she felt for him than to pay for it later. There was no room in her life for Jackson Dubchek. She could only hope that in Springfield, clear of Temporal Projects, he'd be safe. "I can't afford to care about you. Maybe I don't even want to. Is that clear enough?"

"Absolutely. When's the next train to Springfield?"

"They run on the hour, around the clock. As soon as you're steady on your feet, we'll get you on one."

"I'm steady right now."

"Let's see."

Jackson quickly discovered that he wasn't as steady as he wanted to be, but with the help of several cups of coffee, a hot shower, and more than a little grim determination, less than two hours later he was sitting beside Suzanne in her tiger-striped Singapore Sling on the way to the train station.

"Why did we use this fake badge with Security?" he asked.

"Just in case. This way, it will be a while before anyone here knows for sure that you came back from 2183 and left TP."

"What about the library? Will they take me back?" He had no intention of going back right away, but she didn't need to know that.

She never took her eyes off the road, unwilling to look at him for fear he would see how much she really did care. "I cleared your return with the library while you were in the shower. As far as they're concerned, you were on temporary loan to us, and now you're coming back full-time. They expect you at work the first of next week. I thought you might want a few days to yourself before . . ."

Jackson sighed. "Thanks." For a long time they rode in silence. Only when he saw the lights of the KC train station did he feel free to speak again. "Thank you, Suzanne. I mean it. For everything—especially for rescuing me. I don't think I'd have survived very long back there on my own."

"You're welcome."

"I wish we were richer, though."

She shot him a questioning look. "What?"

"So we both could afford a relationship that didn't end at the KC train station."

"No sense wishing for what we can't have."

"Right. Why don't you just drop me off out front? No need for you to see me to my train."

"I have to validate the ticket with TP's card," she said, driving up the ramp into the parking garage.

"You could have done that from your office."

"Then maybe I just want to be there to say goodbye. Can't you accept that?"

He could, but it messed up the plan that had been

forming in the back of his head. He had no intention of going back to Springfield. Not yet. There were some things he wanted to know about Temporal Projects and the Time Police and Captain Laszlo Slye, and the answers weren't in the New Nineveh Library in Springfield. They were in Kansas City with Lester Wu.

True to her word, she saw him not only to his train, but to his seat. Only as they stood there did she break the tension between them. On impulse, she gave him a hug and a quick kiss.

He returned her hug, and they stood there silently holding each other until the overhead announced departure.

"You're a nice man, Jackson Dubchek," she said as she pulled herself from his arms. "Stay that way."

"I'll try, Suzanne Brelmer. You stay as nice as you are, too."

"Right. And you stay in Springfield, you hear me?" She squeezed his hand then turned and quickly left the train. Moments later the doors slid shut and the train pulled out of the station. Suzanne watched it go with a mixture of relief and sadness before heading back through the station.

At least he's safe, she thought, and you can take credit for that. A trembling smile played on her lips as she walked toward her car, and she dared hope only that it was true, that he really would be safe back in Springfield, and that Temporal Projects and Laszlo Slye would exercise no more claim on him.

Jackson sat quietly for a long time after the train departed before forcing himself to plan his next step. When the train stopped at Butler, he got off, changed his ticket, and waited for the return train to Kansas City. Lester Wu had introduced him to Suzanne and encouraged him to join TP. Now, after all that had happened, Jackson felt Lester owed him some answers and explanations about what Temporal Projects' real aims and goals were, and Jackson intended to collect the answers in person.

Chapter Nine

Jackson caught the Westport local train at the loop interchange and chose to the walk the six blocks from the station to Lester's old apartment house. The early morning air invigorated him. Even though his jacket was a bit too thin for the coolness of the weather, he enjoyed the walk through Kansas City's most genteel of slums. When he reached the familiar brick-and-glass building, he rang the outside bell for Lester's apartment and waited.

A woman's sleepy voice answered. "Who rings?" The view screen over the speaker stayed blank, but its camera, behind an iron grill, recorded him.

"Lois? This is Jackson Dubchek. I need to see Lester. He hasn't left yet, has he?"

"Lester who?"

"Lester Wu."

"Lester who?"

Alarm bells went off in Jackson's head. What kind of game was she playing? "Lester Wu. Isn't this Lois?"

"We beg your pardon, sir, but we know no Lester Wu at this address. What apartment number did you mean to ring?"

"Seventeen." He knew the number by heart. He had been there a tenset of times before. "Come on, Lois. Release the door."

"Unfortunately, young man, I must inform you that there is no one by the name of Lester Wu living in apartment seventeen—nor in any other apartment in this building, as far as we know. Furthermore, you have not had the pleasure of speaking to Lois. We are quite sorry. Good day."

Jackson knew that the woman had cut off the intercom, but he stood there staring at it as though somehow expecting Lester to come on and tell him it was all a joke. It took him a full minute to realize that it was no joke. Almost in a panic, he turned to the directory next to the call board. It held no listing for Lester Wu.

Was he in the wrong building? Surely not.

Quickly, he stepped outside and looked. The address was correct. It was the right building.

"May I help you, sir?" a uniformed Oriental woman asked as she climbed the outside steps toward him. She wore a large black pistol and carried a stun stick menacingly in her hands. Her tone was polite, but suspicious.

"I'm looking for Lester Wu," Jackson said.

"Wu . . . Wu . . . No one here by that name, sir. Are you sure you have the correct address?"

"Uh, of course. He lived here last week. I visited him."

The woman frowned. "I've been working this door for near on three years, sir, and although the name is slightly familiar, to the best of my knowledge, no one named Wu has lived here during that time." She tapped her stun stick against her leg as she moved between him and the door. "You probably have the wrong building.

Lots of these old Westport buildings look alike, you know.''

"Well, uh, I guess so.'' Jackson walked sideways down the steps, looking up at the address, at the building, knowing that he hadn't made a mistake.

"Have a good one, sir,'' the door guard said. "Hope you find the right building.''

"Thanks.'' As he turned to walk up the street, Jackson almost stepped into a wild-eyed man wearing a black overcoat and an orange stocking cap, from under which hung greasy locks of yellow hair.

"You know 'im, don't you?'' the wild-eyed man demanded.

"Excuse me.'' Jackson attempted to step around the man. He was too confused about what had just happened to concern himself with a derelict.

The man grabbed Jackson's jacket. "You know Wu, and you know where 'e is and where they've got my wife.''

"Let me go!'' Jerking himself free of the man's grasp as fear and panic surged through him, Jackson looked for the door guard. She was gone.

Again the man grabbed his jacket. "You have to tell me where she is,'' he said. Despite the wild tone of his voice, his eyes were clear and lucid. "Where they've got Rosita. I've been going crazy without 'er, and Wu was my last lead.'' Sudden tears streaked down the man's dirty face, but his grip tightened. "You 'ave to help me, dammit.''

"You're crazy. Leave me alone. Let go of me.'' Jackson tried to pry the man's hand off his jacket. "Let go! I don't know what you're—''

"I'm not crazy, and you know it. You 'ave to help

me. You've been there, and I know it. You 'ave that same look in your eye as Lester Wu and my Rosita 'ad."

As he struggled to break free, Jackson backed up the sidewalk, pulling the man with him.

"You've been there—at Temporal Projects. They did things to you like they did to Rosita, and now she's gone, and Wu's gone, and you're the only 'ope I've got, mister." The man snuffled and cried and held to Jackson with both hands.

"Dear Buddha, leave me alone!" Jackson shouted, pounding now on the man's arms. "You're crazy!"

The man wiped his eyes and gazed at Jackson almost gently. "I'm not crazy, mister. I'm not. I'm really not. My name's Homer Alvarez, and I'm just trying to find my wife, Rosita. Those animals from Temporal Projects, they won't tell me what they've done with her, but they can't stop me. I'll stop them, and I'll find Rosita, believe me. So, you've got to help me. You just have to!"

Without warning Homer Alvarez let go. He held his face in his hands as huge sobs wracked his body.

Jackson backed away, ready to turn and run, but something stopped him. Under the man's babble ran a current of truth and sanity that held Jackson where he stood. "Why would they want to do anything to your wife?"

"She knew too much," the man sobbed.

"What did she know? What did your wife have to do with Temporal Projects?" Hundreds of other shapeless questions swirled through Jackson's head.

Alvarez blew his nose on a wadded handkerchief. "She was the director until six months ago. Then she disappeared. And everybody acted like they'd never 'eard of 'er."

"Colonel Brelmer's the director. Has been for a long time."

"Don't you believe it. Wu knew. He worked with her. Now he's gone." Alvarez cocked his head and stared past Jackson before stepping toward him.

Jackson stepped back. "You just keep your distance."

"Police. Walk with me," Alvarez said. Urgency and anger filled his words. Fear colored their tone. "Maybe they won't notice us."

More afraid of police than Homer Alvarez, Jackson turned up the sidewalk with him as two police cars slid down the street with their turbos in descending whines. One pulled to the curb behind Jackson and Homer. The other pulled to the curb in front of them.

"Stand, citizens," an amplified voice commanded.

"Run," Alvarez said.

Jackson stopped and held Alvarez's arm. "No. Stay calm." His own heart pounded insanely in his chest.

Three helmeted police officers climbed out of the cars, two men and a woman. A glance back at Lester Wu's old apartment building revealed the door guard standing arms crossed at the top of the steps, grinning.

"I've run the old one off three times in the last week," she called to the police. "Now he's got the young one asking his questions for him."

"Identification, please," the tallest of the two male officers said. His eyes were shielded by the visor of his helmet.

Alvarez handed his to the officers, then sat down suddenly on the sidewalk, looking totally defeated. All his previous fire had died.

The female officer took Jackson's ID and led him

by the elbow up the sidewalk. "You stay right here and don't talk to anyone. Understand?"

"Yes, ma'am." Jackson thought of the police back in New York in 2183 and wondered if they would have been so gentle if they had caught him. He stood patiently, watching Alvarez cry, feeling sorry for the man, but more concerned with his own safety. Two of the police officers conferred over their computer while the third kept watch over Alvarez.

It occurred to Jackson that he might be able to run if he wanted to, but how far? Not very far—he was sure of that. And where would he run to? He had nowhere—not there in Kansas City.

What would he do if they arrested him? Who would he call for help? Suzanne? That would put him back in the hands of the Time Police, which would only make things worse. For the thousandth time he wished he understood what was happening to him. Back in 2183, Rankin had failed to tell Jackson *why* he had been displaced, and Jackson still didn't know why TP would want . . . What did he know, anyway? Nothing that could hurt TP, did he? Lester might have known something, and Rosita Alvarez, if she really was a director, but Jackson was sure *he* didn't.

The female officer emerged from the police car and walked over to Jackson. "You are Citizen Jackson Elgin Dubchek?"

"I am."

"Would you tell me what you were doing here this time of day, Citizen Dubchek? And look right here when you speak, please."

He stared directly at the camera lens built into her helmet. "I, uh, I was looking for a friend of mine I, uh, thought lived here." He pointed toward the building. "She said I was wrong, that my friend didn't live there and I—"

"What is your friend's name?"

"Lester Wu."

"Spell it."

Jackson spelled it slowly, forcing himself to keep his eyes focused on the camera lens.

"So what did you do after you found out you were in the wrong place?"

Over her shoulder Jackson could see the other two officers questioning Alvarez and shaking their heads. Cold sweat ran down Jackson's spine.

"Well?"

"Uh, I, well, uh, I started to leave, and that man stopped me and started talking crazy about his wife. Then you came."

The officer frowned and her right hand came to rest on the butt of her stun stick. "Tell me exactly what he said."

"Uh, I don't know," Jackson lied. "It was all crazy— at least it sounded crazy to me. He thought I knew where his wife was, or something, and thought I could help him. I was too busy trying to get away from him to pay close attention."

The woman shook her head. "What are you doing in Kansas City, citizen?"

"I was here on business," he said. "I was going to stop by and see my friend—Mr. Wu—before going back to Springfield, today."

"The computer says you're on extended leave from the New Nineveh Library in Springfield. Is that correct?"

Jackson saw one of the other officers put forearm cuffs on Alvarez and felt sorry for the poor man. "Yes, uh, yes—well, not exactly. I have to be back there next week.''

"It says extended leave.''

"My leave's over next week.''

They helped Alvarez into one of the police cars. "Corliss,'' one of them called.

"Wait here, Citizen Dubchek.''

"Yes, ma'am.'' He stood as still as he could, hands in his pockets, trying to look as innocent as he could, but every few seconds his eyes focused on the police car and Homer Alvarez's hunched form in the prisoner's seat. All of Alvarez's accusations flooded through his mind, all linked with Lester—the missing Lester—his friend who had . . . disappeared . . .

Or been displaced, he thought. Not only was he gone, someone else was living in his apartment and the door guard didn't remember him—almost as though he had never lived there at all. Was that what had happened to Alvarez's wife? Could the Time Police really have displaced them both? Why not? They had displaced Jackson—for no apparent reason at all.

"Citizen Dubchek, we cannot reach the New Nineveh Library to confirm your story. We have instructions to take you to the station so you can catch a train back to Springfield.''

He stared at her as though not comprehending. "Well, that's okay, I guess, but I really don't need you to.'' The first police car pulled away from the curb with Alvarez still hunched down in the back seat. "It's a nice morning. I haven't had breakfast yet. I think I'll just walk.''

"We have instructions, citizen. Since we have no

records on you here, we are sending you home . . . for your own protection.''

Jackson knew better than to resist. Everything in her tone said it would be foolish to do so. He wasn't surprised when she opened the door to the prisoner's seat for him. ''But . . .''

''Sorry about that, citizen, but rules don't allow you to ride anywhere else.''

The prisoner's seat had a peculiar, antiseptic smell, and by the time the officer's partner started the car, Jackson was sure the smell was going to burn the membranes out of his nose. By the time the car pulled into traffic on skyline beltway, he felt dizzy and faint. But when he tapped on the plex dividing his seat from theirs, they ignored him. Then he keeled over in the seat and it didn't matter what it smelled like.

Chapter Ten

Suzanne shut down her reports file and stared at the computer terminal, feeling all the while as though someone were staring over her shoulder.

No one was, of course. She was alone. Her office was locked. The security screens were all up. But ever since she had returned from taking Jackson to the station, she had felt as though she were being followed and watched. On top of that, she needed to talk to someone about what was happening at Temporal Projects, but she had no one at the moment in whom she could confide.

Her natural choice would have been to talk to her father, but he was in Moscow. Even if he had been there, she wasn't sure she was ready to burden him with her concerns. However, there was no one else she trusted and who had all the security clearances necessary to listen to her questions.

"On your own, Suz," she said aloud. "Might as well get your brain in gear and see if you can't figure out what's really going on around here . . . Or . . . you could talk to Paress." She smiled. "Yes, you could talk to Paress."

The thought of taking Paress into her confidence

cheered Suzanne considerably. Crazy Paress, some people called her, but that didn't bother Suzanne. She liked Paress, and although Paress wasn't cleared for all the classified information Suzanne had, Paress, at least, had sufficient knowledge about Temporal Projects because of her costumer's duties to know what Suzanne was talking about. Paress also had a keen eye for human behavior and a way about her that told Suzanne she was sharper than most people gave her credit for.

Without further hesitation, Suzanne went looking for Paress Linnet. She found her, as usual, in the costume shop sitting behind one of the computer-assisted industrial sewing machines.

"Well, Ms. Brelmer, what brings you here? Another trip?" Paress asked, her long face folding into the permanent creasescaused by fifty years of constant smiling.

"You alone, Paress?"

"Quite alone. The crew worked very late last night and just went home a few hours ago, but I wanted to get this project laid out before I left."

Suzanne looked around. "Can you come to my office for half an hour or so? I have something I need to discuss with you, but it has to be in a secure area."

"About what, Ms. Brelmer?"

"About Temporal and what's been happening around here lately, Paress. Haven't you noticed some unusual things?"

Paress's smile disappeared. "Maybe."

"I thought you might have." Suzanne sighed. "Please, Paress, won't you come to my office? I have a hundred questions I can't answer, and I need your advice and good sense."

"Did Captain Slye tell you to question me?"

Suzanne shuddered. "No. Absolutely not."

"All right. We can use my cubby. It's secured, though prob'ly not as fancy as yours."

"That's fine. Yours then." Suzanne followed Paress past the sewing and gluing machines through a maze of racks, bins, and shelves, flanked by banks of drawers and closets into a neat four-meter-square room whose walls were laden with shelves of old-fashioned books and holo-tanks. The center of the room was dominated by a one-by two-meter worktable. Paress went through the security sequences—flipping switches and adjusting pots—until her board showed a steady row of green lights.

"Your board's more complex than mine, Paress," Suzanne said, her voice betraying her surprise as she sat in one of the straight-backed chairs at the worktable.

Paress sat in the chair opposite Suzanne and shrugged. "I wouldn't know about that, Ms. Brelmer. I don't get to see much outside the shop."

The sight of Paress leaning on the table all smiles and curiosity left Suzanne at a sudden loss as to where to start her probing. "Uh, Paress, you've been with the project since it started, haven't you?"

"Yes, ma'am, since Dr. Alvarez hired me away from the Missouri Theater, oh, seven years ago it's been now—or is it eight?"

"Who was Dr. Alvarez?" The name meant nothing to Suzanne.

Paress's smiling creases turned to frowns. She leaned back and crossed her arms over her full breasts. "Why do you want to know this, Ms. Brelmer—and what do you want from me?"

After a moment's hesitation, Suzanne said, "I wanted to talk to you because I've had this feeling for a while now that things—events—are happening that shouldn't be happening, and that Temporal is somehow responsible. And other than my father, you were the only person I felt I could talk to . . . Who was this Alvarez? Was he the first head of personnel?''

"*She*—Dr. Rosita Alvarez—she was the first director, Ms. Brelmer. But you weren't here yet, of course. That was before they, well, before she was, uh, you know . . .''

"No, Paress, I don't know. Before she was what? What happened to Dr. Alvarez?''

Paress waited a long time before meeting Suzanne's eyes with her own steady gaze. "Same thing they tried to do to that nice Mr. Dubchek. They displaced her. Lost her. Ditched her someplace in time . . . At least that's what *I* think happened. I couldn't prove it, of course. Who could? It's like she never existed. Like she was never here at all. And now there aren't but one or two of us who really remember her.''

The warm air in the room made Suzanne loosen her collar. "Who else remembers her?''

"Oh, nobody important.'' Paress shook her head sadly. "A couple of the maintenance people used to play lectrogolf with her husband, but he went crazy after she disappeared, and me, of course, and Janet, my assistant, because Dr. Alvarez really liked her, and who knows, maybe some others too.''

"What happened then? I mean after she disappeared?''

"That's when Dr. Minor took over, and suddenly everybody forgot Dr. Alvarez, like she never existed. Then the senator's barrel mates kicked Dr. Minor out, and that's when your father took over.'' She said it all simply, as though anyone with a clear eye and mind would have understood it.

Suzanne shook her head, feeling suddenly overcome by the intensity of Paress's information. "Why haven't you told the administration about this—or have you?"

"I did. I tried, at first, but then I gave up. I could tell that either people thought I was crazy, or else they knew I wasn't crazy, but didn't want to hear about it."

"Why are you telling me?"

A smile softened her face for a brief moment. "Because I know I'm not crazy. Because I think you're willing to listen. Because I think you want to know the truth. Because there are some things I want to know, too. Because in the end I've got nothing to lose if you don't believe me. I'm just that crazy old Paress Linnet, costumer to the wandering travelers. She knows her costumes, but she's as nosynco as they come."

Under other circumstances, Suzanne might have laughed, but there was a look in Paress's eyes that denied the humor in her smile. "Do you know what they tried to do to Jackson—Mr. Dubchek?" Suzanne asked.

"I know. It was Captain Slye's doing, no doubt."

"Who else, Paress? I mean, who else has gone into the past and not come back?"

"That, I don't know, Ms. Brelmer." Anger and frustration tinged her voice. "I'm not privy to departures and returns, normally—just clothes and time periods—and sizes. Everybody's a different size. Sometimes clothes are returned to me and sometimes they're not. Your records should tell you something about people who were here and then disappeared."

Suzanne shook her head. "Classified. I can't talk to you about my records, only about—"

"Oh? You can query me, but you can't tell me anything, is that it? Hell of a deal."

"It's a matter of clearances and security, Paress. You know that. You don't have the necessary clearances or a need to know, so I can't tell you even if I want to."

Paress stood, arms crossed, brow furrowed. "I have to leave now, Ms. Brelmer. I'm on my own time."

Suzanne stood also, with a feeling of losing her grip on something important. "Paress, I'm sorry. You know I can't—"

"Sorry won't patch the pothole, miz."

"What do you want from me?" Suzanne asked, knowing in some intuitive way that she needed Paress as an ally and a friend. "I'll tell you whatever I can."

Paress put both hands flat on the polished surface of the worktable and leaned forward. "All right. Here's a question for you and your records. What happened to Lester Wu? He's gone. Has been for almost a month. I costumed him for Russia, 2102, and haven't seen him since. I don't think he came back."

"That's impossible. I just saw him not . . . not . . ." Suddenly she couldn't remember how long it had been.

"Are you sure, Ms. Brelmer? When? Where?" Paress straightened up and folded her arms again. "Give me a date, an exact date. When did you last see Lester Wu?"

Suzanne closed her eyes and tried to concentrate, but every thought surrounding Lester seemed to have blurred at the edges. "I can't. I don't remember exactly when I saw him last."

"Right." Paress pointed at her. "And tomorrow the date will be vaguer, and the day after that vaguer, and eventually you won't be sure there ever was a Lester Wu, and if you go looking for him, people will stare at you like you're crazy, and eventually you'll quit thinking about him altogether unless you force yourself to remember him.''

"You said you costumed him for Russia, 2102? That's the year of the republican revolution, isn't it?''

"Yes. Red hammer and sickle on a blue star on a red field.''

"And he never came back?''

"I didn't say that. I don't know if he came back or not. But I didn't get the costume back and I never saw him again.'' Her face softened. "I liked him, Ms. Brelmer. I really did. I liked Rosita Alvarez too, and Rishary Owens. And they're all gone.''

"Rishary Owens? Who was she?''

Paress shook her head and a sudden tear ran down one cheek. "Rishary was the first one I know of who disappeared. She used to have your job—or one like it. It's hard to remember her.''

"I'll find out, Paress. Or I'll do my best to try, anyway,'' Suzanne said. "I'll dig into the memory banks for as long as it takes until I find out what happened to all of them—Rishary, Dr. Alvarez, Lester Wu, and the infinite only knows who else.''

"You'll have to be careful.''

"Of course.''

Paress's security board flickered to red as she unlocked the system. "If I can help, you tell me.''

"I will.'' On impulse Suzanne gave Paress a quick hug that Paress returned. "If you'll lead me out of here, I'll get to work right away.''

When she returned to her office Suzanne was surprised to see the message light blinking on her private line. Deciding it could wait, she immediately secured her office and her terminal, then keyed in Rosita Alvarez's name for a general query. To her great surprise, a dossier came up immediately.

    ALVAREZ, ROSITA LUCIA ALEXIS, Suspected Felon, Classified Data Level VIII-K. Enter Clearance Code.

    As she entered her code, her private line chimed. Thinking it would be a call from her family, she turned the receiver on.

    "Suzanne? It's me, Jackson," his face said from the corner of her terminal screen.

    "Did you get home safely?" she asked.

    Suspected of felonious activities with Mnemosyne Historians and other anarchist groups, the screen read.

    "I'm not home. I'm here, in Kansas City. I came back looking for Lester Wu, but he's missing."

    Suspected of attempts to alter history.

    "Where are you?" she asked, thinking she should be angry with him, but realizing she was not.

    "At the train station. The police left me here."

    "The police?"

    Suspected of further illegal activities under classification XI-Relocation. Enter classification code.

    "Yes, the police. Where's Lester Wu?"

    She shook her head. "I'm not sure. Can you meet me here in an hour?" Again she entered her code.

    "Why?"

    Relocation Program. Need to know, only. Enter secondary clearance code and name of traffic.

    "Because I need your help, Jackson." Traffic? she thought. Wasn't that what Jackson said they had referred to him as back in 2183? "Just come here. Security will let you in.'' She entered her secondary code, then on a hunch, *Wu, Lester.*

''That seems stupid after all the work you went through to get me out of there.''

WU, LESTER, 2102, X-ref, Russia, Brezhnevgrad, traffic relocated successfully. Further data deleted.

''Do you want to find Lester? Get here as fast as you can. Or leave me alone. I'm too busy to cope with you now.''

''All right. I'm on my way.''

ALVAREZ, ROSITA LUCIA ALEXIS, 1964, X-ref, Cambodia, Kampuchea, 1968, X-ref, Czechoslovakia, Prague, 1968, X-ref, Wheeling, W.V. Relocation probable. Further data deleted.

Chapter Eleven

"She did what? When? Where? Brezhnevgrad?" Brelmer cursed softly under his breath and was relieved that the UltraSecure communications line in Senator Voxner's Moscow home was in a room separate from the office where he and the senator had been discussing future Temporal Projects for the past day and a half. He would need some time to compose himself before facing Senator Voxner with the news.

"Yes, sir, Brezhnevgrad," Sergeant Garrison said, her face wavering on the screen. "That much and the date we've confirmed."

Brezhnevgrad? Brezhnevgrad? Why was that important? Brelmer couldn't be sure, but he knew there was a connection with Brezhnevgrad that he should remember.

"Very well," he said to the technician in Kansas City, "I understand. Captain DeVere can stand vigil, but have Captain Slye contact me as soon as you locate him, and I will instruct him for command of the situation." He pressed his right thumb against the screen so that his print could be verified and his orders certified. "Yes, thank you, Sergeant Garrison. I'll remember this."

For a long moment after the communications console went blank he sat staring into its depths, a terrible ache building inside him. Brezhnevgrad?

Why? Why had Suzanne gotten involved? It was bad enough that she had gone back to 2183 on her own to get that interpreter, Dubchek. But now to have sent him to 2102? Why? What earthly motive could she possibly have for breaking regulations, for endangering him and everyone else connected with Temporal Projects? And why Brezhnevgrad?

Sending Dubchek to 2102 made no sense—period—Brezhnevgrad or not. Yet Brelmer knew there had to be a logical explanation for her actions. There just had to be. With a long, low sigh, he stood, straightened his back and his uniform, and returned to the senator's office.

"Disturbing news, Friz?" the senator asked.

Brelmer knew there was no sense in trying to hide anything from Senator Voxner. The senator had eyes and spies of his own, as he had already proven, and trying to hide something from him would be the height of foolishness. "Yes, sir—at least news that could be disturbing if there is no good explanation for it," Brelmer said as he sat opposite the senator across the leather-topped desk.

Voxner frowned. "Explain."

"It's my daughter, sir, Suzanne. She has apparently sent Jackson Dubchek back to Brezhnevgrad in 2102, for reasons that are a mystery to me at the moment."

The senator's frown deepened. "That is not the kind of news I like to get from my director of Temporal Projects. What was her explanation for this unauthorized action?"

"We don't know, Senator. She has apparently secured the secondary transmission and receiving room, and we won't know anything until she emerges."

"Which will be when?"

"Within the next nine hours, sir. At least that's what we have to assume. It's the normal time frame."

"And I may assume that you will be going straight back to Kansas City on the next government flight, Praetor Centurion Brelmer?"

It was a command, not a question—a command made odious by Voxner's use of Praetor Centurion as a singular title without referring to Brelmer's rank. Brelmer knew he had to do his best to quiet the senator's concerns as best he could before returning to North America.

"Senator, I understand your anger, but let me assure you that it is no greater than mine. All I can say is that if my daughter felt it necessary to make an unauthorized foray into the past, she must have had an excellent reason for—"

"A second unauthorized foray, Centurion."

"Yes, sir, but she did not make this foray. She sent the interpreter, Dubchek."

One eyebrow cocked. "Is that somehow an ameliorating factor so far as you are concerned?"

"Only in that I have to believe that she chose to send an interpreter into a situation in Brezhnevgrad 2102 that required his presence—someone with his expertise—and that as soon as they both emerge, we will have a reasonable explanation for her actions." He was thinking aloud, and he knew it sounded lame.

"Dammit, Friz! Do not try to make excuses for her solely because she is your daughter. I will not stand for such nonprofessional behavior on your part or anyone else's. You should know that by now. There can be absolutely no excuse for your daughter's actions, and regardless of her explanations, she will have to be disciplined. Do I make myself clear?''

Brelmer's stomach twitched in an internal wince. ''Certainly, sir, but may I at least suggest—''

Senator Voxner held up his hand, and a long pause built between them like a thickening wall. ''What are your feelings about Kampuchea, Friz?''

''I beg your pardon, sir?''

''Kampuchea, nineteen sixty-something. Is that not where our beloved Dr. Rosita Alvarez resides?''

Suddenly Brelmer knew exactly what the senator was thinking and resented the implications—and feared them for Suzanne's sake. ''Nineteen sixty-four, sir. Dr. Alvarez was supposed to be displaced in 1964—it was called Cambodia then.'' Had the senator forgotten what really happened? Or was he playing some game Brelmer hadn't figured out?

''However, sir, we don't know that Dr. Alvarez actually ended up in Cambodia. According to the data crystals, there is some possibility that she was deposited in Prague in 1968.''

Without warning the senator laughed. ''Ah, yes, I had forgotten. The 1968 loop.''

''Nineteen sixty-eight and sixty-nine, in all accuracy, sir.''

''And Wheeling, West Virginia?''

''Yes, sir. Seventy-three percent of errant loops dump our teams in Wheeling.'' Brelmer hoped the senator's laughter was a good sign, not a bad one. ''Fourteen percent have looped to Prague. The others seem quite random.''

The senator's laughter and smiles stopped. "And you still have the loop? Your people have failed to find the cause, and consequently, you have failed to correct it?"

The accusation was all too clear to Brelmer. Senator Voxner held him personally responsible—even for phenomena fully beyond Brelmer's control. "Unfortunately, yes, the loop still gives us problems. The techs review every data crystal for every errant trip looking for the cause, but hardware or software, we still haven't found the cause or the solution." He heard the defiance in his voice and hoped the senator did, also. Brelmer wasn't about to apologize for something that wasn't his fault.

"So, Friz, what is your emotional relationship with Wheeling, West Virginia, 1968?"

"As a destination, sir?" Brelmer felt his back automatically straighten and felt anger and resentment burn in his cheeks. With practiced restraint, he forced himself to breathe more slowly and deeply. "I think not, sir."

Again the senator's eyebrow cocked. "You think not? Pray tell, what do you mean, Praetor Centurion Brelmer? If I should decide that you need to go to 1968, you will most assuredly end up in 1968."

Again Brelmer straightened. "I should think you would be better off eliminating me, sir, than by displacing me. I know too much."

This time the senator's smile was cynical. "Yes, but who would believe you in 1968?"

"No one need believe me, sir. I need only know what to do and whom to do it to in order to make your future a less pleasant place than it is now."

The senator waited a long moment before responding. "Are you threatening me, Centurion?" He looked cruelly amused.

"Most certainly not, sir. I'm merely suggesting that if you find it necessary to remove me from my position, you might want to give serious consideration to a more conventional means of doing so than displacement."

"That sounds like a threat to me, Centurion, and I must remind you immediately that I do not take kindly to threats."

"No threat intended, Senator."

"Perhaps." Voxner rubbed his pointed chin. "However, since I find it difficult to accept that there is not at least some implied threat in your position, let me remind you also that you serve solely at my pleasure. You do what I want done, when I want it done, how I want it done, and you do it without questions or opinions if I so choose. You do whatever I tell you to do, regardless of personal feelings, or so-called philosophical concerns about the fabric of time and history. Does that help you reestablish an understanding of our relationship?"

Brelmer kept his eyes riveted on the senator's. "Most assuredly, sir. There can be no other interpretation of our relationship, and I would be the last person to—"

The communications buzzer interrupted him. The senator listened for a moment on his earphone, then said, "It is your Captain Slye requesting instructions. We will talk to him in the Secure Room."

Together they went to the Secure room, and in no uncertain terms Brelmer instructed Slye to go to Brezhnevgrad and bring Dubchek back alive. The senator observed without comment until Brelmer was about to break communications.

"Captain," the senator said, "I want there to be no mistakes on this operation. You are to locate Mr. Dubchek, and bring him back—without harm if possible, but alive in any case."

"I will do my best, Senator. There is always the Clio factor involved here, however."

"Exactly what does that mean, Captain?"

Slye looked surprised. "Well, sir, perhaps Colonel Brelmer should explain. I thought you knew."

Only then did Brelmer make the connection that had eluded him before. "Wu," he said simply.

"Correct, sir."

"Understood, Captain. I will explain to Senator Voxner."

"You most certainly will," the senator said softly.

As soon as he closed the communications line, Brelmer said, "I knew there was a reason Brezhnevgrad was important, sir, but, well, I'm sure you remember the problem we had with the historian Lester Wu concerning Project Clio and the alteration of Texas history. He was displaced in Brezhnevgrad in 2102."

"Why?" the senator snapped.

Brelmer hesitated only for a second. "Because you suggested it, Senator. You said you thought it would be amusing to—"

"And you actually did that? Because of what I said? That is not a very professional approach, Friz."

"No, sir. Of course not." Despite the frown he saw on the senator's face, Brelmer was sure the tension had broken between them.

"What problem will Wu's presence cause?"

"It shouldn't cause any, sir. Assuming that he is still in Brezhnevgrad, he is probably in the hands of the authorities on one side of the civil war or the other."

"Yes, well, it would be nice to know that Wu will not be causing us further concern. When will you be leaving, Friz?"

"On the next sonic out, sir."

"Excellent." The senator stared unfocused over Brelmer's shoulder. "You will keep me informed in real time, of course."

"Of course, sir."

"I shall be returning to Kansas City in two or three days' time, and we will meet again then."

"Yes, sir. Goodbye, sir," Brelmer said, backing toward the door.

"Yes, Friz . . . goodbye for now . . . Oh, and Friz"—his eyes snapped into focus—"you will remember our discussion earlier, I am sure . . . the one about Cambodia and Wheeling."

"Most certainly, sir."

"Good. I would not want you to forget."

There was no mistaking the tone of Senator Voxner's voice, and Brelmer understood that he had been foolish to think that the tension between them had broken. Giving the senator a sharp salute, he turned and left the room.

Two hours later he was buckled into his seat as the sonic roared over Europe at mach four, when the intercom in his headset buzzed.

"A message just came in for you, Colonel," a metallic voice said in his ear. "It reads, 'No one home at 2102 Brezhnev Platz.' That's all it says, sir."

Brelmer sighed in frustration. What was that supposed to mean? Had Slye failed to find Dubchek? Was Suzanne no longer in the secondary? The sigh was replaced by a low growl. He was ready to reach home and find out what in Gautama's name was going on at TP.

Chapter Twelve

Jackson's stomach grumbled and rolled over several times—empty, but still unhappy. Time travel could starve a man to death. His head ached. His eyes refused to hold focus on anything for more than a second. He finished wiping his face and stared somewhat sickly out the window of his time machine.

A jolt of panic propelled him up in the seat. Time machines! As far as he could see . . . time machines!

Hundreds of them, stacked on top of each other, five or six high, in long rows like terraces down the hill that stretched away in rusty . . . no, they weren't time machines. They were . . . he knew what they were . . . he'd seen them in holos . . . antique automobiles—huge cars, larger, even, than police cars. His time machine sat smack in the middle of some kind of storage area for damaged antique cars.

Relieved that they weren't time machines, Jackson was surprised that so many antiques had been stored in Brezhnevgrad in 2102. Somehow that didn't seem to fit with what he knew about Russian history. Hadn't Russia switched almost totally to two-seat electrics early in the twenty-first century? Or was that the United States that had switched? No, Canada, maybe, or Mexico, but not the United States. They were last to switch over, but who was first? Jackson couldn't remember.

The sun broke through light clouds overhead and fell full upon the mountains and down into the river valley below him.

Mountains? There were no mountains like those around Brezhnevgrad, no deep river valley, no steepled church that looked like a picture out of the North American past . . . and probably no mountainside covered with antique automobiles.

Jackson shivered. He didn't know where he was, but he was certain he wasn't in Brezhnevgrad, and he felt fairly safe in assuming he wasn't even in Russia. Then he giggled. Not only didn't he know *where* he was, he didn't know *when* he was, either. The time readout on the instrument panel of his machine flickered and showed, 17 June 2102. Again it flickered.

03 December 2108
04 April 2036
16 January 1855
20 February 1910
15 October 2077
16 May 1969

16 August 1969. 16 August 1969. *16 August 1969*. Finally the readout stopped flickering. 16 August 1969.

Jackson slowly shook his head in disbelief. Nineteen sixty-nine? How in Buddha's ancient name had he ended up in 1969? And if he was in 1969, *where* was he? Something told him he wasn't in Russia. But where? Where was he?

It didn't matter. All he had to do was roll out the Portable Ovshinsky Energy System the way Suzanne had shown him. Its solar cells would recharge the batteries, and in six hours or less he could go back to Kansas City, 2249. That was all that mattered.

And when he got there, he would tell Suzanne she could take the next trip, because suddenly the idea of finding Lester was less interesting than avoiding any and all further time travel.

As soon as he thought that, Jackson felt guilty. The Time Police had apparently dumped Lester in Brezhnevgrad in 2102, left him there to die, just as they had displaced Jackson in 2183. Now, for the want of a little courage, Jackson was willing to abandon his friend to an undeserved fate. Well, he would face the problem of Lester once he got back to 2249 . . . if he got back.

"That's no way to think," he muttered as he climbed out of the time machine.

It teetered.

Jackson looked down and saw that the time machine rested atop one of the stacks of antique automobiles—rested very unsteadily. How was he going to get the POES rolled out? And what if some of the local people saw him? What would he do then?

Suddenly the enormity of his problems hit him and he lost his balance. Jackson grabbed the door. The time machine rocked while he clung to it for all he was worth. It slid forward. Fear tightened his grip. There he was lost somewhere in the world on 16 August 1969, on a mountain used to store damaged automobiles, with a time machine that threatened to fall and damage itself, thus stranding him forever. "What the hell am I going—"

A noise interrupted him. Far down the hillside two men were walking up a lane between the stacks of automobiles in his direction. One pointed directly up at him.

Jackson froze. Then he remembered what Suzanne had told him, that if the POES was deployed, no one but the imprinted users would be able to gain access to the time machine. The POES latch was less than half a meter from his hand. He grabbed it like a drowning man grabbing a branch and yanked.

The POES popped open and rolled out to cover the entire time machine. The machine tottered. Jackson lost his grip and fell. He hit the ground flat on his back. A growl of pain rattled from his throat.

As he opened his eyes he saw the door to the time machine overhead swing slowly closed. For a second he panicked. Then he realized that all he had to do was climb back up the stack and into the time machine and he would be safe.

Except he couldn't move. He tried, but he couldn't move anything but his fingers and toes. That was a good sign, wasn't it, that he could move his extremities? He thought it was. He prayed it was. Pushing against the burning pain in his back and shoulders, he managed to roll himself over onto his stomach.

The pain ate its way down his back like acid eating through a metal plate. Even though every fiber in him wanted to scream, he somehow had the presence of mind to muffle his curses. In the near distance he heard voices approaching.

Forcing himself up on one knee, he knew he couldn't stand, and if he couldn't stand, he couldn't climb up into the machine. He would have to hide. What other choice was there? But where? Where could he hide? The voices grew louder.

From his hands and knees he could see, six meters in front of him, a vehicle that looked like some kind of dark blue van on its side. There was nothing stacked on top of it, and one of its back doors was open. The approaching voices spoke some dialect of English.

Jackson needed no more encouragement. As quickly and carefully as his pain-wracked body would let him, he crawled over to the blue van. After he dragged himself inside, he pulled the door closed. It squealed and screamed in protest, but it closed.

"Tol' you there's someone up chere."

Through a crack between the doors, Jackson could see very little, but he could hear all too well.

"Well, if hit's them Jurdy boys, I'd uz soon shoot 'em uz near anythin'. They been tol' to stay out of chere."

Twentieth century Scotch-Irish-Appalachian. Jackson felt sure he recognized the dialect from recordings he had studied at New Nineveh. Now at least he knew he was in North America.

"Prah'bly them hippies alookin' for to steal parts."

"M'be, and m'be not. Never caught none of them in chere, but I'z caught the Jurdy boys afore. Le's look down seben an' eight."

To Jackson's surprise, the voices moved away until they faded from hearing. More to his surprise, he yawned and his eyelids drooped. He was afraid to give in to sleep, but he didn't have the energy to resist, and for the time being he had nowhere else to go and nothing to do. He was as safe as he was going to get until he climbed back up into the time machine, and he wasn't ready to risk that, yet. Moments later, with his head resting on his arms, his eyelids closed and his mind drifted.

SCRANNNNNK!

Jackson jerked away from sleep fighting to flee from the darkness of his fear. Every muscle in his back screamed in pain as his eyes popped open. An old man stood in the sunlight at the open door with what looked like a double-barreled weapon pointed directly at Jackson's face.

"Well, damn, you sure was asnorin' loud, boy. Found him, Fratcher," he called over his shoulder. "Get out chere, boy."

Slowly, painfully, Jackson climbed out of the van.

"What's them clothes you're awearin'? Ain't that a Commie patch? You a Commie, ain'tcha? If that don't take all." He poked Jackson with the weapon and they started walking down the hill. "I got me a walkin' Commie hippie in my junkyard."

Jackson still wore the armband with the black hammer and sickle on a blue star on a red field. Paress Linnet had insisted it would help protect him in Brezhnevgrad. "N-n-no," he stammered. "It's part of a costume." Would this man kill him? Jackson had seen *Easy Rider* and *Texas Chainsaw Massacre* and *Mercy Killin' Mama* in holo and remembered, now, that the twin-barreled weapon was a shotgun, and people in this time in America often killed other people whose looks they didn't like.

"You talk strange, Commie. You from Russia or what?"

"J-j-just a traveler from Missouri."

"Like hell. Fratcher! I caught me a Commie!"

The man, Fratcher, joined them a few moments later, and the two of them talked as they followed Jackson all the way down the hill to an unpainted building where they led him inside and sat him in a ladder-backed chair with a rope seat. Jackson was too frantically trying to figure out what to do to pay much attention to what they were saying. He had to escape. He had to get back to the time machine and lock himself in it until it recharged and he could get his butt back to Kansas City in 2249.

Sound from a small wooden box in one corner of the cluttered room distracted him, and Jackson stared at the blurred, off-hued, flat images on the tiny screen on the box for a long few seconds before he realized that it was some primitive form of holovision. The voice over the two-dimensional images demanded his attention.

" . . . estimate five hundred thousand young people at the outdoor concert. Marijuana is being smoked openly. People are reportedly walking around naked and committing sexual acts in public in the name of free love. Rock and roll musicians from all over the country, including Jimi Hendrix, Janis Joplin, and Paul Anka, are scheduled to perform for the growing hordes of—"

"Purty good pi'chur, ey, boy? Ran nigh eighteen hunered foot of antenna war up the mountaint to get that pi'chur."

"You Commies have pictures that good?"

"I ain't no Commie," Jackson said, trying to echo the sound of their accents.

"Them hippies at thet Woodstock party is sure awallowin' in hit like Commies. Why ain't you with them? They's asmokin' hemp growed right chere in West Virginny. Fratcher prah'bly sold hit to 'em." They both laughed.

Jackson jumped from the chair and ran out the door. "Hey!"

"Catch his ass!"

"Call the sheriff!"

"The gun! Take the gun!"

He ran up the hill between the rows of stacked cars. Lost. He was lost. But he dared not stop, dared not pause and try to get his bearings.

"Get back chere, you damn Commie!"

Up. He ran up the mountain. Panting. Heaving. Legs screaming in pain. Eyes unwilling to focus, unable to locate his time machine among the stacks of rusted cars.

Boom!

Jackson turned a corner and ran harder. They were shooting at him. Shooting at him! Just like in the holos!

Suddenly he was faced with a Y in the lanes, both branches going up. He stopped, fighting to catch his breath, forcing his eyes to scan up the mountain speckled by the many-colored cars.

Nothing. No time machine. No POES glistening in the sun.

Boom!

He ran up the right fork.

Boom!

He charged down a narrow aisle. His lungs ached. Right between two stacks. His throat burned. Left at a cross stack. His legs screamed. Back up the hill.

Pain. Crying. Then he saw it—through his tears. Not the time machine. The truck. The truck he had hidden in. He was sure that was the one.

BOOM!

There! The POES!

Jackson scrambled up the stack of antique cars and jerked the door to the time machine open. The machine teetered.

Metal ground against metal. The stack shifted.

Jackson threw himself into the machine and pulled the door closed behind him.

The stack slid sideways with the sound of rending metal and breaking glass. Jackson braced himself.

The time machine tumbled forward, down the junkyard mountain in Wheeling, West Virginia.

Chapter Thirteen

Metal screamed. Jackson braced himself against the seat. Rough surfaces ground out coarse groans as gravity dragged them down the mountain. The time machine tumbled back over front. Inside it, Jackson tumbled like a child in a box. Someone cried. Jagged, vibrating edges sawed the sound into painful moans of protest. Someone else shouted.

Ever so slowly, the time machine stopped sliding. A low hum filled the air. Jackson opened his wet eyes and was more than a little pleased to discover that the time machine sat upright in the middle of the dirt lane between the rows of stacked cars. He was less pleased to see Fratcher standing outside in the settling dust pointing the shotgun at the side window.

"Get out chere, boy!" Fratcher shouted, his eyebrows bouncing over the dark frames of his glasses. Brown stains marked the corners of his mouth like blood on the mouth of a feeding dog. "Get yourself out chere right now. Right now. I don't know what you done to that Buick, but you're in big trouble, boy. *Biiiiig* trouble."

The hum persisted. Jackson looked carefully from

Fratcher to the instrument panel. Under the label SE-CURITY SYS/OP a green light glowed. Only then did he wonder if the security system would stop a shotgun blast.

A blue light blinked on the row above SECURITY SYS/OP. A green light blinked beside the blue. The hum rose through the alto clef.

"Get out chere, now, boy, or I'm gonna pull this trigger and blow you out."

A yellow light blinked beside the green one.

Suddenly Jackson understood. The time machine was about to go somewhere! The hum hit middle C.

Jackson didn't know where. He didn't know why—except that maybe the slide down the mountain had triggered—

Boom!

The window rattled. Jackson snatched his mask off the seat and wrestled it on, gulping hard to force his face past the smell of his earlier nausea.

Boom!

Again the window rattled. Through its pocked surface, Jackson saw Fratcher shaking his head and staring from the shotgun to the time machine and back again.

The hum rose quickly through the treble clef.

Fratcher backed away, shaking his head and trying to load the shotgun at the same time.

The ready light pulsed ten or twenty times, then held its red glow. The universe spun out of control, slamming Jackson down into darkness.

He saw blind men and beggars and women with two guns. He felt the cold weight of a million icebergs. Then he heard the sweet strains of mountain dulcimer playing that old-timey Lennon and McCartney song "Eleanor Rigby," and his fall eased to a soft bounce on a slow-motion cushion that rolled his stomach over and over in queasy loops that he kept in a car by the gore, making it snore, all the only people, where . . . where . . . do the balls come from? Father McFrenzy, writing the Germans that—

"Jackson? Jackson, are you all right? What happened?" His skin was pasty and cold, and for a brief moment she feared for his life. "I'm going to give you a simstim patch."

The voice was familiar, but he wasn't sure why, and he wanted to throw up all over it. His mask popped off with a loud wet chomp of the gorse . . .

Something stung his arm. Electricity. Hot electricity. Burning electricity flowed from the sting through his body. His eyes banged opened to see Suzanne bending over him holding a disposable hypo patch.

"What happened?" she asked, pleased to see color returning to his cheeks.

"My eyes itch."

"What happened?" Her voice was angry and insistent.

Jackson tried to remember. For her. For her he tried to remember what had happened. "Uh, I, uh, I, uh"—he rubbed his itching eyes—"I, uh, landed in Wheeling, West Virginia. Yeah, in Wheeling, West Virginia in the old United States in August 1969."

Suzanne shuddered, wondering if she should tell him.

Whatever simstim she had given him was running through his veins like a squirrel running from a fire. He felt its every step. "Some old man was shooting at me—with a shotgun! Then the machine went crazy."

"How did you get back?"

"I don't know. It started itself and . . . here I am."

Suzanne shook her head as she handed him a wet-towel. "The Wheeling loop." She couldn't lie to him—not about that.

"What's that?"

"It's what happened to you. That's what we call it."

"You mean it's happened before?" He wiped his sour mouth on the wettowel.

"Several trips—more than several, actually—have looped through Wheeling in 1968 and 1969 when they were on their way to other times and places." She tried to gauge his reaction, but he was staring hard at her.

His eyes held hers only for a second. Then she glanced away. "Oh, great," he said. "That's really great. I ended up in some kind of automobile junkyard—a lovely place to end—"

"We have to get you ready to go again."

He barely thought for a second. "Not a chance, lady. I'm not about to—"

"Dammit, Jackson, you wanted to find Lester Wu." She handed him a clean mask and an unopened packet of wettowels. "Well, that's what you're going to do. I've put my career on the line—and maybe more than that—so you could find Lester, and that's at least what you're going to do."

"Oh, no. Uh-huh. Not me. I quit." He neatly folded the used wettowel, then tossed it out of the time machine. "This is for idiots only."

A tear ran unbidden and unexplainable down her face, but she refused to wipe it away. "Jackson, you have to go. I found out that Slye has gone back looking for Lester. You have to find Lester first."

"Wait. Wait a minute." Jackson couldn't believe

what she was saying. "How am I supposed to find Lester first if Slye's already gone?"

"We send you back sooner. It's time travel, remember?"

Jackson felt the same dizziness he had felt on the escalator in New York in 2183 when he realized his parents weren't even alive then.

"Slye must be working behind my father's back, and I have to stop him if I can. If you go back for Lester, that will help. I'm sure of it." She wasn't sure of anything by that point, but she wanted to give Jackson as much positive reinforcement as she could. "Please? Lester needs you. So do I." She put a cool hand on his warm cheek.

His face smiled at her for reasons he didn't begin to understand. Within another fifteen minutes of his return to Kansas City, she had talked him into trying again. Even as he sat there with the time machine's capacitors whining up toward high C, he couldn't quite believe he had agreed to try to go back again.

Blackouts. Spinning stars. Mad vibrations. Twirling death. Nausea. They all convinced him.

He gagged and coughed as the machine came to—

"Jackson? Is that you, Jackson? What's going on? Who's there? Jackson Dubchek? What in the name of the holy Time Police are *you* doing here?"

The voice and the face peering in the window of the time machine belonged to Lester Wu.

"I came looking for you," Jackson said as he swung open the time machine's door.

"You're a capital idiot. The revolution rages around us and you come whining in here, chariot afire, to rescue me, me? When all else fails, you should go—"

"Who's that?" Jackson asked, pointing to a figure huddled against the rough brick wall of the large room. The look on Lester's face and the tone of his voice frightened him to the center of his bones.

"My ancient and faithful companion, the good squire Captain Laszlo Slye, time's policeman extraordinaire, hero of many Russian revolutions, Brgermeister of Brezhnevgrad, et cetera, et cetera. Ever meet him?"

Jackson was startled. "Yes. What happened to him? Is he sick, or what?" It was hard to tell in the dim light, but—

Lester grabbed Jackson's left arm just above the elbow with both hands and clutched it. His bright eyes darted around as he talked. "I've tied him to a pipe and knocked him out, and with any luck he'll die right there or the Rosies will find him and haul him off to one of their—do you know how long I've been here, waiting for—and that's not all, I can tell you they won't find him, because—"

"Easy, Lester. Easy." Jackson tried to calm his friend, knowing it was probably too late. Lester was already far beyond any help Jackson could give him. Lester was mad, crazy, driven insane by forces Jackson could only guess at.

"—coming through the doors. Rosies. Listen." Lester's grip on Jackson's arm threatened to cut off the circulation.

Muffled by walls and distance were the sounds of gunfire and angry voices. "The revolution?"

"Chinese New Year." Lester laughed, slapped Jackson on the arm, and laughed harder. "The Rosies are coming!"

Gunfire echoed closer.

"Hear them? Hear them? The Rosies are acomin' and spring is in the air."

Rosies. Jackson remembered them from his history books. Rosies were what the forces of the Second Republic had called the Communist resistance forces. The Rosies had lost the war, but not before they made sure there wasn't much left for the Republicans to win.

"Lester!" Jackson shook his friend's arm. "We have to get out of here."

Lester doubled over in laughter. "Nowhere to go, Jack. Rosies . . . Rosies everywhere."

Something crashed overhead. Unintelligible voices shouted back and forth.

"Do you know, Jack? Do you have any idea how scary it is?" For a moment the insanity cleared from Lester's eyes. "To be dumped in a time you know nothing about, with no one around to listen to what you're trying to tell them?"

"Why, Lester? Why would they dump you back here?"

The crazy smile came back to Lester's dirt-streaked face. "To feed me to the Rosies, of course."

"Then let's cheat them of their dinner." Jackson looked around and realized that they were in a basement of some sort. Briefly he wondered what there was about underground locations that the time machines liked. "Come on, Lester. Let's get Captain Slye in the machine and get the karma out of here."

An explosion rattled the building and shook dust from the pipes above them.

"Recharge!" Lester shouted. "Too late! His machine's in Xanadu. Follow me." He turned toward a closed door.

"We have to take him with us." Jackson bent over Slye and began to loosen the rough rope that held Slye's hands to the pipe.

"Why? Who says?"

"Because he tried to kill both of us—you and me—and he has to face the—"

"Leave him. Let him die here."

"We can't. He has to answer in the future for what—"

"All right. The skies are falling cozy and the Rosies are acomin' through the rye." Lester opened the door and went through, leaving Jackson alone with Slye.

"Captain? Can you stand?"

Slye looked at him with clouded eyes.

"Stand, Captain. You've got to help me. You're too heavy for me to carry." With Jackson's help, Slye struggled to his feet, and the two of them staggered after Lester Wu.

The door led to a short hallway that opened into another basement room slightly smaller than the first. In the center of the room sat a time machine that could have been the duplicate of Jackson's. Lester was sitting in it, cursing.

"What's the matter?"

"It's set for Slye's security code and won't let me override."

"So we press his palm against the plate and be done with it."

"No," Slye said. "Self-destruct. Kablooey." His knees buckled and he fell to the floor.

"What?"

"He says it will self-destruct."

The sounds of automatic gunfire rattled down on them through the basement ceiling.

"All right, Captain," Jackson said, "you're going to have to get us all out of here. Help me get him in, Lester."

"I hate this," Lester said, climbing out of the time machine. "Why can't we just leave him?"

"Just help me."

Together they pushed and pulled Slye into the time machine.

Chapter Fourteen

A muffled explosion shook the floor and echoed hollowly through the building above them.

Slye gave Jackson a sick grin. "The Rothies are going to get uth all," he said, the words coming out slurred. "Chuck the Second Republic."

"You ride in back." Lester elbowed Jackson out of the way and climbed over Slye to sit next to him on the controller's seat. In Lester's hand was a large pistol that was pointed directly at Slye's chest.

"What difference does it make?" Jackson asked, not wanting to see the pistol, unable to take his eyes from it.

"You want to make sure we get where we're supposed to with our wings on, don't you? Well, I do too, and you can bet your baby's bootchka I'm not going back to the Time Police, crazy fox. I'm going home—to my place—my apartment, in Kansas City. In my time, Jack'o'lack. My time." His eyes gleamed.

"I'm not sure that's such a good idea." Jackson remembered all too clearly what had happened at Lester's old apartment just, uh, when? Earlier that day—just 148 years from now. Back in *their* time. Lester's gun looked larger and more menacing, and it never stopped moving, but always pointed in Slye's general direction.

"Ya dance with who brung ya."

"Did he drug you, or what, Lester?" Jackson asked as he climbed in the rear seat and closed the door, wanting to be out of the line of fire as much as he wanted Lester to calm down. Sweat rolled freely down his spine. "Uh, Lester, look, some of what you've been saying hasn't made much sense, you know. Are you sure you can—"

"Eleven days I've been living in Brezhnevgrad, speaking only Northern Modified Serbo-Croatian garbage to revolutionary idiots, fighting for food and holovision, and the boy wonder wants sense out of cabbages. I've set the destination. It's a home run," Lester said, slapping Slye's hand away from the controls like a parent would slap a child, holding the pistol steady all the while. "Listen to that."

Jackson listened. The fighting sounded like it was in the next room, but he didn't know quite what to do. Slye was obviously still not functioning very well and Lester sounded crazier every second.

Slye groaned and rubbed his oversized ears with his hands.

"Look at you! Look at you, you mutated Time Police slime. Oh, the Rosies are completely rusted through tonight. I could blow you from here to Moscow in a split trillionth of a second, you know that, Slye?"

"Come on, Captain, get this thing going," Jackson said, ignoring Lester's threat.

"We're going to my apartment." Lester grinned.

Slye shook his head very slowly. "Hard to remember.

Hard to remember what we do. Old Lester here fogged up my log when he bumped me on the clump . . ."

"I'll do it, then," Lester said, flipping the safety cover off the start-up switch.

Jackson looked with dismay from one to the other of his companions. They were both crazy.

"Good. Good, slant. Do that. Blow us three to ABC. Kablooey. Kalamazoo and Timbucktoo."

Lester hit the switch.

A klaxon wailed under the seats. Jackson's heart stopped for a full second, then beat like a roadhammer. The first blue light of the ready-light sequence blinked furiously on the instrument panel, but Jackson had no idea why the klaxon was wailing.

Lester and Slye looked at each other and broke into hysterical laughter.

Their laughter only reinforced Jackson's fear. He was sitting in a time machine in Brezhnevgrad in pre-Republican Russia in 2102 with two men sitting at the controls in front of him who were both out of their minds. One he hated. The other he had come to help. Neither cared a thing about him. He was baggage, freight . . . traffic. Rankin's term finally made sense. He was traffic on a road to insanity with the time machine humming low under his feet. He was going to die.

"Uh, uh, uh . . ." Jackson forced himself to pause and take a deep breath. "Uh, maybe I should take ov— Uh, maybe I should check the settings before we begin," he shouted. The ready-light sequence climbed from blue to green.

Lester switched the klaxon off. "You? You? Do you hear that, Captain Slye?" he asked, waving the pistol at

Slye. "He wants to check our settings." Lester sputtered and they both laughed again.

The floor bounced with a roar. Bricks popped out of the wall. Pipes fell.

Jackson stared in disbelief.

Slye snatched the pistol from Lester's hand. "Out, sucker," he said. "Now."

"No!" Jackson shouted.

The door beside Lester popped open. Slye spun in his seat and kicked Lester in the ribs in the same motion. Lester tumbled out of the time machine and disappeared from Jackson's sight.

"You, too. Out!" Slye pointed the pistol at Jackson.

He saw the ready light blink yellow and all too clearly heard the capacitors humming louder and louder and louder and—

Armed men broke through the doorway, shouting something unintelligible.

"Out!"

One of the men sprayed the time machine with automatic fire. Bullets drove Lester's door shut. The ready light blinked red.

Lester reappeared in midair, diving back toward the machine, terror graven on his face. An invisible wire jerked through the middle of his gut, yanking him backward, ripping red clumps of life out of his body and splattering them in a grotesque pattern against the dirty brick wall.

The time machine pulsed and shook. Jackson vomited. The world went black.

It went white seconds later, too white—

White with the cold glare of lights and the hot blare of horns—

White with the wet smell of death and the flash of grinding wheels—

White with the line that stretched from his body into a broken infinity of white lights, bright lights charging both sides of his body, roaring by within centimeters, blaring, glaring—

White!

Jackson vomited again. He forced himself to his hands and knees to get his face off the cold, wet street as his empty stomach emptied itself yet one more time.

Street? Street?

It took a few seconds for him to realize that he was kneeling in the middle of a street. The glaring white lights were turbocars, and he was going to get run over if he didn't get out of the traffic. At the thought of traffic, he almost laughed. Then he remembered Lester dancing in front of a shadow of blood on a brick wall somewhere in the past. His stomach turned the laughter into a wretch.

More cars roared past him. Jackson lurched to his feet, spun in the bright confusion, then ran . . . ran toward darkness because there was nothing else to do.

Horns cursed him with wordless screams. Someone called his name. He ran faster and hit a fence. He scaled the fence like a welfare cheater and ran, stumbled, fell, and ran faster. Every instinct to escape drove his legs, his body—away, down, away downhill, past the State Line sign, across another street, running for the dark, the safety, the shadows, sliding, into a creek, scrambling up the bank, clutching roots and plants, running, squishing, running, turning always toward the darkness, praying for safety to the unnamed One.

Suddenly he stopped in a deep shadow and leaned against a tree. His lungs gasped in sharp, ragged drafts of biting air. His gut twisted in pain. Hands on wet knees, eyes watering, nose running, cold water dripping into his soaked shoes, he fought to get enough oxygen to live one more second—enough oxygen to live ten seconds, maybe twenty, maybe even a minute—sure in his pounding heart that the terrible sounds of his struggle to survive would bring the authorities down on him at any moment.

As his breathing slowed from desperate gasps to ragged panting, he stared across an oddly familiar open expanse of lawn at a lighted building he recognized immediately, but couldn't place. What was that building? Why was it familiar? He couldn't remember. He knew he should, but he couldn't. And even if he could remember what it was, *when* was he there?

Something had obviously gone wrong with the time machine, because it hadn't duplicated itself at the destination—and surely neither Lester nor Slye had sent it to a street.

Tears ran down Jackson's face as he shivered against the cold creeping up his wet legs. Everything had gone wrong. He had gone back to 2102 to try to help Lester and ended up watching Lester die. Now he was lost in time and place, standing he knew not where, he knew not when, crying, gasping, cold and wet, praying that something, someone would save him, and knowing, like Dorothy in the great *Oz* holo, that no one could save him but himself.

The stupid machine had dumped them in the middle of State Line Street and . . . State Line Street. Fresh tears ran down his face, tears of relief. State Line Street. Kansas City. He was in Kansas City.

The building. Old Museum Golf Club. Quiet laughter

welled out of him even as he tried to calm his frantic breathing. He was on the golf course, the Old Museum Golf Course where only the grand high government muckety-mucks—senators, secretaries, and regional governors—were usually allowed to play. It was a famous golf course. Jackson had played it on hologolf in the library rec center at New Nineveh.

I know this course, he thought. This is the ninth hole. Why, if I had a hovercart and some night glasses and a set of those new double-weighted Heller Dynasmack plastinium clubs, I could play a real round right here and now and maybe even break a hundred.

More laughter welled out of him. Why, if he had a caddy who knew the true course and some eleven-dollar-a-pop Alan & Wayne 94.65 compression Starlight night balls, he might even break ninety. . . . No, he would never break ninety, not even with all that help. Ninety-five, maybe, but never ninety. Not on the *real* Old Museum course in Kansas City! He laughed harder.

The sound of his own laughter echoing across the golf course frightened him into shivering silence. When was he in Kansas City? What day was it? What year? He patted his pockets. He had no money—no real money. Rubles, he had rubles, old rubles, and if he could find a currency dealer in the morning, he might be able to sell them for their collector's value. That might give him enough money to get back to . . .

Suppose the time machine had really malfunctioned? Suppose it had gone backward instead of forward? Suppose he was in 1969 in Wheeling, West Virginia, again, and this golf course just happened to look like the one in Kansas City?

Holy Buddha. Jackson shivered and wrapped his arms around himself. Nineteen sixty-nine? Ugh. He never wanted to even here about 1969.

"Time to get moving," he said, "or we're going to freeze to death out here." Turning away from the museum clubhouse, he started walking in a direction he hoped was west—back toward Shawnee-Mission, or Mission Hills, or West Mission-Whatever, he could never keep them straight. But he knew some people there, some people who might be willing to help him without asking too many questions, people who—

Spotlights flooded the grounds around him. Instinct plastered him against the nearest tree. It was too young and thin, but Jackson dared not move.

"This is state museum security. We know you're out there," an amplified voice said. "Just show yourself and save us all a lot of trouble."

Jackson stopped breathing. He heard several hovercarts moving down the fairways behind him and saw lights splashing through the trees.

"We have the local police coming," the voice said. "It will be much easier if you surrender to us. They play a lot rougher than we do. We'll give you five minutes, then we're setting the dogs loose. They'll chew you a new one." Several voices laughed.

Jackson cursed silently and let himself breathe. Peering around his tree, all he could see were lights flooding every fairway and green. If they had dogs . . . What choice did he have? He didn't really know where he was, and the last thing he wanted was to be chased—attacked by dogs. A shiver ran through him as he stepped away from the tree.

"All right," he shouted. "I'm coming out. Where are you?"

"Over there, Ezra, by seventh green."

"You just walk into the light and stand still," the amplified voice said. "We'll find you."

Jackson walked shivering to the nearest patch of light—the seventh green—and stood perfectly still. First he heard a hovercart approaching. Then he heard the dogs.

Chapter Fifteen

Jackson turned in time to see a charging silver dog flashing through the mottled light under the trees. It frothed at the mouth like the rabid monster in *Rambo vs. Cujo*, the old horror holo—the one that had frightened him so much as a child that he never again wanted a dog for a pet.

His heart jumped and his muscles tensed. He knew not to run. He knew that running would only make things worse. But he couldn't stand still. Sprinting legs and pumping arms drove him across the green, away from the devil at his heels.

Another dog charged from his front, then a third from his side, and he stopped. Then a fourth and a fifth until from every direction dogs charged him—silent dogs—deadly dogs—killer dogs.

A spotlight cut through them all, washed them out, faded them into silver shadows—holo dogs—fake dogs—phantom dogs used to trick him into—

"Stand!"

The voice nailed his feet to the ground—froze the water in his knees. It was a different voice from the first one he had heard. It was a female voice full of certainty, a command voice that left no room for dissent, not a voice Jackson was going to argue with under the circumstances. Phantom dogs or not, he was too helpless under all that had happened. A violent shudder swept up his body from the cold, wet trousers clinging to his legs.

"Put your hands atop of your head and don't you move, until I tell you to move. We'd be bringing some real dogs here, mister, so don't be stupid."

Jackson heard the hovercart approach him from behind, but resisted the urge to turn around. His body vibrated with cold and fatigue. His heart pounded with fear and adrenaline. His mind trembled with despair. He wasn't going anywhere or doing anything she didn't tell him to go and do.

"Don't flinch," her voice commanded, close behind him. A gloved hand grabbed his left wrist and jerked his arm down behind his back. It hurt, but he only grunted. A second later she jerked his right arm down and attached his wrists together with the backs of his hands touching.

"All right, turn around."

He turned and found himself facing a gray-uniformed policewoman who couldn't have weighed more than fifty kilos even with all her equipment on.

"Don't know why you'd be grinning, mister. I'd be the police. You'd be the trespasser. And the law says you'd be in a meg of trouble. Show me your identification, please."

"I don't think I have any."

"You don't be carrying any identification?"

"Probably not," Jackson said with a shiver.

"Don't smart out on me."

"I'm not, uh, officer. I'm just—" The look on her

face in the artificial light would have glared the paint off a wall. "No, officer, I don't have any identification."

"You've got rights, and in a minute I'd be going to put you in my cart and be showing you a holotape of those rights, but before I do, I'd be going to ask for your fingerprints. Law'd be saying if you got no identification, I don't have to ask permission to fingerprint you, but I'd be asking anyways."

He couldn't see her eyes clearly under the visor of her helmet, and thus couldn't read the expression on her face, but the set of her mouth said she would accept no challenge. "Yes, certainly, I mean, of course you may fingerprint me, but I don't understand how"—she took him by the elbow and started walking his trembling body toward the hovercart—"uh, I mean, uh, what are you going to do with me?"

"Never you be worrying about that, young man. Here. Stand still while I'd press this against your hand . . . like that. Good. Now turn around. Step up and sit on this side of that seat, ankles together. That'd be it." She fastened a clamp around his legs, attached a safety harness over his shoulders, then pushed a button on the back of the front seat. "Now you should be watching this holo real careful, 'cause it'd be going to explain all your rights."

A holo six inches tall appeared standing on top of the seat. "Greetings, Citizen. I am Counselor Coxlane from the Republican Civil Liberties Union and I have been asked to advise you of your rights under the laws of the Second Republic, the provinces of the United States of North America, and the state of Kansas, and if applicable, the city of Mission-Mission."

The holo figure of Counselor Coxlane in her ugly blue

one-piece suit explained in great detail that Jackson was required by law to give the local authorities nothing more than his name, social receipt number, and fingerprints, and that he was entitled to speak to a counselor within one hour of his arrest. Provincial and Republican governmental authorities, however, could require him to give additional information—address, communications code, names and addresses of living relatives, employment rsum, social vita, et cetera.

Something about holo counselor Coxlane bothered Jackson. With her long red hair lightly streaked with silver and the dimples perfectly placed in her freckled cheeks she was somehow too sweet . . . too virginal . . . too radiant with a perky kind of nurturing spirit. It was almost as though she were telling him contradictory things that—

Of course! He'd seen the techniques before. The whole implication in her tone, in her body language, in everything except her words said it: A good citizen would want to tell the authorities everything, immediately, without benefit of counsel, because that was what was best for the Republic as anyone who loved freedom and democracy could perfectly well understand.

Jackson closed his eyes with a shuddering shiver and ignored the remainder of what Counselor Coxlane's holo had to say. Seeking some comfortable position, he let his body relax in a forward curl leaning against the safety harness, and almost immediately felt the urge to sleep.

"We'd be going now, Citizen Dubchek," the officer said.

He didn't care. For a brief second guilt and shame washed over him as he thought of how his family would feel about Jackson the criminal. But his parents were dead. His brother was gone to Texas. The shame and guilt didn't matter, and Jackson didn't care.

The hovercart moved and Jackson swayed with it, mind drifting on the dark edge of awareness, body suspended on the heavy ropes of fatigue. When the hovercart stopped, he was barely surprised at being helped off directly into a police car. The car was warm, and he slept even better, slept all the way to a building where they made him stop sleeping long enough to change out of his Russian revolutionary costume into fluorescent green prisoner coveralls with knitted orange booties, long enough for them to pry his name and social receipt number from his brain, long enough for them to take his fingerprints again, long enough yawn after yawn for him to refuse to tell them anything else—not long enough to walk to his cell. He fell heavily back to sleep head down on a table in a gray little room.

When he awoke, he lay on a bed in an even smaller gray room. Room was too generous a word. Box—he was in a box, a gray box two and a half meters long, two meters wide, one and a half meters high—like an Origato Hotel room he had stayed in once in Saint Louis. As he threw off his blanket and sat up, he realized it was more than a box or a room. It was a cell. The door at the foot of the bed had no handle. The toilet had no handle. The sink had no—

"Good afternoon, Mr. Dubchek," a synthetic female voice said from a grill in the wall. "You will please listen carefully as the guidelines our clients are expected to follow are explained to you. After initial sedation, processing, and orientation—"

"Let me out of here." If they had sedated him, the

drug was wearing off, because Jackson felt anything but sedate.

"—to the facility, the client will act in an orderly and—"

"Let me out of here!"

"—sanitary manner at all times. When spoken to by staff, the client will respond promptly and honestly with all due—"

"Let me out of here!" He couldn't believe the shouting voice was his own—but then, his world had filled with things he found difficult to believe.

"Please, Mr. Dubchek, calm yourself, compose yourself," the synthetic voice said. "Think of a warm, comfortable place where you would feel most at home. There is no cause for hostility. Further sedation will be provided for your convenience in due course of the approri—"

"Out! I want out of here!"

"—ate schedule. As soon as you have received your orientation, a staff member will attend to your questions and medical needs. *Eeerrrk*—respond promptly and honestly with all due courtesy. Clients will follow any and all directions given by staff to—"

The door at the foot of the bed opened, and the speaker went silent. "Outside, please, Mr. Dubchek," a male voice said. "Please exit your abode with hands together in front of you."

"No sedation," he said.

"No further sedation is authorized at this time," the voice answered. "Hands together in front, please."

Jackson climbed out of bed and, after a moment's hesitation, exited through the low doorway as instructed. His wrists were bound together even before his body was fully out of his box. "Where are we going? What's going to happen to me?"

"Not my job," the stubby gray man said, taking Jackson by the arm and guiding him through a maze of hallways and locked doors to a cubicle three meters square where two men—an older and a younger—wearing almost identical one piece green business suits waited for him.

"Citizen Dubchek, I am Counselor Anderzy," the younger of the two said, "representing you at the behest of Temporal Projects. This is Junior Assistant Underprosecutor Anderzy, representing the state on behalf of the aggrieved museum." His eyes were hidden behind dark glasses.

Jackson looked from younger to older and saw the family resemblance even as he wondered why Temporal Projects had sent a counselor to represent him.

"Your sarcasm is unnecessary, Danny," Underprosecutor Anderzy said. "Pardon my son's rudeness, Citizen Dubchek. Do you understand the charges that have been brought against you?"

"No. What are the charges?"

"I shall file for immediate release and file suit on your behalf, Citizen Dubchek, for false arrest, illegal detention—"

"Shut up, Danny."

"Yessir."

The prosecutor turned to Jackson. "Citizen Dubchek, according to the information presented to me this morning, the charges against you were fully explained and you signed an affidavit indicating same approximately seventy-two minutes after your arrest on the Johnson-Mission Republican Historical Golf Museum and Course. Is that incorrect?"

"I, uh, I think I was asleep."

"Father, I shall file charges if my client was—"

"Shut up, Danny, and stay shut up." He frowned and the younger Anderzy looked away. "Now, Citizen Mr. Dubchek, you should understand that the state has little interest in when and where you sleep, so long as it is not in public. Is this or is this not your signature?"

Jackson looked at the screen built into the surface of the table. "I think so, yes."

"Good. Then you were informed of your rights and the charges against you. Now it is your turn, Danny."

"Thank you, Father. Citizen Dubchek, you have been remanded to the custody of Temporal Projects until such time as you will be called for trial. You may come with me."

"Uh, what about my clothes?" Jackson wasn't sure he wanted to go anywhere with young Danny Anderzy.

"Evidence," Prosecutor Anderzy said, opening the door. "You will be issued clothes before leaving here."

"Suppose I don't want to go?"

"You have no choice. The judiciary has decided, Citizen."

Jackson swallowed hard. "Temporal Projects, uh, doesn't, I mean, look, you're the prosecutor, and I don't have any idea what that means, but Temporal Projects . . ." He didn't know how to say what he felt.

"You have been remanded to their custody, Citizen Dubchek. According to the information supplied to me, you are or were their employee when this unfortunate desecration of an historical monument occurred."

"Alleged desecration, Father."

"I didn't desecrate anything. And I wasn't their employee."

"Well, that will have to be sorted out later, Citizen. For the time being, you have been assigned to them, remanded to their custody, and are now probably in debt to them for this legal wizard whom they have so graciously supplied. You will be given police escort to Temporal Projects Center and there you must stay until your trial."

Jackson shook his head. "No. I won't go."

Prosecutor Anderzy left the room and the door clicked shut behind him.

Young Anderzy's smile was malicious. "You will come with me, Citizen. Besides, don't you want to save your parents' lives?"

Jackson stared into the dark glasses. "They're dead. My parents are dead."

"Not necessarily. If someone went back to the right place in time, they might be saved."

Chapter Sixteen

"So," Slye said, leaning in close to Jackson's face, "you thought you could dump me and the project all at once, didn't you, *Citizen*?"

Slye's breath stank with the cloying smell of mouthwash and toothpaste hovering over other odors too rank to identify. Jackson glared back at him, mentally rehearsing his rights as a citizen under arrest, and knowing that they would do him absolutely no good whatsoever. Only the local police and TP security people knew Jackson had been brought there.

Still, so long as Anderzy was present, Jackson felt sure that Slye wouldn't do anything . . . anything what? Violent?

Slye straightened up, his fists balled at his sides.

As Jackson glanced at Anderzy for help, a shudder of fright ran up his spine.

"Well, *Citizen?*" Slye asked, "did you or didn't you try to get me killed?"

Shaking his head, Jackson finally understood that what was missing in Anderzy's eyes was compassion. Then Jackson knew he had good reason for fright. Anderzy was one of them. His eyes lacked compassion because they were artificial eyes. Anderzy was a Time Policeman. That explained why he had said what he did about Jackson's parents and why—

"It would be best," Anderzy said with a smile that revealed low rows of peglike teeth that also looked artificial, "if you answered all of Captain Slye's questions . . . even those questions you might believe require no answers." In that moment, everything about Anderzy looked artificial.

"I—I don't—I mean—There's nothing I can tell you. I didn't do anything." Jackson looked from one to the other, not knowing what to expect, daring to expect nothing positive.

"We don't need people like you in this society," Anderzy said. "And we won't tolerate you and your kind of disruptive influence . . . unless, unless, of course, you should offer to make some satisfactory contribution necessary to our current projects."

Slye leaned toward Jackson again and grinned. The tips of his ears twitched. "I know a contribution you can make. You can take another trip for us—a permanent farewell trip, you might say, to some special place in time where you—" He stopped and turned sideways as he straightened up.

Jackson followed Slye's gaze to the open door where Colonel Brelmer stared at them a moment before marching into the room, resplendent in his dress uniform.

"Ah, I see you started without me, Captain . . . Counselor," Brelmer added with the barest of nods toward Anderzy. "And under what regulations do you anticipate displacing Citizen Dubchek?"

Brelmer read Slye's defensive posture all too easily,

but he couldn't read Anderzy's attitude and he wasn't sure why Anderzy was there or what his presence meant. Anderzy usually only showed up doing his dirty work when Senator Voxner had a problem. But why would Senator Voxner have ordered that be Dubchek displaced? Brelmer had already lost confidence in his relationship with Voxner, and now, to find Anderzy there with—

"Good to see you, Colonel," Anderzy said. "I'm afraid this situation is totally unacceptable."

Disgust flashed across Slye's face as he flicked at some speck of dust on the sleeve of his uniform.

"And exactly what do you mean by that remark, Counselor?" Brelmer asked, his eyes holding Anderzy's artificial gaze.

"I mean, Praetor Centurion Colonel Brelmer, that Citizen Dubchek has refused to cooperate. Consequently, Captain Slye felt it necessary . . ." Anderzy's words trailed off as his eyes jumped from Brelmer's stare to Slye's glare to a spot on the floor.

Brelmer fought the frown clouding his face. The two of them managed to turn his—

"You have no right to hold me here," Jackson said.

"Yes, well, perhaps I should speak with the citizen alone," Brelmer said, using aerobic discipline to control his voice, refusing to let any of them see the intensity of his anger. "If you both would wait for me in the officer's mess, I will join you shortly." He couldn't read Slye's face, but he knew that his subordinate was not overly concerned about having been caught breaking regulations again. That lack of concern was part of Slye's problem.

"You can't hold me here," Jackson said. "I have rights, just like any other citizen."

"Ah, but of course you do, Citizen," Brelmer said

after Slye and Anderzy had left and closed the door. "May I call you Jackson?" He waited until Dubchek nodded. "Thank you. Now, Jackson, I'm afraid there has been an unfortunate series of misunderstandings between us. However, I am certain we can straighten them out." He sat in the chair facing Dubchek, reading the confusion rippling across the young man's face.

"Like the killing of Lester Wu? Was that what you would call a *misunderstanding*?" The bitterness and anger in his voice startled even Jackson.

"Lester Wu, dead?" Brelmer hoped he sounded genuinely surprised. "I am sorry. I did not know that he had died. Truly I didn't. When did it happen?" He saw the uncertainty on Dubchek's face and felt sure the young interpreter had bought the lie.

"Back in Brezhnevgrad in"—Jackson struggled to recall the year through the mist of blood that clouded the memory—"in 2102, I think. Slye pushed him out of the time machine and—"

"Please." Brelmer held up his hand. "I will investigate the details. I promise you. Then we will rectify the situation. In the meantime—"

"How are you going to rectify someone's death?"

Brelmer sighed. "There are certain things you must understand about Temporal Projects, Citizen Dubchek, the most important of which being that we are technically capable of making certain . . . uh, adjustments, shall we say, to history—adjustments that, while they won't severely affect the continuity of the timelines, will serve to correct certain, uh, injustices."

Flags of suspicion waved in Jackson's mind. "Like what?"

"Like saving your parents from the Great Plaza Fire."

Jackson swallowed hard. Rectify Lester's death? Save his parents? Brelmer wanted him to believe that? Jackson opened his mouth, but no words came out. Images of his parents alive and smiling flooded his mind.

"You look surprised, but you shouldn't be. The operational details would be fairly simple. The same for the technical side. We could do it, if we chose to," Brelmer said slowly. "We would most certainly have to be very careful, but we could do it. It is within our power—within *your* power, I should say."

"Mine? But . . . but how?" Words collided in his brain and off his tongue in a Brownian confusion. "I don't—You mean, you mean if you—if I go back, they won't really be dead, and I can get them out of there— before the fire?" He sensed sincerity in Brelmer, but Jackson dared not trust it.

"Yes."

For the millionth time in his mind's eye, Jackson saw the other images, the images from the news vids—saw the pictures of people on fire running from the wall of flames that collapsed on the plaza, heard the silent screams, felt the rage of helplessness knowing his parents—so many people—had died in that holocaust. "What about the others?"

"What others?" Brelmer asked. The look on Dubchek's face filled him with suspicion.

"The other people—the other people who died in the Plaza fire—what about them? Can't we get them all out?"

"Of course not. Don't be stupid."

Jackson thought Brelmer's frown lines looked like black lines across his forehead. "What's stupid about that? If we can save my parents, why can't we save everyone?"

"Because history won't stand for it. Too much would

change. Saving your parents would be dangerous enough
in and of itself. Saving more could cause . . . could cause
we don't know what.''

"Then you could save them. You're just afraid to."

"No! Absolutely not," he added in a softer tone as
he looked away. "Just your parents." Something in Brelmer's tone gave the secret away and he knew it.

"You've never done this before, have you?" Jackson
waited until he was almost sure Brelmer wasn't going to
answer.

"No, we've never gone back to save anyone's life
before.''

"Then you don't know if it will work or not."

Brelmer met Dubchek's accusing gaze. "There's no
reason to think that it wouldn't work."

"So why can't we rescue them all?"

"No!" Again the word came out sharper than he intended. "It's too dangerous, far too dangerous."

"You mean there's no big political gain," Jackson
said, his anger swelling with an undertow of frustration.

"I mean what I said. There is a great deal you don't
understand about this business, Jackson."

"Like what?"

Brelmer let a faint smile bend his lips. "Well, for one
thing, we're not the only people in the temporal business."

"Surprise, surprise."

"You knew that?"

"Of course. I met some of the others in New York
when Slye and his crew dumped me there.''

"Then you know there are rebels from the future who
are trying to destroy the Second Republic?"

Jackson suddenly understood how much he didn't
know, but he wasn't going to let Colonel Brelmer see his

ignorance. "Sure," he lied, "they knew all about us—about you and the Time Police, I mean."

"Like what? What exactly did they Know?"

"More than they would tell me."

"Did they mention Radek?"

"Who?"

"Radek, Karl B. Radek. Didn't you learn any Republican history in school?"

"Of course, but . . . oh, that Radek. No, they didn't mention him. I mean, the people I met in New York didn't mention him." What did Karl Radek have to do with anything?

"Those people were rebels from the future. They've destroyed his papers, you know—the future rebels have." Brelmer shook his head. "Why should they care? Why should you? He was only the intellectual grandfather of the Second Republic."

"What about my parents? Are you serious? About saving them?"

"Certainly I am serious."

"There's a catch, isn't there?"

"I don't know that term."

"There's a deal you have in mind, something else you want from me."

"But of course."

"How foolish of me to think otherwise." Jackson sucked in a tight breath. "What is it? What do you want?" Unexpected tears burned the corners of his eyes, and he brushed them away with angry swipes of his hands. "What do I have to do to get you to save my parents?"

"Make one more trip for us."

"No."

"They're your parents, Jackson." Brelmer knew

from the look on Dubchek's face that he would make the trip.

"You're a real bastard, Colonel."

"Perhaps."

"Where? Where do you want me to go?"

"Geneva, 1930. There was a Congress of Socialist Writers held there and Radek had several of his working manuscripts there with him. We want them—or copies of them."

"What good will they do? They're just—"

"You don't understand yet, do you? Without Radek's writings, the foundations of thought that helped form the Second Republic are altered, thus our present is altered. Do you realize that today, here in the North American provinces, a criminal suspect is considered innocent until proven guilty? That is the most bizarre notion in the world. Yet it's true. It's true because those damned rebels destroyed Radek's works. You're going to keep them from being destroyed and thus . . . well, we'll move them to the right people at the right time and the Republic will be the way it always was, the way it was meant to be."

Jackson shook his head. "You're crazy. You're all crazy. You're toying with history—with our very lives. Buddha only knows what could happen if . . . if . . ."

"If we save your parents? True. But we're willing to risk it because putting history—our history—the history of the Second Republic back the way it was, is absolutely essential. The dangers of leaving those changes are far worse. . . . But as I said, they're your parents."

When his mouth opened, no words came out. There were no words for the agony Jackson felt. But part of him already knew that if making a trip to Geneva in 1930 would save his parents, he would do it.

Chapter Seventeen

Jackson rinsed out his mouth for the fifth time since he'd stumbled out of the time machine. He spit the water out on the grass, careful to keep the cool Swiss breeze to his back. Even though he hadn't eaten for six hours prior to the trip to Geneva, his arrival sickness was just as bad as it had been every time before.

Geneva, Switzerland, 1930—a simple trip from 2249. simpleminded was more like it. How had he let Brelmer talk him into something so foolhardy?

His parents. They were the key, the key to everything. For the chance to save their lives, for the chance to make—let them—live again, he was willing to risk one more trip. He had known he would do it for that reason—and probably for that reason only. Brelmer had known it. Even Slye and Anderzy had probably known it. Suzanne probably even knew that.

Jackson cursed softly, then cleared his mouth a final time. What none of them had known was what he was going to do when he got to Geneva. They didn't know how he was supposed to find Karl B. Radek, socialist theoretician/writer/journalist, other than the name of the hotel where the conference was being held. And they certainly didn't know how he was supposed to talk Radek out of his manuscripts.

Brelmer and Temporal Projects had left those minor details up to Jackson, although they had given him two hundred thousand Swiss francs to help smooth out any problems he had. Jackson had no idea how much that many francs was worth in real money, but they assured him that Radek should certainly be willing to sell him the manuscripts for far less than that amount. Radek had a reputation for being a paranoid personality, and thus TP's researchers had assured Jackson that Radek had made several copies of every manuscript he ever wrote, just in case something happened to the originals.

Writers, Jackson thought with a shake of his head. He looked around the sunlit clearing where his time machine had come to rest and decided he ought to unroll the Portable Ovshinsky Energy System before doing anything else. By the looks of the sun over the mountains, the time was somewhere between late morning and early afternoon. With any luck the POES would have the machine charged enough for the return trip by nightfall—or at least early the next day.

Suddenly he wondered where in Geneva he was—if, in the name of the great Daruma, he was in Geneva at all. More importantly, he wondered if his premodern French would be intelligible to the citizens. Might as well go find some answers, he thought after making sure the POES was functioning properly.

Jackson followed a narrow dirt path down the hill from the clearing to a paved road not much wider. The first person he met—a boy of ten or twelve pushing a bicycle up the hill—tilted his head quizzically when Jackson asked directions to the Woodrow Wilson Memorial

Hotel. The boy said something about *habit drôle*, then pointed down the road and laughed.

"Merci. Merci beaucoup," Jackson said several times before the boy continued up the hill. *Habit drôle* . . . funny clothes. Jackson hoped his clothes weren't as amusing as the boy seemed to imply they were.

The steep road switched back and forth down past neat stone houses seemingly built into the mountainside. After a kilometer or so, the road leveled off for a short distance where it ran between a tenset of buildings. There Jackson stopped at a café and asked directions of a thin man wearing an old tweed jacket who had risen to greet him when he entered. After a long pause during which the man seemed to expect something, the man shrugged and gave Jackson a look of annoyance.

It took Jackson a moment or two to realize that the man worked in the café and apparently expected Jackson to order food as prepayment for an answer to his question. Only then did Jackson stop to think that the francs TP had given him were all in one-thousand-franc bills. He suspected that the man in the tweed coat would not be amused if Jackson ordered something to drink and then offered payment in a one-thousand-franc banknote.

"S'il vous plaît," he said, continuing in French, "I must find the Woodrow Wilson Memorial Hotel."

"What would please you, monsieur?" the man asked.

"Café au lait," Jackson said after another brief hesitation. It was obvious that he would have to order something to get directions from the pinch-faced man.

"But of course, you are American, *non?*"

"Yes, I am. You speak very good English."

"I learned in England. Would you not like something to eat with your café?"

"I am very embarrassed, monsieur," Jackson said,

"but I have just been paid a debt owed to me for a long time, and the smallest bill I have is a one-thousand-franc note."

"That is no problem for an American friend. Please, be seated, and I will bring you some café and kuchen."

"Thank you." Jackson sat at a table by the window and hoped his stomach would accept the food when it came. To his great relief, his stomach took the food quite well—well enough for him to order more of the delicious kuchen, a light cake with poppy seeds sprinkled over it. He was thoroughly enjoying the second piece when he glanced out at the street just in time to see the passenger in a passing automobile.

Jackson choked on the cake. The passenger was Laszlo Slye—or his twin in time.

The kuchen turned to ashes in his mouth, and his stomach rolled over. Quickly he put the cake back down on his plate and took a gulp of the coffee, holding the hot liquid in his mouth and letting it trickle slowly down the back of his throat. Do not throw up, he told himself. *Do not throw up*.

He closed his eyes for a long moment and breathed deeply to calm himself. What in Buddha's name was Slye doing in Geneva? If Brelmer didn't trust Jackson to do what he'd been sent back to do, why send him at all? Why create the elaborate charade of saving his parents?

Slowly Jackson opened his eyes again and looked back at the road. Slye's car had disappeared around a bend, leaving only a faint black cloud of exhaust in its wake. Jackson watched the foul-smelling smoke drifting upward, thinning out, and disappearing above the tidy buildings, and wondered why he couldn't disappear with it.

Why not stay in the café forever? What would it matter? The Time Police obviously intended to get rid of him one way or another. But if he stayed in 1930, he could lose them forever. He probably had enough money, and Geneva looked like a much more peaceful place than the other times he might have been stranded in. It was certainly better than Wheeling.

But then the old familiar holo images flashed across his mind again, and he saw the wall collapsing on all those people in the Plaza. And he knew he would never have the chance to save his parents if he didn't go down that hill and try to find Radek.

Something pushed him out of the chair. He handed a thousand-franc note over to the man in the tweed jacket, collected his fat handful of change, and listened automatically to the man's directions. Then he stepped off down the hill and into the city, his mind blank, his thoughts frozen, unable to focus on the hotel, or who he might find there. He just walked.

After a while he heard himself humming, turning the rhythm of his steps into a little tune. Then he began to sing under his breath, nonsense words to match his nonsense world. The song kept him moving.

> *Up and down, up and down,*
> *I am walking up and down.*
> *Up the hill, down to town,*
> *I am walking up and down.*
> *In and out, round and round,*
> *My whole world is upside down.*
> *Anytime, I'll be found*
> *walking, walking up and down.*

It was a stupid song, and he knew it, but somehow it pleased him. He remembered all those summers he'd

spent at Camp Arrowhead making up hiking songs with
his campers—songs that helped them overcome the
steepness of the trails and the fatigue in their legs—and
he wished briefly that he could get himself stranded in
some time like that.

A low rumble behind him resolved itself into the roar
of an automobile engine, then the blare of a horn, and
Jackson jumped to the side of the street. A long black
limousine rushed past, with barely enough room for Jackson to get out of the way. He looked around, realizing
that he'd come much farther into the city than he'd
thought. Houses and shops crowded right down next to
the street, and there were more people, crowds of people
in *habits drôles*, laughing, talking, the general flow of them
heading down the hill in the same direction the car had
taken.

Jackson walked on down the gently sloping street,
breathing shallowly against the exhaust fumes of the
growing automobile traffic, and wishing this city, with its
narrow sidewalks, had developed hovercars sooner. The
street took one more turn then opened out into a little
plaza in the middle of several impressive buildings. Plaza,
place, *platz*, piazza, square—this was one of the nicest
he had ever seen.

The buildings rose all around him like magnificent
relics. Marble facades were decorated with columns and
cornices, and massive wreaths and cupids and lion heads
adorned the windows and ledges. Jackson momentarily
forgot about the exhaust fumes and took a deep breath,
awed by the time and effort and money it must have taken
to create elaborate buildings like those. Then he shook
himself, and looked around the little square for some indication of where he was.

On the other side of the plaza a narrow red banner

had been stretched between the front columns of one of the buildings. Though the writing was small, Jackson made out the word *camarades* and suspected it was the place he was looking for. The banner hardly seemed in keeping with the staid facade of the building, but the black limousine had pulled up by the front steps, and a uniformed doorman was opening the car's door and helping the occupant out.

Jackson fumbled in his pocket for the picture Brelmer had given him of Radek and compared the face in his hand with the face of the man from the car. It wasn't Radek, but there was something about the man's beefy build and jowly face that reminded Jackson of all the cartoons of Russian Communist leaders he'd seen in his history books.

"This must be the place," Jackson muttered. He watched for a break in the traffic then stepped out into the square and crossed to the building he hoped was the Wilson Memorial Hotel.

The limousine had pulled away by the time he reached the steps, and the doorman was out of sight inside the building. Jackson took the steps two at a time, suddenly eager to get it all over with. He reached for the door handle, but before he could pull on it, it was pushed outward, tipping him off balance. He took a couple of steps back down the marble stairs as the doorman came out.

"Monsieur needs assistance?" the doorman purred.

"Ah, I . . . is this the Wilson Hotel?"

"Monsieur is not familiar with Geneva?"

"I'm here from America." Jackson suddenly realized how obvious that must have been, since he was speaking English. "Is this where the Congress of Socialist Writers is meeting?"

"Does monsieur have identification?"

"Uh, what?" Jackson had no idea what the doorman was talking about. "I . . ."

The doorman looked politely embarrassed. "Monsieur must understand. The writers are most interested in tranquillity for their conference. They do not wish to be disturbed, and so I have been asked to carefully check all credentials of people who wish to be admitted. Therefore, I repeat that it is necessary to see your identification."

"I just . . . that is." Jackson groped for a logical-sounding excuse. "I'm here to cover the convention. I'm a reporter, not a delegate. Isn't there somewhere I can register? My editor told me to check in and they would issue me credentials once I got here." His lie sounded weak even to Jackson.

The doorman only smiled, sadly shaking his head. "Perhaps monsieur would like to have me check at the desk. If you will tell me the name of your publisher?"

"Gannett. *USA Today*," Jackson blurted out, grabbing for the first old-time newspaper name he could think of. He already knew he wouldn't get in the door this way, and all he could hope for was that the doorman would go back in and he could make an escape before someone called the police. He took another step backward, smiling in a way he hoped looked reassuring.

The doorman acted satisfied—whether he believed Jackson or not—because he went back up the steps and opened the door. For one moment Jackson got a glimpse of the lobby, full of opulent carpets, dusty palm trees, and quietly gleaming brass. Then his eyes focused on a man standing just inside the door.

Laszlo Slye. Slye smiled and nodded ever so slightly in a way Jackson didn't find reassuring at all.

Chapter Eighteen

"Perhaps I may be of assistance, sir," a man's voice said in English from Jackson's elbow.

He turned to see the smiling face and outstretched hand of a blond man who stood a head taller than Jackson.

"Reed, John Reed, fellow American and fellow journalist. Why don't we get some coffee at that little café over on the corner and talk about your newspaper?"

Behind Reed's smile and simple suggestion lay other implications that Jackson didn't understand.

"Don't worry. We won't be noticed over there. They're used to tourists—especially Americans."

A shiver ran up Jackson's spine as he stared into the man's washed-out blue eyes. "Who are you?"

"Just a fellow American who wouldn't want to see anything happen to"—he took Jackson's arm in a firm but friendly grip—a compatriot. Why don't I explain it over coffee. The gendarmes are paying too much attention right now.

Suddenly Jackson spotted a man in uniform watching them, and allowed Reed to guide him down the steps and across the side street to the one empty table in a small sidewalk cafe. "You're one of them, aren't you?" Jackson asked as they sat down out of sight of the local policeman.

Reed laughed, showing a mouth full of yellow teeth. "If you mean that I'm a Communist, of course. It's still the rage, isn't it?" He signaled a waiter, who nodded as though he had served them many times before.

Jackson heard cynicism behind the laughter. "That's not what I meant. You're from . . ." He let the thought hang unfinished with his words. Maybe Reed wasn't another time traveler. "What do you mean, it's still the rage?"

"Oh, you know. Everyone still wants to be Communist—thanks to me. I helped spread the gospel. Wrote a couple of books about it. Equality for all. From each according to his ability, to each according to his need. The people are the government. All that stuff. The evangelist of Communism, the *New York Times* called me. Catchy, but hardly true."

"Those are noble goals you set forth, John Reed, but I don't understand what you want from me." The words sounded stupid to Jackson even as he spoke them. But suddenly Reed's name rang a distant bell in Jackson's memory. Reed . . . John Reed . . .

Again Reed laughed with unmasked bitterness. "Noble goals? Ah, but yes . . . yes. They all had noble goals. But only goals. Ideas may improve, but people don't."

"What are you talking about?" Then Jackson remembered. *Ten Days That Shook the World*—that was it. That was the book he had read about the Bolshevik Revolution in Russia in the early twentieth century written by one John Reed. But that Reed had died young—before 1930—hadn't he? Young? Jackson couldn't remember.

But if that Reed had died young, and this was an older Reed, older than the one who had died, then Jackson knew that they were in another of those alternate versions of history.

The waiter set down two cups of coffee and a small plate of glazed pastries. Reed handed him a one-hundred-franc note, then turned back to Jackson. "You don't look too good. In fact, you look sick. And if you annoy that doorman over at the Wilson, and you'll look even sicker. They don't want you in there. Hell, they only let me in part of the time"—he grinned oddly—"and I'm supposed to be one of them."

Jackson shook his head slowly, afraid. "I don't understand what's going on here. What time are you from?"

"What time?" Reed pulled a battered watch out of his vest pocket. "Eleven-fifteen, by my watch, if that's what you mean by your question. And what's going on here—if you really want to know—is that the revolution's gone sour. It stinks like a sty and there are worms in the meal."

"No, I mean here, right here and now. Would you please tell me what's going on *here?* In Geneva? Now? With you and me? Why did you bring me here? What do . . ."

Reed smiled darkly, and that smile held Jackson like a vise gripping his mind. He had never met a man like Reed before.

"You told the doorman you worked for *USA Today.* There is no such paper. Then you didn't or wouldn't show your identification. For all I know you don't have any identification. That's it, isn't it? I'd bet Zinoviev's socks you're some kind of spy, for the Trotskyites, maybe . . . except you look too lost to be a spy. Who are you?"

"My name is Jackson Dubchek."

"And?" Bushy eyebrows arched over the pale, pale eyes.

"And what?"

"And what are you doing here, Jackson Dubchek?" Reed leaned across the table, squashing a piece of pastry under one elbow as the eyebrows dropped to hood the eyes, giving them gray shadows. "Is that your real name? And who sent you? And what is it exactly that you want from the Socialist Writers? Publication? Influence? Money? What?"

"Information, uh . . . information. I need some information from Karl Radek."

Cccccsssuuu. The whistle slid between Reed's teeth. "Where did you—"

"Do you know Radek?" Jackson asked.

"Of course. Everyone knows him, or at least knows who he is. Doesn't mean he'll talk to anyone, though—not me, and certainly not to you."

Jackson tensed. "Why?"

Reed started to lean back, then shifted conspiratorially toward Jackson. "Because Karl Radek's a big man. You understand what I mean? A big man, a powerful man, a man of respect and knowledge, but one of the suspected intelligentsia in a national cage full of proletariat simpleton bears, so he's suspicious. He's scared of every stranger and every acquaintance. You'd have an easier time getting to see Uncle Joe Stalin himself."

"I don't have to see him—Radek, I mean. I only want to buy something from him."

Reed's eyes narrowed and his brow folded in an expression of surprise or disbelief. "Buy something? Did I hear you correctly? Buy something? You want to buy something from a Bolshevik socialist theoretician who doesn't believe in owning anything? You want to . . . God!''

Reed looked down with closed eyes and shook his head before looking up at Jackson again. ''You're one of President Hoover's boys, aren't you? Or J. Edgar's. The good old government of the U.S. of A. sent you, didn't they? Damn Republicans are—''

''No. They didn't send me.''

''Then who did?''

''I, also, would be interested to know the answer to that, monsieur. First, *s'il vous plaît*, your passport.''

The policeman standing beside their table was not the same one who had watched them in front of the hotel, but he was a policeman, nonetheless, and Jackson had absolutely no idea of what to say to him. TP had sent him with only minimal tools. A passport was not one of them.

''My friend left his passport at the hotel,'' Reed said. ''I was just explaining to him the necessity of carrying it at—''

''And which hotel would that be?'' the policeman asked in heavily accented English, looking straight at Jackson.

''The Woodrow Wilson—''

''The Alexandria,'' Reed interjected.

''Ah, yes, well then, perhaps you had best come with me, monsieur, for I fear that you are required to carry your passport at all times.''

Jackson's legs froze. His eyes snapped from Reed to the policeman and back to Reed. The expression Reed's face was indecipherable.

''Check your pockets again,'' Reed said as he stood.

For some reason Jackson realized that Reed wanted

him to stand also, and he did, patting his pockets, wondering how far he could run by jumping the low wall
around the café. He knew it was a stupid notion, but he
didn't know what else to do. The boundaries of his world
had slipped over some unseen horizon, and the bottom
had dropped out like the floor on one of those spinning
carnival machines.

Reed softly said something to the policeman in Ger-
man. The policeman's eyes widened momentarily and he
looked away. *"Nein!"* he barked after a long hesitation.

Jackson fought the urge to jump the wall even as his
stomach turned over on itself. That wouldn't do. That
wouldn't do at all. If he got sick, how would he escape?
And if he did escape, where would he run to?

"You will come with me," the policeman said.

"We will ride in my car," Reed insisted.

"That is not necessary."

"Ah," Reed said, towering over the policeman, "but
I insist."

"Very well, then, in your automobile, monsieur, but
do not trifle with me. I am an officer of the government,
and your friend is in serious trouble."

"This way," Reed said, walking out of the café.

The policeman gestured like one of those materdees
in an old holo, and Jackson followed Reed. The policeman
followed him, and single file they walked a block and a
half past the stares of curious pedestrians to small, battered black automobile.

"You first," Reed said to Jackson, holding the door
for him.

Jackson's queasy stomach did not like the smell of
the old car. He wedged himself onto the narrow back seat

as the policeman sat in the left-hand front passenger seat. Only then did Jackson realize that the car's steering wheel was on the wrong side.

"You will follow my directions precisely," the policeman said after Reed started the car.

"But of course."

As the car rattled through the streets of Geneva, Jackson had to swallow hard to keep his stomach from turning itself inside out. It seemed like all he had done since getting involved with Temporal Projects had been to run from police. So where does he end up? Going to jail in 1930's Switzerland. And for what? For not having proper identification. The impulse to laugh made him gag.

"Are you sick, monsieur?"

"Yes," Jackson moaned.

"Pull to the curb," the policeman said. As soon as the car stopped, the policeman jumped out.

Jackson started to follow. The car jumped forward in a rattling squeal of tires. His head banged the low roof.

"Hold on," Reed said. "We're going for a ride."

"Where?"

"Where else? To send you home."

Clutching his stomach with one hand and covering his mouth with the other, Jackson wasn't sure if . . . what . . . who . . .

Quickly he rolled down the window and barely got his head out before losing his breakfast.

"Ah," said some cynical voice in the back of his head, "the joys and glories of time travel."

Only after he had spat several times and pulled his head back in did Jackson realize that the voice had been Reed's.

"What did you say?"

"I didn't say anything. Where do you want me to take you?"

"Uh . . . uh . . . the road to Bern."

"Why that one?"

"Will you take me there or not?"

"Of course."

"Who are you, mister?"

"John Reed, like I told you."

"The same John Reed who wrote about the Russian revolutions?"

"The same."

"But you're a time traveler too, aren't you?"

"Nope," Reed said, acceleratining around a corner away from the stranded policeman. "But I know about you time travelers. Some of your people saved my life."

"They're not my people."

"Doesn't matter. That's how I recognized you. They saved my life because they wanted me to write a book for them . . . the bastards. So I'm alive now and I wrote the book thay wanted, but it was their book, not mine. *Toward a Second Republic,* it's called. Could have been a great book—or at least a damn good one, but by the time the illiterate editor they used finished mutilating the manuscript, I was ready to blow up the publisher."

Jackson looked through the rear window, but no one seemed to be following them. "I work in a library . . . and I don't think I've ever seen *Toward a Second Republic.*"

"Doesn't surprise me. Book distribution is one of the least logical systems in the world. It's a wonder any books are ever available anywhere, much less in libraries. What library do you work in?"

"New Nineveh," Jackson said without thinking.

"Never heard of it."

"You wouldn't have."

Reed laughed. "Not in my time, huh?"

"No . . . There. I think that's my road."

"You're right." Reed turned up the road, drove though the village where Jackson had eaten, and—after two wrong turns—finally stopped at the path to his time machine.

"This is it," Jackson said.

"I want to come with you."

"You can't You can't go into your own future. It would kill you. At least, that's what they told me."

Reed laughed. "That's what they told me, too. But look, I'm already in my own future and I want to go with you. T've got to get out of here. It isn't my time any more than it is yours. These socialist conferences are driving me crazy. My publisher is driving me crazy about the deadline for the new book. The idiot editor is driving me crazy. And my old editor is too buried in work to—"

"Okay. Okay." Jackson heard a klaxon in the distance. "If you're willing to risk it, it's all right with me."

When thry reached the time machine its gauges indicated only the minimum charge of necessary power, but he didn't care. He showed Reed how to strap in, entered the coordinates for Springfield, Missouri, and adjusted the date to his personal limit. "Are you sure?" he asked Reed.

"Absolutely." Reed gave him a lopsided grin. "There are some publishers, even socialist publishers, you'd die for."

"Okay, then hang on. That bag is for you to be sick in, and if you make it, you will be sick. I promise."

"We'll see."

Jackson set the sequence on automatic and flipped the warm-up switch.

The machine whined to life. A policeman ran into the clearing, carrying a large pistol. The whine climbed toward the inaudible. Reed laughed, then gagged, then shimmered. Time hung still for a long moment before everything swirled into infinity.

Chapter Nineteen

His body tumbled through gravel and wet weeds down a shallow incline. His empty stomach turned noisily, but either the nausea wasn't as bad this time, or he was getting used to time travel. Either way, the results were the same—less nausea, but no less dizziness.

For long moments he lay in the damp grass staring up at black fields of sky sprinkled with bright stars. Lights from five or six aircraft tracked slowly across the spectacle of the Milky Way. Something told him he wasn't in Springfield—unless he was in the old Confederate Cemetery Historical Monument. But even from the cemetery the stars hadn't looked so bright in Springfield for several hundred years.

Jackson shivered. Several hundred years? Had he missed coming home by a hundred years? Slowly he rolled to his stomach, then got up on his hands and knees before forcing himself to his feet. His stomach rolled with a growl, but he was so preoccupied with where and when he was that he pushed the nausea aside.

Jackson didn't know. All he did know was that the bottom of his carnival ride really had fallen out. He was lost some*where* and some*time*, and there were no guides to tell him where and when. To his left, across the narrow road, spots of light receded into the darkness. To his right, the horizon glowed with light. Wherever he was, he was in the midst of people—many people with lots of power. That put him somewhere between 1950 and 2249 in *any* civilized part of the world.

Hysterical laughter doubled him up. He plopped his hands on his knees, and laughed harder. Waves of pain and fright swept over him and sucked at the foundations of his mind in a dark undertow of despair.

Suppose he had bounced into Russia, or Spain, or Bangladesh, or Australia? Suppose he had fallen short in a time before he was born? Suppose he was still in 1930 in Switzerland? Tears ran from his eyes, but the convulsive shaking of his body only worsened.

"You're crazy," he gasped. "Crazy, crazy, crazy. Out of your effing mind."

A sound startled him. He straightened as a vehicle topped a rise not too far from him. It raced down his side of the road and held him in its headlights until it hummed past, its turbine never hesitating. The glare of its lights had briefly revealed a small sign before the darkness swallowed truck, sign, and road again.

"Hey, Jackson," he asked himself, "when did they switch to turbines in North America? Does that narrow it down for you? Turbines came when? Twenty eighty? Twenty ninety? Sometime in there. Now you've got yourself to within a hundred and sixty years of the right time. All you have to do is find your way home."

Only then did he realize that the time machine hadn't come with him. "Not enough power," he muttered with a shiver. "Might as well find out if that sign will tell me anything."

The sign was farther away than he thought it would be, but when he got close enough to read it by starlight, he whooped for joy, ran up, and hugged it.

GREENE COUNTY
BB

"Home," he whispered to the cold metal pole. "Or damn close to it." If this was Greene County Road, BB, the bright lights on the horizon could only be Springfield. He was a fair distance north of the city, but if he kept the lights on his right and followed the road, it would either take him to New Z or Highway 13 and either of those would get him back to Springfield. He marched off toward the east with a lightness in his step that he wouldn't have thought possible ten minutes earlier.

He knew *where* he was. If the *when* was close enough . . . well, he would learn soon. Only as he walked did he realize that if he had actually made it back to his own time, he was going to look very odd to anyone who saw him. The rumpled wool suit he wore was of a style that had been out of fashion since before his father's day. And what was he going to do for money?

Jackson didn't care. If he was home, in his time, in his place, he didn't care.

After walking almost an hour and being passed by fifteen or twenty cars and trucks, he came to the intersection of BB and New Z. There was a fair amount of traffic on New Z, but no one stopped to offer him a ride as he trudged south. Each familiar landmark cheered him up, and at every store he passed he thought about going in, asking to use the caller, and calling Chrys and having her come pick him up.

But he didn't. He couldn't. He was too afraid—afraid to find out that even though he had come back to the right place, back to Springfield, Missouri, the time would be wrong. What if he was off by six months? If he was six months early, would he find another version of himself living in his apartment? He didn't know the answer to that and too many other questions. For the moment he had to remain alone.

Another hour of walking brought him to International Highway 44, and an hour and a half after that he stood on the doorstep of his Strawberry Fields apartment on West Sunshine trembling with anxiety.

Cautiously he raised cover the off the ID plate and pressed his hand against it. Without hesitation his apartment door swung partway open and a gust of dry, dusty air escaped. He pushed himself through the opening and closed the door to find himself standing in a large slide of envelopes, circulars, fliers, and catalogs, sixth class mail so worthless that it wasn't worth sending on postalnet.

Jackson kicked it aside with the sheer joy of being home. One envelope, a green and yellow striped one the size of a microbook flew higher and farther than the others. On impulse Jackson picked it up and flipped it back into the pile. Then he bent over and picked it up again and looked at it. First-class private carrier postage. A return address in New York, F.D.

He had never seen such an envelope. "Later," he said, tossing the envelope onto the table by the door. Next he sat at his terminal. The date read, 21 April 2249. He'd been gone how long? Four weeks? Three? Suddenly he couldn't remember. And again he didn't care. At least no other Jackson Dubchek had been living in his apartment while he was gone.

Punching up the messages menu, it quickly became obvious to him that most of the calls on his terminal had come from Chrys. He almost laughed. Chrys Calvino, his acrobatic partner in sex and recreation, had barely entered his mind in weeks. Not only had he not missed her, he hadn't thought about her. Yet the sudden thought of Chrys aroused him in a totally unexpected way.

On impulse, he called her.

"Do you know what time it is?" she asked sleepily, her video off so he couldn't see what she looked like—or if she was sleeping alone.

"No. I'm sorry. I just got back and I'm starving and I got your messages and well . . ."

"Now, Jackson? You just got back now? From Kansas City?"

"Not exactly."

"Then where have you been?"

"You wouldn't believe me . . . Listen, Chrys. I'm starving. I'm sorry I woke you, but I'm going to send out to Wu Wing's for cashew cat and a gallon or two of hot chianti. You want to join me? Should I order double?"

She giggled, part of the sleepiness gone from her voice. "You know what cashew cat and hot chianti do to me, Jackson. A gallon of hot chianti and your body won't be safe anywhere within my reach."

He hadn't thought about that—about the effects of hot chianti on her—but . . . "It's yours to command. I'll order, you get yourself over here."

After ordering Jackson took a quick shower. The

cashew cat, hot chianti, and Chrys all arrived at the same time. She paid because he didn't have any real money or his credit standard, which he supposed was still at Temporal Projects in Kansas City. They both ate voraciously—Jackson surprised all the while at how good the food was and how much he was looking forward to having sex with Chrys.

"Are you ready?" she asked before he had finished eating.

"Ready for what?"

"To go for a ride," she said, with false coyness as she stood up and gave him a sideways glance.

He hated her little euphemisms, but his body told him he was indeed ready. "Almost."

"I'm ready now," she said, pulling her sweater up over her head to reveal the unencumbered swell of her flesh.

"I, uh, I . . ." He realized he was staring and stuttering, but there was something else going on. His body was responding to the sight of Chrys's, but his mind was visualizing Suzanne Brelmer, wondering what she would look like naked, what her skin would feel like under the press of his fingers.

"Hurry," Chrys said. "I want to have sex. Now."

He hurried to swallow what he was chewing and follow her into the bedroom.

They had sex. She had it several times in that explosive way of hers. He had it once to coincide with her final convulsive explosion. She went to sleep.

Jackson floated on the little pond of endorphins sex had released in his brain—floated aimlessly, thinking, wondering, worrying, and finally, slipping quietly out of bed to wander naked into the living room where he absently began sorting the pile of mail as he nibbled on the remains of the cat. Amid all the fourth-, fifth-, sixth-, and eighth-class plastic junk mail, he found three green and yellow striped first-class private postage envelopes.

Two had no return addresses. The third was from Temporal Projects, and he opened it first. They had sent him official notification that his contract with them had been violated, that same contract was thus null and void, and consequently, that he was indebted to them for a sum—including interest and penalties—to be specified later as reimbursement for the cost of the training they had given him. The letter was postmarked April 14, before they sent him on his first trip.

Jackson tossed it aside. He was about to open the second envelope when Chrys wandered into the living room. Much to his surprise, his body responded instantly to the sight of her.

"Oh, good," she said, looking down at him. "I thought you'd forgotten me."

She held out her hand, and he took it, following her back to the bedroom again with a mixture of anticipation and annoyance. His body was obviously ready for the sex, but all the while Chrys straddled him and pushed him relentlessly toward orgasm, he saw flashes of Suzanne Brelmer.

Would she be as good as Chrys? Would he care? Could he care? Could sex be something more than a physical act of sterilubed bodies grinding against each other for physical relief?

At the moment of orgasm, he didn't care. But Chrys wasn't through with him, and by the time she had worked and stroked and coaxed him into a third orgasm, all he could think about through the tender aching pain of it was that there had to be something better than this between two people. There had to be something more than sex and release, something more than lust to be fulfilled—something more than bodies and flesh and orgasms and emptiness. There had to be. There just had to be. He fell asleep with tears in the corners of his eyes.

When he woke up, Chrys was snoring loudly beside him. He had to stifle a giggle. Once when they were watching an old holo movie they'd seen a diesel tractor and Jackson had told her it sounded just like she did when she snored. It was two weeks after that before she offered him sex again. But he had never mentioned again how loudly she snored.

According to the clock it was two in the afternoon. Jackson was hungry again. A trip to the cupboard brought out a freeze-dried lasagna. The addition of a little water and ten minutes in the waver made it hot and chewy. The aroma of it brought Chrys out of the bedroom wearing one of her silk robes.

"Lunch?" she asked with a yawn.

"Whatever. You eat this one and I'll do another."

"Thanks."

She ate while he wetted and waved another lasagna, then as he tried to eat, she knelt beside his chair and began running her hands over his body. "I've missed you, Jackson."

"You've missed the sex."

"I *had* sex while you were gone. I missed *you*."

"Why?" He was genuinely curious.

"You're different. You hold me afterward. I don't know. It's just better with you."

"Compliments accepted." His body had begun to respond to her hands and he ate faster in spite of himself.

"That's not a compliment. It's the truth." She had a firm grip on him, but her voice never changed pitch. "So where have you been? You were going to tell me last night, but we got interrupted."

"It's too hard to explain. New York, Geneva, Brezhnevgrad, but in a way . . . well, it's crazy. You're driving me crazy."

"Then let's do something about it."

Again they went to the bedroom. Again they had sex. But Jackson faked an orgasm after she had three, just so she would quit rubbing him raw. In five minutes she was asleep again, snoring like his favorite tractor.

He lay beside her, aching, unhappy, unfulfilled, frustrated, not knowing what to do, until he remembered the mail, the two first-class envelopes with no return addresses. Quickly he pushed himself out of bed, threw on some clothes, and went back to the living room. Under the cashew cat box he found them.

The first envelope he opened contained a computer microdisk and nothing else, no note, no name, nothing.

The second envelope contained a brief, handwritten letter from Homer Alvarez. It took Jackson a moment to remember who Alvarez was. Then he did. The husband of the missing Rosita Alvarez. Homer's note was written on the stationery of the Grandview Psychiatric Institute in Mountain Home, Arkansas.

Chapter Twenty

The note was signed by Homer Alvarez. The handwriting was ragged, but legible.

> *Dear Mr. Jackson,*
> *Please accept my apologies for any trouble I might have caused you concerning my past problems. You will be pleased to know that I am now under medical care and receiving fine treatement. You may direct all correspondence to this address.*
> *Sincerely,*
> *Mr. Homer Alvarez*

Jackson didn't believe for one minute that Homer Alvarez had written the letter by himself or for himself. It was too simple, too neat, too pat . . . too phony. The very paper stank of Temporal Projects and Brelmer and a lot of coaching—

Or maybe even someone else writing it. Jackson certainly had no idea what Homer Alvarez's handwriting looked like. The whole note could be a complete forgery, and Jackson would have no way of knowing. Then why had they sent it? Why send him a note from some distraught man he barely knew well enough to get arrested with? What purpose did it serve?

Jackson took a long deep breath and let it out slowly. If they—Temporal Projects—had wanted the letter to look like the real thing, why hadn't Homer mentioned his wife? After all, her connection to TP and Jackson's connections to TP were the only tenuous link between them . . . other than Lester Wu's apartment.

Shaking his head, Jackson laid the note aside and picked up the unlabeled computer cartridge. After staring at it for a long moment, he slid the stiff magnetic strip into the proper slot on his terminal. The screen flickered several times before turning a deep blue. Sharp-edged, pale yellow letters rolled in from the side of the screen.

"This program now has closed access control of your terminal. No external data will be admitted. Any attempts to copy, further transmit, or alter the data will destroy the data and infect all networked systems with destructive virus. Press your thumb on the recognition plate for further information," the message on the screen said.

Jackson pressed his left thumb on the plate and was startled when the screen flashed from blue to pale green.

RECOGNITION COMPLETE

FROM: LESTER WU   TO: JACKSON DUBCHEK
Jack—This is my insurance cartridge.
Things here at Temporal Projects are not what they appear to be, nor what the charter calls for

*them to be. It looks to me like someone is trying
to tamper with history—and that someone is us.*

Jackson laughed at the old cliché: we have met the
enemy and he is us. But the laughter tasted bitter in his
mouth. Lester was dead in Brezhnevgrad somewhere in
the past. There was nothing funny about that.

Quickly reading the rest of Lester's message, Jackson
looked for some clue, some small hint, anything, that
would help him understand what had happened to Lester
or what was happening to him or why TP was trying to
alter history.

Lester didn't know. At least, that's what he said on
the cartridge. But at the end of the cartridge's message
was a list of EBB numbers and addresses Jackson could
contact if—as Lester's message said—"I am no longer
available. These people might be able to assist you."

Jackson shivered, but for want of any other leads,
he copied the numbers on a piece of the junk mail, then
punched up the numbers for the first of the electronic
bulletin boards on Lester's list. Before he could call the
first address, however, out of the corner of his eye he
saw Chrys walking down the hall—naked, as usual, her
athletic body in top physical form.

"What's the matter, babe?" she asked as she came
up beside him and kissed him on top of the head.

"Nothing."

"Then what are you doing up?"

"Wasn't sleepy."

"Who you calling?"

"Oh, just a bulletin board."

"Why?"

At that moment, Jackson did not want to tell Chrys

anything, but neither was he good at lying to her. Instead of answering, he ran his hand down her tautly muscled thigh.

"What's so important about a dumb old bulletin board?"

"It might have some information I can use."

"For what?"

He looked up into her face and saw something he had never seen before—real curiosity . . . and something else, something he couldn't name. "It has to do with the Temporal Projects thing I was working on."

"Are you going to tell me about it?"

"I don't think I should." Her skin felt cool under his touch.

"Why? You don't think I'm smart enough to understand what—"

"Security. Top security. I swore not to say anything on penalty of my life."

"I don't believe you."

"It's true, Chrys." He wrapped an arm around her muscled legs and leaned his head against her hard abdomen. Fifty miles a week she ran to keep her body hard. Every once in a while he had wished she had a soft stomach he could burrow his face into. The scent of her made him twitch.

"What about us?"

"What do you mean?"

"Well, if you're going to sit there all day and fiddle around on your terminal, what am I supposed to do? It's my running day, you know."

"So go run." She smelled of sex, and sex was the last thing he was interested in at the moment. Unfor-

Warren Norwood

tunately, sex was the one thing Chrys was always interested in.

As she stroked his hair, she shifted her body so her right breast hung just above his eyes. "Come with me."

"You know I can't. I can't keep up with you . . . and you won't go slow. Then I end up running by myself. I hate running anyway. I really hate running alone. Pain, boredom, mindless—"

"I'll go slow, I promise."

"Chrys, please, if you want to run, run. If you want to go swim, swim. If you want to go to the sexatorium and find somebody better than me at sex, go. I know I don't always—"

"You're an uppity effing jerk." She pushed herself away from him and walked back down the hall. "And a really simple sexual," she called back to him. After a moment he heard the bathroom door slam.

It was just as well. Maybe she would go do her running and leave him alone. He liked Chrys. She was a nice girl, decent, kind, sexy, of course, but boring . . . very boring. Her list of interests beyond sex and athletics was limited to three things: oriental food, especially cashew chicken, cat, and dog, of which Springfield had an abundance; clothes, of which Chrys had an abundance; and *cine verde*. Chrys loved cine verde, the so-called green movies, pointless, plotless, senseless video montages highlighting beautiful bodies, bucolic sex, exotic food, strenuous exercise, and—usually at the finale—the modeling of clothes.

The thing Jackson hated most about cine verde was the music. He could close his eyes when Chrys dragged him to see one at the Landers Theater, or rented one of

185

the cine verde vids for her wallscreen, but he couldn't shut out the music. It was mindless, tuneless, hopeless orchestral imitations of wave sounds and wind through the trees and babbling brooks and undifferentiated chirping birds that, unlike real birds, knew no real songs.

With a sigh he punched in the first address.

LEAVE RETURN ADDRESS, the screen read.

He cursed softly, canceled the call, and punched in the next number.

LEAVE RETURN ADDRESS.

After more than a little hesitation, Jackson hit his return address button, then punched up the next number on Lester's list.

LEAVE RETURN ADDRESS.

"Damn."

"Same to you," Chrys said from behind him. He turned to see her dressed in her fluorescent blue Skintite running suit and orange Speedflasher shoes. Over her shoulders was her red duffle bag, crammed full.

"Where you going to run?"

"I'm leaving, Jackson." Her mouth was set in a firm downward curve. The duffle looked heavy.

"That's obvious. When will I see you again?"

"I don't know. Not soon. You make me mad."

That didn't surprise him in the least. Except when they were having sex or eating, almost everything he did irritated her in one way or another. "You leaving just because I wouldn't run with you?"

"Yes, and because you won't trust me." Her lips pulled into their natural pout.

"And because I won't say I love you," he added just to poke at her sore point.

Her face reddened. "Keep your stupid old love. I

don't want love from you. I told you I didn't want love the first day I met you in the sexatorium. You're the one who keeps bringing it up. Why can't we just have sex and a good time like other couples? Why do you always have to talk about love and all that?''

"All that meaning babies, I suppose?"

Her lower lip trembled.

"I'm sorry," he said, almost immediately. He had jabbed the biggest conflict in her life.

"No you're not."

He stood and walked toward her. "Yes I am. That wasn't fair of me and we both know it."

Her body stayed stiff when he hugged her. "You want to leave that laundry for me?" he asked softly, his lips close to her ear. Suddenly he wanted to have sex with her again and he didn't know why. "I'd be glad to do it while you run." He pulled his head back enough to see her face.

"You're horny again, aren't you?" she asked.

"Maybe."

"You are. And you're horny for me, Jackson.'' She did a slow pelvic grind against him. "Too bad. Sounds like a personal problem to me."

"I've heard this before." He put just enough disappointment into his voice to tell her he was willing to play their old game.

"Work it out yourself."

"Not as much fun that way. No fun for you."

"And what do you think you can do for me?" She let the duffle slip to the floor.

"Oh, I don't know. Give you an endorphin fix to start your run with."

She put her hands on his hips and pulled herself tight against him. "That would be nice. How long will it take?"

"As long as you want." He leered, surprised by how much lust had welled up in him. Could it be another of the side effects of time travel?

"All right, but I'm still leaving afterward."

"I understand."

They hurried to the bedroom, but took their time having sex. Jackson made sure the sex was most pleasurable to her, and was surprised again by images of Suzanne Brelmer atop him instead of Chrys. Afterward, they both fell asleep. When Jackson awoke, the house was dark and Chrys was gone. So were her duffle bag and almost all her clothes.

Jackson smiled to himself as he dressed. She would be back, but not too soon. He would get some time to himself, but not too much. Then Chrys would come to him for sex and the world would be closer to its old balance.

Except that it wouldn't. Everything had changed, and Jackson knew it could never achieve its old balance. For all he knew, there might never have been a true old balance. Chrys wanted children, but she refused to put her body through pregnancy. She saw pregnancy as something vulgar and nasty, but she longed for a baby of her own. That was the old balance . . . and it had never included images of Suzanne Brelmer riding him to ecstasy.

Nothing stays the same but food, he thought as he called his second most favorite eatery for a pizzamax.

"McSalty's Three Hundred," a young female answered. "Pizza for Springfield for three centuries. What can we cook for you, sir?"

He ordered a Kodiak Bear Pie, their largest size with the most ingredients. As he waited for his pizzamax to be delivered he called up the next address on Lester Wu's helplist.

Chapter Twenty-one

"You have to trust me, Suzanne," Brelmer said, wondering all the while what had possessed him to include his daughter on his staff. He had neither anticipated nor prepared himself for the anger under the surface of her words—but he should have prepared himself for it. Experience should have taught him—

"And you have to trust me, Father." She carefully controlled her breathing in an attempt to keep the emotion out of her voice. "What good am I to you if you don't trust me with the truth about Temporal Projects?"

His artificial eyes stared at her unblinkingly, reflecting a flat blue glare from the overhead lighting. "The truth is never as simple as we want it to be. If anyone should understand that, you should. The truth gets complicated all too quickly and usually cannot be explained in a brief discussion, regardless of how much I trust—"

"Father, don't. Don't play word games with me, please. I'm not your baby girl anymore and I'm not one of your retarded mutants. I'm not going to—"

"Watch your mouth, Suzanne. I am one of those so-called *mutants*—in case you have forgotten."

"No," she said, leaning back and crossing her arms over her chest, "I haven't forgotten that you let them mutilate you for the cause of—"

"I was not mutilated."

"—the Republic and the glory of peace."

He stared at her, seeing in her all the things that made her most difficult for him to cope with, things she called the Brelmer traits—stubbornness, self-assurance, and a relentless drive to understand and control their relationship. "You are not being very fair today, are you?"

"Fair is as fair gets. Why should I be fair with someone who doesn't trust me?"

"Fairness is its own reward."

"That's pretty hypocritical coming from you."

Brelmer flinched, but turned the action into a slamming of his palm flat on his desk. "I do not have to put up with this, from you or anyone else. I can and should treat you as I would treat any other employee of Temporal Projects. Consequently, in light of your unauthorized trip with Dubchek, I warn you that—daughter or not—I am totally prepared to dismiss you if necessary for the good of Temporal Projects . . . especially if you don't cease your insubordination."

"Oh, forgive me, Papa," she said, shaking her head in mock dismay. "Is wanting to know the truth now insubordinate? Good, Papa, good. Fire me. Live with that. You'll like it. You'll like my reaction, and Mother's, and maybe even your own. Papa flexes his muscle. We'll all cheer for you."

Beyond her sarcasm, he heard bitterness in her voice that slowed him down. Furthermore, her calling him Papa brought a snap response he had to stop before it reached his tongue. She never used that title with affection. Perhaps he had been too harsh with her.

"I am sorry, Suzanne. I did not mean to upset you. However, you must understand that my position requires certain controls—"

"You don't understand yet, do you, Father? Your bureaucratic junktalk isn't going to do anything for me. I don't like it, and I won't buy it, and I don't believe it, and I'm insulted that you would keep trying to use it on me."

"What do you want? What's really bothering you?"

"I've told you." She paused for a long, deep breath that she let out slowly. "I want the truth. Please? I want to know what's going on—what's really going on. What is TP trying to do that I don't know about? What are our real goals? I can't help you if I don't know what you and Senator Voxner are trying to accomplish."

"It is Top Secret, Suzanne."

"I'm cleared."

"Yes, but you don't have the need to know."

"Dammit, Father, I, I—" A sudden insight and the stern expression on his face made a smile play in the corners of her mouth. "Uh, oh, never mind. There are other ways to find out what you're doing."

Brelmer didn't like the sudden smug look that crossed her face. "I beg your pardon?"

She stood so he had to look up to her if only for a moment. Even a moment could be an edge. "You're not the only source of information in this business, Father. Despite all the impressive security, Temporal Projects is a sieve. It is riddled with holes in time and space—holes that leak information. If you won't tell me the truth, I'll just look elsewhere." Suzanne paused to give him an opening to respond, but his face remained impassive and he said nothing.

"Of course," she continued, "if the information I get from other sources is inaccurate, or incomplete, I won't have any way of knowing that for certain, but at least I will have better basis for making judgments on—"

"Not better, just different, probably worse."

His answer surprised her. "Is that what you want, then? You want me to seek the truth somewhere else?"

"It might prove interesting . . . might even help security plug up some leaks."

"Like the pope?" Suzanne asked without hesitation. "How are you going to plug up Pope George Ringo II? You going to displace him in time?" A brief twitch of her father's facial muscles told her she'd scored a point.

"What does Pope George Ringo have to do with anything?"

Suzanne shook her head. "That's classified. If the security people haven't told you, I certainly can't. You obviously have no need to know."

The rush of anger he felt was swept away by a wave of laughter. "Wrong, but good," he said. "I have a need to know everything. So tell me."

"Tell you what, Father? I don't understand the question." She watched with spiteful pleasure as the smile faded from his face.

"Do not play games with me, Suzanne. What does the pope have to do with security leaks here?"

"I can't recall, Father."

"Suzaaaaanne . . ."

"Perhaps you could help jog my memory." She gave him her best smile, knowing he was angry, and knowing she had pushed him almost as far as she dared, but knowing also that if they didn't find a path to resolve this problem, it could be a wedge between them that might never be removed.

"And what would that be? What would help jog your memory?"

"The truth. That's all I've ever asked from you. Why was Jackson Dubchek abandoned in New York in 2183? Why was he sent to Geneva in 1930? Why was Slye allowed to destroy Lester Wu? Where is Jackson now? What's going to—"

"One at a time, Suzanne. One at a time. The problem in 2183 was an operational error of judgment on the part of the—"

"Slye screwed up."

"If you insist on the vernacular, yes." He sighed softly. Suzanne's questions only aggravated his own, yet he dared not let her know that. "As for the unfortunate death of Lester Wu," he continued, "we have conflicting reports from Dubchek and Captain Slye and the follow-up evaluation team. But of course you know that already."

"Why did Slye screw up in 2183? What I want to know—what I need to know if I'm going to help you—is what made Slye believe that Jackson Dubchek had to be displaced?"

"I do not think that was Captain Slye's intention."

"I do. And I don't think he screwed up, Father. I think he thinks he was doing what you would have wanted him to do for the good of Temporal Projects." She watched his face carefully for some sign of what he was feeling.

"That evaluation," he said slowly, "seems unfortunately accurate to me. Captain Slye did, indeed, assume that he was helping the projects. The scouting reports have revealed a whole list of persons—''

"The scouting reports are rubbish, Father. You should have been able to spot that as soon as you saw the first set. They're predicated on futures that may never happen." Even as she said that, a disquieting shiver ran through her.

Again Brelmer sighed, this time more noisily, not caring if she saw his frustration. "You understand our official goals, do you not?"

"Of course. To preserve, protect, defend, and improve the Second Republic for the good of all its citizens."

"Correct. But how do we accomplish those goals? It seemed simple at first. Send observers back in time for firsthand accounts of historical events. Retrieve copies of important documents. But what did we find? Other time travelers—from ten years from now, and fifty, and unknowns. And what did we learn from them? . . . That there are no simple answers. The past changes the future and the future changes the past and there are more paradoxes than a brain—or a computer—can cope with."

Her father's sudden openness only made Suzanne want to hear more. "And so?"

"And so, the Department of Time Police. There are people from the future whose only purpose traveling back is to destroy the Second Republic. Time rebels, if you want the senator's term. People who want to destroy everything we have sworn to defend."

"And paradoxes, as you said."

"Yes, daughter of mine, paradoxes. The first trip back created a new past, a past which contained a visitor from its future, which meant that our past before then was a different past than the one we now have. Or was it? And if one of our teams observes the assassination of the Persian ambassador in the Federal District of New York in 2183, but our current history books do not mention it at all, what happened? Whose past were our observers in? Did someone from another future go back and stop the assassination?'' Brelmer rubbed his temples, suddenly weary.

"But we knew all this in theory before going back."

"Correct again. However, coming nose to nose with the reality behind the theory is something else. Do you know exactly why Temporal Projects was started—what the original impetus was?"

"Professor Mylius's proof of the ability to send objects back in time."

"Wrong. A visit, a visit from a future time traveler, a woman whose name should be familiar to you—Cassandra Yossarian."

Suzanne started. "The woman who was killed by the welfare mob in Westport?"

"Yes. They refused to believe she could be from the future, and when she told them that they were stupid and ignorant for supporting the Second Republic, they killed her. The official autopsy revealed that she had an organic artificial heart, and a synthetic filtering system to replace her kidneys."

"Then she was from the future."

"Absolutely. Now, we have reason to believe that Jackson Dubchek is in league with the same people, the ones out to weaken and destroy the Second Republic."

Something, something she couldn't specify or name, told Suzanne that her father was still not telling her the whole truth, but no matter how hard she pressed him, he wouldn't come to the heart of the matter—solid proof against Jackson. He had no evidence—at least none he was willing to share with her. However, when they reached their impasse, he agreed to talk to her more about it the next day, so she left him with a quick kiss on the cheek and headed for her office where much work remained for her to do.

After she left, Brelmer shook his head sadly. He had hated lying to her, but at the same time, the less Suzanne knew, the safer she was. At least that was what he hoped. There were no guarantees anymore—no guarantees that radical changes were not already happening in the past, changes that would require new adjustments to history even as he sat and thought about it. What frightened him was that someone would make an adjustment to history that would kill them all. And what frightened him even more was that there was nothing he could do about that.

Suzanne reached her office deep in thought, wanting to believe that she and her father had made some kind of a breakthrough, knowing that what had happened between them had been a compromise based on what remained of their mutual respect. She loved her father, and she wanted to believe in him totally, but if Jackson Dubchek had a revolutionary bone in his body, she would grow alligator feet and swim down the Missouri River.

Perhaps the time had arrived for her to do what she had threatened her father with—develop her own source network for information. And in the process . . . maybe she could find out what had happened to Jackson. Maybe she would start with that project first—but where? What if he had died in Geneva?

To her surprise, a tear rolled down her cheek.

Chapter Twenty-two

After eating half the McSalty's pizzamax, Jackson put the remainder into the refrigerator, knowing it would be just as delicious later, hot or cold. Then he returned to the terminal and punched up the last address on Lester's helplist. The response was immediate, but once more he read the message and shook his head in frustration. All seven of the addresses on the Electronic Bulletin Boards had given him exactly the same instructions.

LEAVE ADDRESS FOR RETURN MESSAGE.

"What's the point?" he muttered to himself. "And what's the use? You can sit here and play with these numbers, or do something constructive, like get in touch with the library and see if you can get your old job back."

A muscle in his jaw twitched hard enough to hurt. He turned his head back and forth, opened his mouth and moved his jaw around, but the twitch persisted. Now what? he wondered. Is the body treacherous going to start acting up on me? A low growl rose from his throat.

The muscle kept twitching like a silent painful met-
ronome marking time for a melody he couldn't hear.

"Relax. You have to relax," he said, getting up from
the terminal. The desperation in his voice was as obvious
as the ache in his jaw. If he didn't stop the twitching fairly
soon, he knew from experience, his jaw would hurt for
a week. "Odar'a," he whispered. "Play Odar'a."

He went to the corner and took his dulcimer case out
of the closet. For the briefest moment it looked unfamiliar
to him, almost alien. It had been too long since he'd played
Odar'a, too long since her beautiful antique body had
rested in his lap. Yet as soon as he took the dulcimer out
of the case, he felt an intimacy and eagerness that gave
him almost instant comfort. The twitching eased a little.

Jackson tuned Odar'a's four strings quickly, and no
sooner had he put the tuner down than he started to play
"Martha's Christening Song," an old tune that had been
the first one he had ever learned to play on her. His fingers
knew the song and the dulcimer better than they had ever
known any lover.

Odar'a had "Baird" branded behind the bridge, and
the signature of her maker, Joe Sanguinette, still faintly
visible inside the sound box—visible after almost three
hundred years. The dulcimer had been a gift from his parents on his sixteenth birthday, and along with Odar'a, his
father had given him a laminated slip of paper found inside
the sound box by her previous owner.

The paper said, "This Baird Mountain dulcimer was
made by Joe Sanguinette of Branson, Missouri, in 1987.
Her name is Odar'a, and as long as you love and play
her, she will provide you with the sweetest of music."

That was it. No signature. No date. Nothing else.

Jackson had done his best to love and play her because she gave him a pure emotional outlet without comparison. In return over the years, she had provided him with thousands of hours of beautiful music and a form of meditation deeper and more soul-satisfying than any of the many others he had tried. Playing Odar'a brought him internal peace.

His fingers moved almost without pause through "Martha's Christening Song" and "Missouri Violets" to "Hymn to Buddha," where in the momentary hesitation before the final chorus, he heard the low chime of an incoming call on his telephone. Unwilling to interrupt the song, he played through to the end. By the time he put Odar'a down and walked over to the phone, the caller had disconnected and left no message. Then as he started to turn away, he noticed a triangular symbol in the lower lefthand corner of the terminal screen.

What did it mean? Had he ever seen it before? Jackson didn't know. "More pizzamax, first," he said. His jaw muscle twitched again. When had it stopped? Why had it restarted? He reheated the pizzamax, then sat down at the table to eat it as he worked his way through the terminal's user manual. Finally, in a sub-subappendix of the manual under "Additional Symbols" he found the explanation for the triangular symbol on his screen. It meant his terminal was being or had been monitored.

For some reason he didn't understand, that information neither surprised Jackson nor upset him. If the Time Police knew he was back home, he would expect them to monitor him. If it wasn't them, he didn't—

The telephone rang again.

As he stood up to answer it, someone knocked on

his door. Unsure of which to answer first, he stood paralyzed between the two. Then his terminal signaled an incoming message.

Jackson went for the phone. The knocking grew louder. He punched the receive button on the terminal and picked up the phone at the same time. "Hello?"

"Is that you? Jackson, is that really you? Are you all right?"

"Who is this?"

"It's Suzanne—Suzanne Brelmer. Isn't this Jackson Dubchek?"

"Suzanne? How did you, I mean, how in the world—"

"I know you're in there, Mr. Dubchek, so you might as well open the door," a muffled voice called through the door.

"You have to be careful—very careful," Suzanne's voice said in his ear. "I'm sure you're in serious—"

"Can you hold a minute?" he asked, only half hearing her. "There's someone at the door."

"—danger. Don't answer it. Get out of there, Jackson. Grab whatever you need to live and get out of there. The Time Police are—"

The line went silent.

Everything went silent. The knocking had stopped, also. For the longest moment Jackson stood perfectly still, waiting, wondering what would happen next, fearing something he couldn't name or explain. It was as though Suzanne's words and the insistent visitor at the door had conspired to freeze him in place, then leave him there unable to move except for the twitching of the muscle in his jaw.

Finally, with great determination, Jackson straightened up, took a deep breath, let it out slowly, then forced himself to take a step forward. He tiptoed to the door, each step slow and cautious, each breath long and ragged. All the other muscles in his body trembled in sympathy with his jaw as he leaned forward and peeped through the spyhole in the door.

A man stood on his landing—a large man at least two meters tall—wearing mirrorshades and a pullover cap that failed to hide his oversized ears. A Time Policeman.

Jackson swallowed hard. His eyes flicked from corner to corner of the door, and in each corner saw a green security light glowing. The system was completely locked. If the Time Policeman wanted to force the issue, he would have to destroy the door to get in. If there was a—

"I know you can hear me, Mr. Dubchek. Look, I'm not here to harm you or do anything disrespectful to your person. I'm only here to assist you. In fact, you don't even have to leave your apartment if you don't want to. But we have to talk, Mr. Dubchek. That's my job, you see, talking to you, so you might as well let me in and get it over with, because I'm prepared to wait here as long as necessary."

Even as the Time Policeman talked, Jackson backed away from the door, the trembling of his body aggravated by a fear of what now was no longer nameless and faceless. His fear had a menacing presence outside his door. He knew that the first thing he had to do was to take Suzanne's advice—pack a few necessities and get out of his apartment.

With exaggerated caution he forced himself to walk down the hall to his bedroom, almost as though he expected the Time Policeman to break through the wall and grab him. Out the emergency chute, he thought, staring at its door beside his closet, I can escape out the emergency chute. Using the chute would set off the building alarms, but even that might help cover his escape.

"Oh, you're brave," he whispered as he pulled his old backpack out of his bedroom closet. "Yeah, you're real brave now," he muttered under his breath while beginning to fill the pack. "Grab your stuff and run. Socks. Toilet kit. But will you stay that way? Will you stay brave? Underwear. Toothbrush. Shirts. Pants. Probably not." Suddenly he couldn't think of anything else to pack. What else did he really need?

"Food? Should I take food? . . . No. Then what?" He zipped the pack closed. Books? he thought as he tiptoed back into the living room. Only then did he see the blinking light on his screen and remember that along with Suzanne and the Time Policeman, a message had come in for him. The light went out as he called up the message.

> *PER YOUR REQUEST FOR*
> *ASSISTANCE. A TIMEPOLICEMAN WHO*
> *IDENTIFIES HIMSELF AS BRYAN WILL*
> *ARRIVE AT YOUR LOCATION WITHIN THE*
> *HOUR. YOU CAN TRUST HIM. HE WILL*
> *LEAD YOU TO US AND WE WILL GIVE YOU*
> *WHATEVER ASSISTANCE WE CAN. DO*
> *NOT ATTEMPT FURTHER CONTACT.*
> *TYSONYLLYN*

Jackson stared at the message almost without comprehending it. He had no idea who Tysonyllyn was or why—

Then he remembered. Tysonyllyn was Satan—the

man in New York in 2183 who looked like a cheap holo's idea of Satan, anyway. But where is he now? Jackson wondered. Here in Springfield?

Of course. Tysonyllyn was in charge of moving people—traffic, Jackson recalled Rankin's terminology only too well—in charge of moving traffic through time for the Mnemosyne Historians. Why couldn't Tysonyllyn have come from the Federal District of New York in 2183 to Springfield, Missouri, in 2249? No reason. None at all.

"Mr. Dubchek, at least have the courtesy of talking to me. You can do that, can't you?"

And no reason *for* Tysonyllyn to come to Springfield, either, Jackson thought, ignoring the voice at the door, no reason for him to come unless, unless . . . what? Jackson wasn't sure what.

Then the reality of the problem hit Jackson in a totally unexpected way, and he had to stifle the urge to giggle. Assuming that Tysonyllyn had access to his own time machines, he could go or be anywhere in time he pleased. He didn't have to be in Springfield to send for Jackson. Suppose the Time Policeman—what was his name? Jackson checked the screen. The message had faded in a process of self-erasure, but he could still make out the name. Bryan—that was it, Bryan. Suppose Bryan wanted to take him back to 2183?

"Do I go or stay?" Jackson asked himself. "Do I trust Tysonyllyn or not? Can I trust a time policeman?" He shook his head. "Oh, Buddha, how did I manage to get myself in this fix? And more importantly, what do I have to—"

Renewed pounding on the door stopped his slide toward self-pity and reawakened the twitching of his jaw muscle.

"Mr. Dubchek! Would you quit playing games? Please? You might as well let me in now so we can get this over with and go on about our business."

A Time Policeman—maybe Bryan, maybe not, probably not—stood on Jackson's landing demanding his attention, but again fear and indecision paralyzed him.

"You have to come out sometime. Delay isn't going to do anything but frustrate both of us," the Policeman said.

Still Jackson didn't move, couldn't move.

"What needs doing?" a voice in his head asked.

"I don't know," he said aloud, but he knew the voice. It was the voice of his old constructive-living teacher asking the fundamental question of Morita-Reynolds.

"Yes, you do. Look at the situation. Accept what reality has given you. Recognize what needs doing. Do it."

Hide the evidence, Jackson thought. He pressed the message-delete key. The screen cleared. With an overwhelming feeling of innocence, he looked around the living room as though it contained more information about what he needed to do.

"I don't know what you think this waiting will accomplish, Mr. Dubchek," the Time Policeman said in his weary-sounding voice.

Odar'a, he thought. Quickly he packed his dulcimer in her case. Now, prepare to run. Taking the dulcimer case in one hand and the backpack in the other, he walked back to the bedroom and set them beside the emergency-chute door. All the while an odd thought rose to the top of his consciousness like a slow bubble rising through a bottle of molasses . . . Mr. Dubchek? The Time Policeman calling him *Mr.* Dubchek? Why? Why so polite?

It didn't fit. The politeness didn't fit with the Time Police Jackson knew, nor did it fit with the man on the landing who again pounded so insistently on his door. It could only mean the Time Police wanted something. Whatever it was, Jackson didn't mean to give it to them.

Chapter Twenty-three

"All right, all right. Quit your banging. I'm coming. I'm coming." As he fought to control his voice, Jackson leaned against the door to steady his body. The screwdriver he'd picked up on his way to the door pressed hard against his leg. What he intended to do with it did not help calm him. "Who are you?" he asked through the intercom.

"You know who I am," the Time Policeman answered.

"No I don't. I don't know anything about you." Jackson could hear the skeleton of his lie rattling in his throat, but he was determined to go through with it. What choices did he have?

"Isn't your spyhole working? Look at me. Look at my face. Look at my ears. What more do you need to know?"

Jackson peered through the spyhole almost as though he expected to find that something about the Time Policeman might have changed. Nothing had. "What do you want from me? Why are you here? Who sent you?"

The man laughed with what sounded like genuine

amusement. "I didn't know you had such a wonderful sense of humor. No one told me that. You're funny. Now, be reasonable, Mr. Dubchek. Let me come in and talk to you. What harm can that do?"

Jackson wanted to take his turn laughing, but the impulse died aborning. "You can do me all the harm in the world, I would guess," he managed to say. As he spoke, his voice climbed an octave higher than normal.

"Like I told you before, all I want to do is talk to you."

"What do you mean, before?" Jackson forced his voice lower again, working for a steady sound that would flesh out the lie. "I've never seen you before."

"When I first got here," the Time Policeman said. "You know what I mean."

"Just now? You mean just now?"

"I mean thirty minutes ago."

"I was asleep."

"Don't lie to me, Mr. Dubchek. I heard you talking."

"Must have been the radio . . . or the neighbors. I've been asleep. All your banging just woke me up."

The man didn't reply. Jackson peeped at him again and was surprised to see the Time Policeman's back to the door. It took him a minute to realize that the man was talking to someone on a small transceiver. When the policeman turned back to the door, his face looked lined and tired.

"Okay, Mr. Dubchek, I'll play the game your way. You just woke up. I just got here. We have to talk. Let me in, please, and we'll talk. If you don't like what I have to say, you can ask me to leave."

"And you'll just leave, right?"

"Of course."

"How foolish of me to think otherwise," Jackson muttered under his breath.

"What? Did you say something?"

"No. . . . No."

"Are you going to let me in?"

"No."

The man sighed noisily. "Mr. Dubchek, don't make this difficult, please. There's no point in it. I can get a warrant, you know. And I can get it without leaving your landing. And I can stand right here till it comes, then force the manager to disable your security system and let me in. Is that the way you want to do it?"

Those words convinced Jackson that the Time Policeman at his door either wasn't Tysonyllyn's Bryan, or if he was Bryan, that he wasn't really there to help. Whichever way the coin came up, Jackson lost. He took the screwdriver from his pocket with a grim smile. "Mister, if that's what you have to do to satisfy your reality, I guess you'll just have to do it."

"What do you mean? You trying to tell me you *want* me to get a warrant?"

"If that's what you have to do, don't let me stop you. I'm not opening this door voluntarily."

"Have it your way, Dubchek, but you'll regret this decision. Things like this make me angry."

"Surprise, surprise." Jackson switched the intercom off before the Time Policeman answered, so he couldn't hear clearly what the man said, and he didn't care.

Using a trick Chrys had taught him, he pried the cover off the security panel next to the door and moved the override switch to manual. Even if the Time Police and the manager disabled the external half of the system, the internal half would continue to function for as long as its batteries lasted. Chrys would never explain why it had been necessary for her to use that trick or who she had learned it from, but she had assured him that if the batteries were any good at all, the security system should remain intact for at least ten hours. Nothing short of explosives would let them in before that.

That gave Jackson sufficient hope to proceed with what little plan he had. Flipping a secondary manual switch slid the tornado shutters over his windows where they locked into place. Sensors turned on lights in each room as the apartment darkened. Once he decided exactly when he would try to make his escape, everything would be ready.

After dark, he thought. Two hours, maybe three. He yawned, suddenly tired. Time enough for a short nap.

No. Have to stay awake. But he went to the bedroom and lay down anyway. "Just in case," he said, setting the alarm for three hours. Once he turned out the lights, his eyes closed and his body grew heavy.

Chrys flitted across his mind, running down the beach under a high Texas sun. A second image followed Chrys, chased her away, drifted, returned, floated down into Suzanne, Suzanne with tea and oranges dark and beautiful sprawled naked across the front of a highly polished time machine. She beckoned to him, her hand moving a flower petal in a gentle breeze.

He responded, moving closer at the same time. No, not naked—she wasn't naked. Not quite. But her blue sunsuit, a slender Y of fabric stretched across the full curves of her glowing skin, left very little to his imagination. His imagination played with the little it had.

Lips nibbled . . . Hands stroked . . . Fingers guided . . . Breath teased . . . Flesh warmed . . . Music played . . .

The sea rocked. Gulls cried. His boat rolled with the swell.

"Swim," a voice whispered. *"Swim hard, hard. Oh, god, swim hard."*

The gulls cried louder. Surf roared up the beach. Salt stung his eyes. A gull screamed in his ear.

Jackson sat up with a start and slammed his hand down on the alarm all in the same motion. The bedroom was dark. Tears wet his face. Had he turned out the lights? He couldn't remember. What had happened to Suzanne? A few moments more and . . . they would have made it. Shivers ran up and down his spine. His clothes clung to him, damp with perspiration.

Then he remembered everything and listened. The apartment was silent. Was the Time Policeman still parked on his landing? Did it matter? Unless he wanted to submit to the Time Police, he had no choice but to run.

But run where? He couldn't go to his brother's place in Texas. They'd look there for sure. So where? He didn't know, but he pushed himself out of bed and began stripping off his wet clothes.

Branson. The name popped into his head as he pulled on a clean shirt. Branson? Yeah, Branson, that would be good. Nice little town—population of fifty or sixty thousand plus lots of tourists in Silver Bullion Center amusement complex and gamblers in the casinos, and little clubs where a dulcimer player might find cash work without being asked a lot of questions. The thought of making a living playing Odar'a brought a brief smile to his lips.

The other good thing about Branson was that Jan and

Pac Verba lived there. They were the only people he knew who might be able and willing to help him hide from the authorities—and since Pac was a professional fiddler, and Jan was a music producer, they had the right contacts.

Branson it was, then. He could take the commuter special and easily get there in time for breakfast. He thought about calling the Verbas, then quickly changed his mind. Someone was monitoring his terminal and phone. Better just to pop in on Jan and Pac, a surprise visit.

After he finished changing clothes, he walked quietly into the living room and stood staring at the front door. The green lights in the corners blinked slowly. The security system was already on manual. Time to get his tail out of there.

He tiptoed back to the bedroom, put on his black leatherette dipyoked jacket and his flat-brimmed ranger hat with its chin strap and pull-down visor. His best pair of cat-skin gloves completed the look he wanted—Ozark conventional. Wearing that outfit, he could blend into any local crowd in almost every town from Tulsa to West Memphis and Kansas City to Shreveport.

Go, he thought. Time to go.

For a long moment he stood staring at the door to the emergency chute, ready to go, but not quite willing. First he wanted to visualize step by step what he would do. He'd been down the chute once before in an evacuation drill, and thus knew he couldn't wear the backpack down the chute.

So, open the door. Throw down the backpack. Hold the dulcimer case close to the chest, and jump down, feet first.

Suddenly he had a bizarre impulse and started digging

in the side pockets of his backpack. Moments later he took out a fuel tablet and his camp lighter. He ran down the hall, set the fuel on his desk on top of Lester Wu's cartridge.

One long deep breath in and out slowly, then he struck the lighter and set the fuel on fire. It caught immediately, the flames eating hungrily at the paper on the desk. He had to resist the impulse to put it out and, instead, turned his back on it and ran back down the hall. Every possession he owned except Odar'a would go up in flames.

With a quick wrench of the handle on the emergency door he flung the door open. In the distance a klaxon sounded. In the living room flames crackled. He threw the backpack down, pleased to see it slide quickly out of sight. With Odar'a clutched in one arm, he climbed into the chute and let himself slide.

He shot around a slick curve. Too fast. Panic grabbed his heart. His throat constricted. Lungs closed.

Moments later the chute dumped him onto the padded dispersal mound in the basement of his building. He tumbled to its edge, gasping for breath, eyes open, expecting to see himself surrounded by Time Police.

The basement was empty of people, but full of the sound of the emergency klaxon.

After a lot of fumbling, he retrieved his backpack from the other side of the dispersal mound, jerked the pack on, grabbed Odar'a's case by its shoulder strap, and ran down the evacuation tunnel out of the basement. The insistent sound of the klaxon followed him down the red-lit tunnel.

Three choices, he reminded himself, as he ran awkwardly down the echoing concrete tube, the dulcimer case banging against his leg, the backpack bouncing against his waist. Sunshine exit, Sad Hammond Road, or Billingsley Park. He glanced over his shoulder. No one behind him. Not yet.

At the first intersection he went left. The sound of the klaxon abruptly faded. At the second intersection, he went right toward Billingsley Park. Jackson figured it was the least likely of the exits they would expect him to use, plus the park offered him more places to hide than either of the road exits.

Approaching the exit door, he had sudden, serious second thoughts. What if they were waiting for him? He stopped and bent over, hands on knees, surprised to hear the harsh gasping of his lungs, dismayed to feel the pain in his legs. If the Time Police were waiting for him on the other side of the door, there was nothing he could do about it. He couldn't go back.

Still panting, he straightened up and pushed the bar handle to open the door. It swung slowly, letting cool air and a flurry of leaves flow in around him. Beyond the door lay a concrete ramp littered with leaves and the dim lights of the park shining through halos of mist.

He waited, for what he didn't know. When nothing happened after thirty seconds or so, he trudged through the leaves and up the ramp. The door swung shut behind him with a quiet thud, but Jackson never broke stride, hoping for all the world to look like he walked up that ramp and into the park three times a day. But with every step he took, his stomach turned over three or four times. When he had walked fifty meters and heard and seen nothing unusual, he risked a glance over his shoulder.

Flames rose from the roof of Strawberry Fields. And someone walked behind him through the shadows.

Chapter Twenty-four

The keening wail of a fire truck's siren filled the night. Flashing, multicolored lights lined the other end of the park. The figure in the shadows behind Jackson moved with a grace and ease Jackson had seen only too recently. He moved like a Time Policeman.

Jackson spun away from the dark figure, away from the fire and the flashing lights—spun away from the past that threatened his future and walked with fast, measured steps toward the far corner of the park. His mind told him not to run, that he would give himself away, but his adrenal gland pumped his system full of the energy of panic.

Maybe I didn't really see anyone there, he thought. Maybe I didn't. Maybe I didn't.

Footsteps ran through the dim light.

Jackson ran, too.

"Dubchek, wait!"

He ran faster. The pack bounced like a living creature, its straps like claws trying to twist him around.

The footsteps pounded closer.

Jackson sensed that he could escape somehow if he

dropped Odar'a, and shucked the backpack, that if he didn't hesitate, he—

"Wait."

As he tried to look over his shoulder to see how close the man was, Jackson's legs tangled with the dulcimer case. It was yanked from his hands, and he tumbled into the wet grass. Even before he stopped sliding, his body scrambled instinctively to put him back on his feet. But before he could get his feet under him, a powerful hand clutched his right arm and pulled him up.

"Easy. Easy. I'm here to help you get—"

"Let go! Let go of me!" Jackson kicked and twisted, catching only flashes of the man's metallic eyes, smelling heavy clouds of the man's stinking breath. Fighting the grip that tightened on his arm, Jackson swung his arms wildly against the man's body. "Let go!"

"Easy, I said!"

His left boot connected with the Policeman's knee. The man grunted before jerking Jackson's arm. Jackson's body suddenly dangled just off the ground.

"Dammit, I'm Bryan. Didn't they tell you I was coming?"

Trying to kick the man again, Jackson twisted around, yet succeeded only in wrenching his right shoulder.

The Time Policeman held him at arm's length like a butcher would hold a cat by its scruff right before hitting it with the stunner. "I said, I'm Bryan. I know you're Dubchek."

But Jackson wasn't stunned yet. Despite the pain in his arm and shoulder, he tried once more to kick the man. A cry of agony echoed through the park—his own agony.

"Listen," the Time Policeman growled, "at least one

of them has seen us and is moving toward us. I may have to fight—more than one of them. But don't you run away. I'm the only friend you've got." With that he lowered Jackson to a sitting position on the ground and turned to face the far end of the park.

A wave of pain swept through Jackson, pushing him down into a dark undercurrent of relief. Tears joined the cold mist on his face. His body swayed. His shoulder burned. His head floated. He held his right arm against himself the way mothers held babies. But the sounds pushing past his lips were moans, not coos.

Grotesque shadows wove in front of him. Someone grunted. A voice muttered dark, indecipherable threats. *Swoosh*. Grunt. Grunt. *Swoosh*.

Jackson blinked back the tears and tried to focus. Dark shadows of giants danced in the haloed mists. Time Policeman.

Suddenly Jackson's head cleared. While they fought, he had to get away. As he pushed himself up to his hands and knees, he swayed like a dog recovering from anesthesia.

More sirens wailed, some approaching, some receding, making the dizzy night swirl with the oscillation of sounds.

Bodies slammed together. The giants growled and grunted.

Escape, Jackson reminded himself. Can't wait. God now. Not god now, *go* now. Go, now. Still he swayed, his eyes searching the ground for . . . Odar'a! What had happened to Odar'a? Where was she? He looked desperately around. How would he make a living in Branson without her? Where was she?

A giant roared. A shot sounded.

Jackson looked up in time to see one of the Time Policemen stagger backward and collapse. The other whipped his body around in a low crouch—dull light in his artificial eyes, guttural sounds stirring in his throat, gun in his steady hand pointing its dark hole of a muzzle directly at Jackson.

The night stopped. The wail of distant sirens hung suspended in a cold B-flat. The air froze in Jackson's lungs. His knees locked. His universe shrank to the ten meters between him and the muzzle of the gun.

Time built up behind the pause like a wave building to a crest before it finally crashed over them all.

Jackson panted for breath. Sirens wailed in the night. His body trembled. His shoulder ached. Then, much to Jackson's surprise, the man spun around again, pausing every quarter of the circle until seconds later he faced Jackson again.

"We've got to get you out of here," the man said.

Before Jackson could figure an answer, the man had put his gun away, retrieved Odar'a from the shadow of a tree, and was helping Jackson to his feet.

"Who are you? Who sent you?"

"I'm Bryan, like I told you, and I've got a tube car over there," he said, guiding Jackson by the elbow toward Sad Hammond Road. "And you should know who sent me. You called for help."

"No I didn't." When Bryan didn't argue, Jackson again found himself at a loss for words. Only when they were strapped in the tube car with Odar'a and his backpack stashed on the jump seat behind them did it suddenly occur to him to ask, "Where are you taking me?"

"To someone who can help you." Bryan made a U-turn and headed away from Billingsley Park and the burning Strawberry Fields toward downtown Springfield.

"You said that already."

"It's true."

"Maybe . . . but who is it? Who can help me?"

"The Mnemosyne."

"That's who you work for, right—the Mnemosyne Historians? Aren't they wanted for all kinds of crimes?"

"Yes, and yes again. But don't worry about that. You have serious problems of your own, young man."

Only when Bryan said that did Jackson take a close look at him in the light from the instrument panel. Despite his bioengineered ears and nose, and his artificial eyes, Bryan looked fifty or sixty years old. Then an unexpected question occurred to him. "When are you from?"

Bryan only snorted in the way that passed for a laugh among the Time Police, and kept on driving. Jackson forced himself to sit back and watch the city lights flicker past him. If I see some landmarks I'll know where I am, and then maybe I'll know how to get out again, Jackson told himself. The car moved almost too quickly for him to focus, but it gave him something to think about besides the pain in his arm.

They headed east, past the back of the old Elfindale Video Palace. Jackson had wandered the gardens around Elfindale often enough to recognize it even through the haze of pain, smoke, and glare of reflected lights. Suddenly their way was blocked by a bright flashing wall and Bryan made a hard right turn to avoid the roadblock. The momentum sent Jackson thumping into the hatch lock, and a new lightning bolt of pain shot down his arm.

As his eyes cleared, he dimly glimpsed the looming bulk of St. John Q's hospital, but Bryan turned again, and Jackson lost his bearings. Then as the car zipped through a major intersection on a pink light, Jackson realized the vast parking lot coming up on the left was the university. They had entered the north side of town, which was considered dangerous, as well as unfashionable, and Jackson rarely went there.

Once past the last dormitory he got confused again. When Bryan threaded the complicated tangle of one-way streets around Boatman's Square, Jackson got completely lost. No one ever came to this part of town except the bankers and financiers, and they had ringed their maxi-security high rises with a sort of no-man's-land of empty buildings. Jackson had seen old photographs of the area when it was a thriving shopping district 350 years before, in the early 1900's. Now it looked like a war zone.

Their speed and the lack of street lights made it impossible for Jackson to read the few battered street signs. He had only the vaguest idea of where they were when Bryan brought the car to a stop in the maw of an old bunkerlike reinforced-concrete parking garage. Customer Parking Only! Violators Will Be Towed! a faded sign read. Jackson giggled in spite of himself to think that there had once been competition for these parking places.

Bryan helped him out of the car, shouldered the backpack, and handed him Odar'a. "Can you walk?" he asked.

Jackson nodded automatically even though his knees shook with a different message. Without another word Bryan turned and led him out of the garage, past the mouth of an alley to a small building standing next to a hole that looked like a bomb crater. A sign in the middle of the crater proudly proclaimed:

Warren Norwood

Future home of
Nouvelle Seville Luxury Hotel
And Convention Center.
Your Republican Tax Dollars at Work.

Jackson glanced around as Bryan led him up the steps of the building, and saw that it was very old—an historical building. He looked past its strangely shaped awning and saw rows of broken-out light bulbs, and above them a magnificent carved marble head, with an elaborate pseudo-Greek headdress. The face's tongue stuck out at him. Jackson stuck his tongue out in response, and giggled again.

Bryan turned to him. "Are you sure you're all right?"

Jackson nodded and cradled his arm closer to his body.

"Don't worry about your arm," Bryan said. "There will be someone inside who can fix it up for you, and give you something for the pain."

The building's double front doors led into a large open room with barred windows all along one wall. Jackson frowned at them, trying to decide whether or not they were some kind of primitive cells. They all had little round holes for speaking through, and small slots for sliding in food, but somehow they didn't look secure enough to hold prisoners, and at the moment they seemed empty.

They went past the cells and through another set of double doors into gloomy darkness. Jackson got the sense of vast space, although a screen of some sort ten feet past the door hid the rest of the room. Wide stairways on the right and the left led to the second floor.

Bryan took the right-hand stair, which led them up to a narrow hallway next to the same sort of screen that blocked the room downstairs. Jackson saw a tiny space in the screen and craned his neck to see beyond it. All he could see were rows upon rows of chairs that ended abruptly with a railing, and beyond that, darkness. Dim lights revealed grotesque golden faces that framed a huge hole at the far end of the room.

Suddenly Jackson thought he knew where he was—the Landers Auditorium and Vandivort Center for the Preservation of Live Performance Arts. The building had been preserved as a historical landmark, and now supposedly housed an odd group of people who persisted in the notion that computer-generated entertainment was not as good as the sort performed by live actors and singers. No amount of argument about the perfect pitch produced by the synthesizers, or the endless repeatablilty of the holoformers, had convinced them that human actors were inferior, so finally the Local Council had agreed to give them this godforsaken little historical building and left them alone.

Jackson had heard that they occasionally produced real plays in the ancient theatrical tradition, but he didn't know anyone who went to see them. He had heard rumors the place was some sort of insane asylum—and the government actually forced crazy people to live there and act in the plays to earn their treatment.

Bryan took him up yet another flight of stairs and down another dingy hall to a poorly lit vestibule where they had a choice of four doors. Strange moaning came from behind one of them, and the Time Policeman opened it without bothering to knock.

Nine or ten people crawled all over a raised platform.

Some hopped like rabbits, others staggered around on their hands and knees like clumsy dogs or horses, and one writhed on his belly like a snake.

Jackson looked frantically around and knew the rumors were true—Bryan had brought him to an insane asylum.

Chapter Twenty-five

"Actors," Bryan whispered, almost in reverence.

Jackson looked from the people on their hands and knees to Bryan and back to the people in disbelief. The people ranged in age from teenagers to old people with white hair, and each made noises in time to his or her movements. When Jackson listened closely the sounds resolved themselves into elongated words.

"Weeeee . . . thuuuh . . . peeeeepole . . ."

"Liiief . . . liiiberteee . . . and thuuuh purrsooot . . ."

"Shalllll not perishhhh from the earrrrth."

Jackson shuddered and drew back. The words made no sense to him, and the contortions of the actors, if that's what they were, frightened him. It all made him feel less steady on his feet.

"Irene around?" Bryan asked.

No one answered. All the actors seemed too absorbed in their weird chants to so much as look up. Bryan shrugged with a grin and backed out of the room, closing the door softly before he turned to the next room.

That one was also full of people, but they were all sitting in regular chairs in front of the little platform stage, listening to a tall man who stood before them. With his eyes closed, he was apparently reciting from memory.

" . . . have information vegetable, animal, and mineral. I know the kings of England and can quote the fights historical, from Marathon to Waterloo in order categorical."

"Very good, Joey," called an older man who sat at the side of the stage in a wreath of smoke. "Who's next?"

Joey opened his eyes and smiled brilliantly as he yielded the stage to a blond woman.

"In July of nineteen forty-five Truman, Stalin, and Churchill met in Potsdam, East Germany, to clarify the terms of the Yalta Agreement, and to—"

"No, no, no!" The older man leaped out of his chair and stormed onto the stage. "You have to open your mouth, dear. Don't clench that jaw. It's clair-i-fieee, not clurfie. Clair-i-fie. Now start again."

Bryan cleared his throat and the man looked around at him impatiently. "And what may I do for you, Bryan?"

"I need to find Irene."

The man looked from Bryan to Jackson. "I haven't seen her since the last break, but she might be in the main classroom. I think she was planning to look in on the beginning interp group."

"Thank you."

The man had turned back to the young woman before Bryan finished speaking. "Now remember, keep those jaws open. Don't swallow your voice. You have a lovely voice." He grabbed her around the waist. "Support it from here, and let your throat relax."

Bryan sighed as he shut the door. "Do you think you can take another flight of stairs, Jackson?"

"What are all these people doing here?" Jackson

asked, more concerned that he had landed in the midst of madmen than that he might not be able to climb another staircase.

"Learning to act. What did it look like? The first room was improvisation, and the second room was Howard's voice improvement class. Some of them are full-time actors. Most are students, I think."

"And the things they were saying?"

"Memory exercises, tongue twisters, elocution lessons, that kind of thing. It's all pretty routine stuff around here . . . I've done a little of it," he added with a hint of pride.

The thought of Bryan twisting tongues reminded Jackson of his twisted shoulder, and it throbbed on cue. He cradled his arm closer to his body. "Who is this Irene you want me to meet?"

"You'll see. Come on. The main classroom is up on the fourth floor."

Numbly Jackson followed the Time Policeman down yet another dimly lit hallway, and up another flight of rickety stairs, into another room where acting students were gathered around a platform stage. A tiny dark haired woman worked with the student on the platform.

"What is it you're saying? 'After the Dictates were lifted in 2099 a new spirit of adventure swept through the fashion world.' Think about the words you're saying. See the color in those words. *New spirit. Adventure. Swept.* Can't you feel the energy, the excitement in those words?"

"Use that. Feel that new spirit. Get excited about that adventure. Let it sweep you away. And carry that into your gestures. Sweep that arm out. Feel that spirit of adventure all the way out to your fingertips." The woman's arm swept out as if trailing a gossamer veil. "Don't let it get out to your elbow and just die." She repeated the gesture, this time letting her arm go limp halfway through. "Would you want to wear a dress like that? Now try it again."

"Excuse me, Irene?"

The woman glanced up at Bryan, and Jackson felt as if she had put them both under a high-power microscope. He had never met anyone with such strength of presence. It was as though she had completely focused on teaching, then switched that same total focus to them. For some reason he tried to clear the expression of pain from his face so she wouldn't see it.

"Is this the man, Bryan?"

"Jackson Elgin Dubchek. I didn't want to disturb you, but he has hurt his shoulder." The hulking Time Policeman seemed to shrink under the tiny woman's gaze.

"Nonsense, it's no bother at all." She turned that electrifying gaze back on the class and smiled. "You're all doing very well, and I've enjoyed working with you. I'll come back to check on you again next week."

Then with no more fuss, she worked her way through the group and led Bryan and Jackson out of the room.

They trailed her back down the hall to a little cubbyhole office where she pointed them toward chairs. Bryan leaned Jackson's pack against an overflowing bookcase, and Jackson set the dulcimer case next to the pack. His shoulder ached with a life of its own.

"Are you hungry, Mr. Dubchek? May I offer you some coffee? Bryan, would you be a dear and go get Cheryl—she's in 314—and ask her to come look at Mr. Dubchek's arm?"

Bryan left the room, and Jackson took the steaming

coffee cup thankfully. After a sip he looked up at Irene and frowned. "I don't know what I'm doing here," he said. This close he could see that she was older than he'd expected her to be—much older, maybe the oldest living human being he had ever seen.

"Don't stare so, young man. You called for our help."

"I did?"

"Didn't you leave your address on our bulletin board?"

Through the fog of all that had happened since his return from Geneva, it finally made a crude kind of sense to Jackson. "Are you really the Mnemosyne Historians?"

"Who told you that?"

"Bryan."

Irene clucked her tongue. "That's one of the problems with altering people. A little bioengineering seems to make them lose their sense of duplicity. Officially, Mr. Dubchek, we are the students and staff of the Vandivort Center for the Preservation of the Live Performance Arts, and I'll thank you not to forget that."

He shook his head. "So, does that mean I've been rescued by a bunch of actors?"

"It's the sort of dramatic gesture that makes good theater, don't you think?"

With a sigh Jackson sank back in his chair. "Please, ma'am, I'm too tired for this kind of game. Could you just tell me why you brought me here, and what I have to do to go home again?"

"Why, you have the power to go home anytime you want to. All you have to do is click the heels of your ruby slippers and repeat, 'There's no place like home, there's no place like home.'"

Only then did Jackson see how confused he had become and recall his burning apartment. Only then did he realize how stupid what he said had been. He had no home to go to. He had burned it down. Dimly he remembered his notion of going to Branson, and dimly it still seemed like a good idea, but when? And how? He didn't know, and he—

The door behind him opened, and Bryan came back in, followed by a tall, thin-legged, hugely pregnant woman in black tights and a maternity smock. Without a word she knelt beside Jackson's chair and began manipulating his arm.

Pain lanced through him. "Hey, be careful!" He tried to twist away. That only made the arm hurt worse, and caused the pregnant woman to look crossly at him.

"Stop that," she said.

"It's very simple, Mr. Dubchek," Irene said. "Something is rotten in the state of Denmark, and you're the only person available at the moment with the knowledge and experience to help us fix it."

"I . . . what?" He turned to look at Irene, unsure of—

The pregnant woman gave his arm another twist.

"Yeow!"

"Relax. Let the muscle relax," the woman said, massaging his shoulder.

Jackson had felt something give way—a muscle, a bone, he did not know and dared not guess. The wave of pain made him nauseous. But he fought to concentrate on Irene's words, sure as he could be that she was preparing a trap for him, a pit as big as the crater next to the Landers.

"As you already know, Mr. Dubchek, Temporal

Projects and their Time Police are actively displacing people in history—a frightening idea if you ever had to face it, which I understand you may have."

Her words came through a fuzz of pain wrapped around his ears, yet Jackson was more sure than ever that he had to listen to her and understand what she was saying.

"But did you also know that Temporal Projects under Senator Voxner's direction, is actually sending teams back to alter history to suit their own ends? And none of us are going to like those ends, I can promise you that. They've got to be stopped, Mr. Dubchek, and I think you can help us do it."

She stopped talking, her eyes alight, boring into his. All Jackson could think of was how to escape her. He knew what she was saying was true—John Reed was proof of that—but he had no more idea of what to do about it now than he'd had in Geneva.

"Why me?" he whispered through his pain and confusion. "First Homer, then Brelmer, now you. Why does everyone insist that I'm the only one who can do anything? I don't even know what's going on. I don't know why the Time Police tried to displace me, or why they killed Lester, or what I can possibly do about any of that now, so why can't you all just leave me alone?"

The fanatic light faded from Irene's eyes, and she reached out to touch Jackson's hand. "It must be terribly confusing for you, Mr. Dubchek. All that time travel— never knowing for sure where or when you'll turn up, or who you can trust."

Just for a moment she looked like the ideal grandmother of the old holos, and Jackson, grateful that someone finally understood the insanity he'd been through, blurted out, "It's been awful—unbelievable. I can't even tell if I'm in the *right* past, or some alternate version of history. I've read a lot about the past, and I thought I knew how things happened, but it's all mixed up. And when I come back I find my friends have disappeared and no one even remembers them. Then sometimes it's so subtle I don't know if anything has really changed at all, or if it's just me."

He looked into her remarkable eyes, silently begging her to understand that there was absolutely nothing he could do. What he saw there wasn't reassuring. Deep beneath the understanding something else glittered like steel.

"We all feel the same way, Mr. Dubchek. We've all had people we love disappear as if they've never existed. And we're all facing the chaos of losing our personal pasts." She patted his hand again and smiled as if she were reading him a pleasant bedtime story instead of sanity's obit.

"Can you imagine what it will be like in a few more years, when no one's personal past is untouched? We'll none of us be sure anymore where we came from, who we are, or what to believe. History will be a total shambles—no longer there to guide us past previous mistakes. We'll have no sense of tradition or heritage, and when that goes our sense of unity will crumble, too."

"None of us is a superman, Mr. Dubchek. None of us knows more than you do about what we can do to stop the chaos. But we all have to try. Don't you understand that yet? If each and every one of us doesn't do the best he can, the chaos and insanity will swallow us all."

Jackson rubbed his dry lips together, wondering if insanity was the inevitable result of time travel. Homer, Lester, and Irene had all messed with time travel, and all were on the edge of insanity. Perhaps he was, himself. He tried to find the words to tell Irene that, but he didn't know how. And on some deep level of his brain a nagging little voice insisted that, crazy or not, she was right.

Fresh pain sliced through his body, cutting off even his feeble attempts to form the words. The pregnant woman worked his arm back and forth, and he thought he was going to faint. Just as he was sure the pain would kill him, he felt a quick jab in the muscle of his upper arm and twisted around to see her withdrawing a hypodermic needle.

"Sorry we don't have a hypo patch, but that should help you feel better. Your arm'll be sore, but if you exercise it, the soreness will go away in a few days."

"Thank you, Cheryl."

"Sure. Exercise, mister," Cheryl said as she left, looking like a parody of pregnancy, a ball walking on two toothpicks.

"Our research indicates that we need to find a certain Rosita Alvarez, Mr. Dubchek," Irene continued, "and we think you can help us find out where to look . . . and then find her."

Jackson's ears fuzzed from the pain and the drugs. He opened his mouth, but only a hoarse croak came out. Irene didn't seem to notice. She kept talking.

Rosita Alvarez, he thought? How in the world was he supposed to find Rosita Alvarez? The thought slid through a gray fog of faint buzzing before it faded away.

# # #

When he opened his eyes, he was surprised to find himself in a bed in a dimly lit room hung with dark curtains and tensets of costumes. Light seeped from behind the curtains. A man he had never seen before sat beside the bed.

"How you feeling?" the man asked.

"I don't know. Who are you?"

"Oh, I just work here. You can call me Ray. I'll go tell Irene you're awake."

"Is it day—what day is it?"

"It's a little past noon, and they said you came in last night. Does that help?"

"Yeah, thanks," Jackson said as the man left. His head was full of questions, but they refused to form up in neat rows so he could deal with them. Part of him didn't care what they were. He felt that if he just closed his eyes, he could disappear and take the world with him, so he closed his eyes.

"Mr. Dubchek? Ray said you were awake," a woman's familiar voice said.

"I am." His eyes opened on their own to see Irene the historian leaning over him. Bryan stood behind her.

"We have to discuss our problem."

"My only problem is how to disappear."

"We can help you with that too, if you'll help us."

"Do what?" Every suspicion in Jackson's brain flattened its ears against her.

"We have to find Rosita Alvarez and bring her back here, if at all possible."

"Why?"

"Because she's the key to understanding what's going on and putting an end to it."

"So send Bryan. He's qualified."

"Not exactly. He's not linguistically trained. We need

someone who can speak Czechoslovakian and Russian, who can ask questions and get answers in—"

"Russian? Czechoslovakian and Russian? What . . ."

"Mr. Dubchek, we have every reason to believe that Rosita Alvarez was displaced in Prague, Czechoslovakia, 1968, during the Russian put-down of the Prague Spring—when your famous ancestor, Alexander, was leader of Czechoslovakia. We need her to fight—"

Jackson shook his head. "Not me. I can't do it. There's no way I'm making any more trips back to—"

"Show him the picture," Irene said.

Bryan leaned past her and handed Jackson a photograph. As Jackson accepted it, his arm hurt. When he remembered why it hurt, he was surprised it hurt so little.

The photograph was old, faded, its color almost gone. It showed three people running from a military tank in an old European city. Two of the people looked like Jackson and Suzanne Brelmer. He didn't believe it.

"You recognize Ms. Brelmer. The other woman with you is Rosita Alvarez," Bryan said.

"But how . . . where?"

"From the TP archives, Jackson. Sooner or later you're going to Prague to find Rosita. You might as well go for us, now. With Bryan's help and ours, you ought to be all right."

Jackson stared at the picture, knowing he would fight and argue with Irene and Bryan, that he would resist, but holding in his hand the evidence that he would finally give in and take one more trip in time . . . maybe his last.

Chapter Twenty-six

Twenty-four sleepless hours had passed since Suzanne lost her connection with Jackson Dubchek. She had tried repeatedly to reestablish it, through the regular telephone coldlink system and the government system, through several computer networks, and finally through the old fiber optics network. Nothing had worked.

Sitting alone in her darkened office she felt the frustration more than the fatigue. I will make one last attempt, she decided, and then I'll rip this lousy phone from the desk and throw it out the window.

The number she punched in was her father's, since she was sure he would have agents watching Dubchek. She was less sure that he would tell her what had happened after the abortive Geneva trip.

Oh, we got our Radek manuscript all right, she thought as she waited for someone to pick up her call. But Slye came back, and Jackson didn't. She drummed her fingers on the printout of the Anomalies Report that had been her first tip-off. The report noted an unscheduled and unmanaged temporal arrival north of Springfield, Missouri, right about the time Jackson should have been leaving Geneva. Didn't take a surge of genius for her to figure out it must have been Jackson. Her call to his apartment had confirmed his return, but then . . .

She stared at her screen for a long moment, then broke off the unanswered call. Her father was unavailable—perhaps unavailable only to her, but unavailable nonetheless.

"Well," she said aloud, "there are always other ways."

She punched up public information for Springfield, and selected a survey of the general news bulletins for the past two days. Seconds later she saw a headline that made her heart jump.

FOUR ALARM FIRE DESTROYS APARTMENTS

A quick scan through the story confirmed that it was Jackson's apartment complex that had burned, but the story also said no one had been killed or injured. In an apparently unconnected incident, the story concluded, an unidentified man had been found shot in a park adjoining the apartments.

Could it be Jackson? Suzanne's heart jumped again. She switched off the report and called up her unauthorized personal copy of Jackson's file. Running rapidly through it, she found the Springfield number she was looking for and punched it into her telephone.

"Hello?" The face that filled her screen was tear-stained, the eyes, puffy.

"Ms. Chrys Calvino, please," Suzanne said.

"That's me. Who are you?"

"I am calling about Mr. Jackson Dubchek, and I wonder—"

"Who are you? Where is Jackson?" The puffy eyes narrowed to an ugly squint. "Is he with you? What—"

"I'm trying to ascertain where—"

"You bitch. Tell him I hate him."

The screen went dead. Suzanne thought about calling back, but decided not to. If Jackson was dead, his steady companion, Ms. Chrystal Carolina Calvino, gymnastics teacher and sexual athlete, didn't know anything about it. Because of the woman's reaction to the call, Suzanne felt just as certain that Calvino didn't know where Jackson was. She didn't look bright enough to put on that crying act just to cover a lie.

"So what next?" Suzanne asked aloud . . . "And why are you letting that stupid little bitch get to you?" The niggling voice of truth in the back of her mind had the answer. *Because you really care about him, idiot. And you're jealous of that overpumped, gonad-driven little* . . . She sighed. "Back to digging."

Suzanne reopened the narrative section of Jackson's file and section by section reviewed everything he had been involved with since his arrival at Temporal Projects. "Since you dragged him in," she muttered. At the sight of Lester Wu's name, she paused and took a deep breath. Lester was dead and Slye had killed him, regardless of what the official report said. That turned her stomach. It turned her stomach that her father felt it necessary to hire and keep people like Slye.

With a shake of her head she went back to reading. The next name that caught her attention was Homer Alvarez. She opened a side bar and called up Homer's file. Rosita's husband. Now in the Grandview Psychiatric Institute in Mountain Home, Arkansas, under government care.

Surely Homer couldn't know anything about Jackson. So why were their names linked? She read further. Because they'd met outside Lester Wu's apartment, when Homer went looking for Lester so he could ask about his wife, Rosita.

Could Rosita Alvarez be the key? Could she be the person with the answers Suzanne needed?

It made sense in a perverted kind of way. Rosita Alvarez had known everything Temporal Projects was doing, had been its director, had . . . had disappeared, become a nonperson, and been smudged in people's memories. She had known . . .

That was it. Her own smudged memory held the answer. Slye and his people had displaced Rosita Alvarez. Suzanne didn't need to know why, just where.

Hastily she shut down Jackson's file and called up all the logged temporal transmissions for the months just prior to the time her father was appointed director. One by one she checked them against the assignment rosters, verifying the justifications for transmissions and the personnel involved.

Hours later she was still digging through the transmission records when her com line lit up, and the front security officer's voice crackled across her speaker. "Ms. Brelmer, there's an Agent Bryan Marthson and a Mr. Jackson Dubchek here to see you."

"Where?" she asked, the excitement jumping in her voice.

"Here at reception, ma'am."

"Send them to my office, immediately," she ordered.

Her excitement turned to dismay when they entered her office and she saw the anger on Jackson's face. Her dismay fell into confusion when she realized that Agent Marthson had a pistol in his hand.

"Jackson! I'm so glad to see you!" Suzanne could hear the quaver in her voice, but she fought it as she tried to ignore the gun and held out her hands to him.

"I'll bet," he said, his hands plunging into his pockets.

Suzanne let hers hang empty in the air for a long moment before they dropped to her side. "What's that supposed to mean? I *am* glad to see you. I thought . . . I thought you might be dead." She couldn't hold his gaze for fear tears would take control of her eyes.

"Don't you mean, hoped I was dead?"

"No, Jackson, I was worried about you."

"You and your father talked me into going to Geneva and then you sent Slye to make sure I stayed there." He was as startled by the strength of his anger as by the wetness of her eyes when she looked up at him. "Why would you be glad to see me now?"

"That's not true. We didn't send Slye to stop you or make you stay there or anything like that."

"Sure."

Angrily she brushed the tears from the corners of her eyes. "Who is this agent? Why does he need that gun?"

"He's just someone who saved my life—after you sent the other one to kill me."

Suzanne shuddered. "Jackson . . . Jackson, please believe me. I did no such thing."

"We need to use the equipment, Ms. Brelmer," Bryan said, "and we may need your assistance with that."

She stared from the gun to his mirrorshaded face, knowing she would find artificial eyes behind those shiny glasses and suddenly hating anything and everyone connected with Temporal Projects. "Why should I care?"

"You don't have to care," Jackson said, "just help me get back to find Rosita Alvarez."

"Who?" Suzanne couldn't believe it.

"Rosita Alvarez. She was director before your father . . . we think. It's not very clear."

"What do you want with her?"

"Answers . . . answers you won't give."

"Dammit, Jackson, I want answers, too. I didn't send Slye after you, and I didn't have anything to do with sending other agents after you." She looked suspiciously at Marthson. "How do you know somebody didn't send him to do something to you?"

"Because he saved my life."

"From whom?"

"An agent who was out to kill me."

"Or out to help you? How do you know this trip you want to make isn't just another way of getting rid of you?"

Jackson looked from her to Bryan and didn't want to let her confuse him, but her words had already had their effect. With a frustrated sigh he flopped into a chair. "I don't know! How am I supposed to know anything anymore? . . . They showed me a photo. You and Rosita Alvarez and I were in it. I said I'd go. . . . There, you happy?"

"Who, they?"

"Never mind who they are," Bryan said. "We have to send Jackson back to 1968, Prague."

So *that* was where Dr. Alvarez had ended up. Suzanne's decision was immediate, and irreversible. "I'm going with you."

Bryan shook his head. "I don't think that's a good idea."

"I'm in the picture, aren't I? Didn't you say so, Jackson?"

Jackson nodded.

"Then I'm going with you."

"Someone has to stay here and guard the machine at this end," Bryan argued.

His reluctance made Suzanne impatient. "So who would you rather trust? Me? The woman who is supposed to be trying to strand him? If I go back then we both get stranded. Think of it as insurance. Or don't think of it at all. I'm going back, and that's the end of it." She wiped Rosita Alvarez's file from her terminal, and stood up.

"Now, when did you say we were going? Nineteen sixty-eight? We'll have to go see Paress. Follow me."

She marched right past them without looking back, daring them to protest. They followed her out of the office and down to the costume shop, where Paress Linnet found the appropriate clothes for them without raising an eyebrow.

Jackson held up the rusty brown suit and wrinkled his nose. "These aren't very colorful. I thought everyone wore rainbow colors in that period of the twentieth century."

"Not in Czechoslovakia," the costumer said. "Not in the Prague Spring of 1968."

Suzanne felt obligated to say something about their mission. After all, Paress had been the first person to hint at what might have happened to Dr. Alvarez and the others. But she wasn't sure she should. It could get Paress in a lot of trouble if she knew too much. "Uh, Paress. . . ."

The costumer's eyes met hers, and she fell silent. Paress's mouth hitched up in the hint of a smile. "Thank you, Ms. Brelmer. I appreciate it," she murmured.

Marthson paced restlessly around the little sewing shop, while Suzanne and Jackson tugged on their costumes. "We need to go quickly," he said.

"I'm ready," Suzanne responded, zipping up her shapeless gray dress. "Jackson?"

"Ready."

With a final squeeze of Paress's hand Suzanne led the others out of the costume shop and down to the transmission facility in the basement. No one was there. They wasted no time sealing off the door and setting the transmitter.

Jackson took a final look around as Bryan shut him into the time machine with Suzanne. He didn't want to think it would be his last view of his own world. Bryan signaled to Suzanne, who initiated the start-up sequence. Jackson closed his eyes, anticipating the now-familiar lurch of free-fall through time, and gritted his teeth as his universe spun out of control around him.

The world spun forever. Seconds later it stopped.

Suzanne opened the door and tugged his arm. "Jackson, come on, we've got to move."

He didn't want to open his eyes. He wanted to throw up and then give the world a few more minutes to slow down before he even thought about moving. Most of all he wanted the noises to go away, wanted the ringing in his ears to fade. It sounded like hundreds of people screaming in his head, while all the walls of Prague rumbled to the ground.

"Jackson, pleeeeease." Suzanne's tugging took on a frantic strength. "We've got to get out of here."

Something heavy bounced off the front viewpanel of the time machine, and the screaming grew louder. The machine vibrated with the rumbling earth.

"Jackson Elgin Dubcek, get out this instant. Or at least open your eyes, dammit. There are tanks out there! Russian tanks! And if we don't get out of here, they're going to roll right over us!"

Jackson's eyes popped open. The tanks were closer than even the fear in Suzanne's voice suggested. He could almost count the rivets on their treads, and their clanking rumble deafened him. In one swift movement he tore open his safety harness and scrambled after Suzanne.

They hit the street running, merging into the panic-stricken crowd fleeing ahead of the tanks. They didn't pause to try to figure out where they were, or where they were headed. All they wanted to do was put as much ground as possible between themselves and the sound of the Russian tanks rolling over their time machine and crushing it to bits.

Chapter Twenty-seven

Senator Voxner's Kansas City office was almost as impressive as his Moscow home, but now Fritz Brelmer was too concerned with where this conversation with the senator was headed to think much about his surroundings. He sat as straight as a riot baton in his chair and formed each word with carefully controlled intonation. He did not want to increase Senator Voxner's anger, but neither was Brelmer willing to emasculate his words nor to modify his position—not unless Voxner forced him to compromise. For the moment, at least, Brelmer was unwilling to entertain the notion of compromise or what that might cost him.

With further control, he took a deep breath, then continued. "As I was explaining, Senator, I see it as an obligatory part of my duty to remind you—whether you or I or anyone else wants to be be concerned with it—that nothing, *nothing* about time travel, nor the activities in which Temporal Projects is engaged—that none of those things have the elegant simplicity of reason or of cause and effect that you continue to insist upon."

Brelmer kept his eyes locked on the senator's. "It

is unfortunate, sir, but totally true. We are no longer in a position where we can keep Pandora's box locked. We can only attempt to control what we have already released and to contain any future releases.''

Voxner waited a long moment after Brelmer finished speaking before he said anything. "You had best watch your tongue, Colonel Brelmer. Need I remind you that there is no iron rice bowl—no long term job guarantee—at Temporal Projects?"

"You made that unquestionably clear when you made me director, sir. I do not expect my job or my employment to be guaranteed. However, neither can I stand here and lie to you in order to protect my job." A muscle quivered under his solar plexus, and he willed it to stop. It did.

"Bravely said, Praetor Centurion. But do not confuse bravery with honesty, nor honesty with loyalty." Voxner paused and steepled his hands under his chin. "The attribute for which I have the greatest appreciation in those who work for me is loyalty. It has a value in this world higher than almost any other." Again he paused. "Your opinion, Colonel Brelmer, is always meaningful to me. I value it above all others. Your loyalty, however, is priceless."

"I appreciate that, sir, but it seems to me that—"

"Let me finish, Friz." Senator Voxner held up one hand.

Brelmer settled self-consciously back in his chair, trying not to let his weariness and frustration show.

"Friz, we can acquire as many opinions and viewpoints as we can tolerate on any subjects that interest us. Opinions are free all over our great republic and they are generously available. But they are rarely worth any more than they cost. Loyalty, on the other hand, is a far less common and far more precious commodity.''

"But, sir, I hope you are not saying that personal loyalty precludes telling you the truth—even when it is a truth you find objectionable.''

"Ah, but what you call truth, someone else might call opinion. Of course I want the truth from you, Friz. But once I have made the necessary decisions for us to act upon''—the senator frowned—"I find no virtue in having those decisions questioned in the light of meaningless dissenting opinions.''

Brelmer swallowed hard. How far dare he push the subject? Or the senator? Not much farther, he knew that, but . . . "You put me in a very uncomfortable position, Senator. Most naturally you want me to keep you fully and openly apprised of our current situation and operations . . .'' Voxner's frown deepened, but Brelmer felt compelled to continue. "Yet you do not want any, uh, negative assessments of our projects or negative analyses of our problems. I do not think I can—''

The chime of the desk phone stopped Brelmer momentarily and broke the immediate tension. Voxner's frown eased as he slipped the private receiver over one ear. "Yes. Yes, I understand. Connect him.'' The frown returned. "This is Senator Voxner, Captain. What—I see.''

Brelmer did not want to know who Voxner was talking to. He only prayed it had nothing to do with him.

"Yes, most certainly. Of course. That is quite correct. However, I think you should wait for Colonel Brelmer. Yes, you are welcome.''

With instincts born in years of service, Brelmer

reached his feet and pulled his body to attention immediately after Voxner had said his name.

The senator slammed the receiver on the desk. His silver brows arched over eyes burning with disbelief. "Again, Friz! Again! What is wrong with your daughter? Is she a damned Mnemosyne or something? Is she in league with those idiots from the future?"

Brelmer flinched, but held his tongue.

"Do you have any idea where she is? Do you? I do. Prague, Czechoslovakia, August 21, 1968—that is right, the date of the Great Suppression, one of the blackest dates in Russian history. And why? Why would she be there?"

The senator was not finished with his rhetorical questions, and Brelmer was not about to say anything until he was. But Brelmer's brain churned with questions of his own and with anger. Questions of "why?" and "how?" struggled for shape in his mind, and anger at Suzanne for doing this to him kept the heat under the questions.

"And who would she go back to Prague with?" Voxner asked, his voice twisted by sarcasm. "Do you know who? Could you possibly guess who she went with? That interpreter! Dubchek! The one who was supposed to have been taken care of. What in the hell is going on in your department, Friz? You have a loose cannon on deck and it is your *daughter!*"

"Dammit, sir," Brelmer said, startling himself and Voxner. "We have a thousand loose cannons on deck! The world—especially the past—is full of loose cannons from the future, our future, not to mention the ones we send there ourselves, and the ones in the past who might have figured out on their own how to use the machines we so carelessly leave behind."

"Listen to me, Friz. You had better—"

"Sir, I have listened to you." Brelmer could hardly believe what he was saying, or the vehemence with which he spoke, but the impulse to continue made more sense than stopping.

"Senator, I make no excuses for my daughter, nor can I imagine what has possessed her to make this unauthorized trip. However, I can do something about Suzanne. You, sir, you who are supposed to be making policy for Temporal Projects, had better decide what you are going to do about all those other loose cannons over which we have little or no control." He paused, fully expecting to be interrupted, but Voxner only stared at him with apparent disbelief.

"Surely, Senator, surely you can see if you do not give us a method of coping with them, one of them—one of those *idiots* as you referred to them—will do something that will kill us one day, something that will kill us all without warning."

Senator Voxner opened his mouth as though to speak, then closed his mouth and turned away, seemingly busying himself with something at the library console behind his desk.

Brelmer stared out the window at the gray spring day and allowed himself shallow even breaths. He had finally said what he had too long harbored in quiet. No matter what Voxner did in response, Brelmer felt much better for having finally said his piece in a way that forced Voxner to pay attention. A faint smile of satisfaction curved his lips.

"You find humor in this, Colonel?"

"No, sir."

"But you smile nonetheless?"

"Do I, sir? If so, it is for no reason I can name."

"Yes, well, perhaps you had best stop smiling and get yourself across town to Temporal Projects where Captain Slye is waiting for you."

"Will that be everything, Senator?"

"No, Praetor Centurion Colonel Brelmer, that will not be everything. However, this is not the time and place to continue. Suffice it to say that you have given me a great deal to think about that we shall have to discuss after you return from Prague."

Brelmer was surprised. "You want me to go to Prague?"

It was Voxner's turn to smile. "But of course, Friz. She is your daughter."

"As you say." Brelmer saluted, spun on his heels, and left, unwilling to wait for a reply or to trust himself further in Voxner's presence.

No matter how he turned the problem, Brelmer realized that Voxner had managed not only to obligate him into going back for Suzanne, but had also quite willingly placed him in mortal danger. Should something happen in Prague, something fatal, well, Temporal Projects would find itself in search of a new director.

On the brief flight across town he resigned himself to that idea in a surprising way. At least by going back to Prague for Suzanne he would be doing something. At least he would be participating instead of fretting on the sidelines. At least he would be . . . doing the very thing he worried so much about, tampering with history.

But perhaps not. If he and Slye could get to Prague

before Suzanne and her renegade interpreter, they could snatch the two of them when they arrived, haul them back to Kansas City, and be done with the project. Voxner would be satisfied. Brelmer would save his job—for the moment, anyway. Suzanne could be dealt with directly, and Dubchek could be dealt with . . . permanently.

By the time Brelmer cleared security, Slye was waiting for him. "Status, Captain?" Brelmer asked as they walked down the hall toward the elevators.

"There's an agent called"—Slye looked at the datacorder on his wrist—"Marthson, Agent Bryan Marthson. He is not one of ours, by the way. At 1527 hours Agent Marthson entered the facility with the proper credentials escorting Dubchek. They went directly to Ms. Brelmer's office, and after a—"

"Status, Captain. What is their current status?"

"Approaching full paradox, sir. Either they're due back very shortly, or they're not coming back."

"Damn. Can we still effect a pickup?"

"Certainly, sir. I planned on that."

An elevator stood waiting for them. Brelmer punched the code for the transmission level, then pressed his hand against the ID plate. Moments later the elevator began its descent. "What about this agent Marthson? Where is he from?"

"From the future, we're fairly sure, sir." Slye paused, then in a tone that betrayed an unusual level of uncertainty for him, said, "He's from our future, sir—TP's future. Analysis of the toposcan of his credentials showed them to be perfect. I mean, perfect. Better than ours currently are."

"Understood. Where is he?"

"Locked himself in Transmission 7-B."

"Recommendations?"

"Capture and interrogate him. Go back and intercept the other two."

"Good. And you have teams ready for both operations?"

"Yes. I will lead the intercept team."

"Excellent. I will go back with you." The elevator stopped.

"But Colonel, is that a good idea? I mean, uh, if—"

"I am going with you, Captain," Brelmer said, stepping off the elevator. "Is this your team?" He gestured to the six or seven armed people wearing ugly green uniforms who stood at attention in the hall.

"Yes, sir. Russian army elite unit uniforms."

"Then we will proceed." Twenty minutes later wearing uniforms matching the team's, he and Slye stood outside the locked doors of transmission room 7-B. "Agent Marthson, this is Colonel Brelmer. I order you to open these doors immediately."

To everyone's surprise, the doors popped open. A smoking object rolled into the hall even as they started to close again.

"Gas!"

The team scattered. Slye dived toward the open doors. Brelmer scrambled after him. The doors slammed shut behind them.

Brelmer's skin burned. His nose ached. His ears twitched uncontrollably. His eyes caught sight of the renegade agent ducking behind the transmission machine.

Slye fired.

Sparks flew.

Just like in the holos, Brelmer thought as he brought his well-disguised pistol to bear on the other end of the transmitter. When Marthson's head appeared, Brelmer squeezed the trigger.

The head exploded.

"Good shooting, sir," Slye shouted.

Brelmer looked at the event timer over the time machine and cursed. Suzanne had been back there for almost the maximum amount of present time. "Let's get going."

"But the team, Colonel."

"It will take too long to clear the gas, Captain. If we do not leave immediately, we will be too late."

To his credit, Slye did not hesitate. "I see it, sir. Load up. I'll get us going."

Less than a minute later the machine whined to life, and Brelmer's stomach turned wild unhappy loops under his belt. Then the universe exploded.

Chapter Twenty-eight

Jackson stared out the window at a city that seemed to be resisting the turmoil of invasion much too passively despite what he had read about it. "We'll never find her, you know. Wherever Rosita Alvarez is, we're never going to find her." An angry kind of emptiness gnawed on him almost as though he suffered from hunger, but felt too nauseous to eat.

Eight Russian tanks, easily distinguished by their low curved turrets, clanked down the cobblestone street with the long barrels of their cannons pointed high in the air. White stripes had been painted on the tops of the tanks— probably so their own fliers won't bomb them, Jackson thought with a shiver.

In front of the building across from the one in which he and Suzanne had taken refuge, stood an equestrian statue whose helmeted rider held a sword pointed straight up in the air and who looked as disconnected from the march of history as Jackson felt. "She could be anywhere in this city—if she is in this city, in this *here* and this *now*." He turned back to Suzanne with a shake of his head. "In the name of Buddha I don't know how or why I let myself get talked into this."

"It was the photograph, you said."

"That was a trick."

"Oh, have you had your picture taken in the past before with Rosita Alvarez? Or are you saying that your friends, the Mnemosyne Historians, produced a fake photograph? That wouldn't surprise me, but what about you? And if they did, where did they get my picture? And why did they put me in the picture with you and Dr. Alvarez?" Suzanne refused to look up from the map she had spread out on the dusty table, afraid Jackson might see that she felt just as unsure as he did, afraid that he had heard it already in her voice.

Instead of looking at him, she kept her eyes on the map. But even with the English notations on it, the map made very little sense to her . . . and even if it had made sense, she wouldn't have known what she was looking for. She took a deep breath and let it out slowly. The room smelled of linseed oil, and a painter's scaffold stood against one wall. "The picture of you and Dr. Alvarez didn't trick *me*. I didn't see it."

He grunted. "If it hadn't been for the picture, I wouldn't have known Dr. Rosita Alvarez if she ran down the street wearing a sign with her name on it."

"So what do you propose? If we don't find her, we may never find a way back to 2249 . . . short of getting old—living that long." Her joke didn't work, even for her, but at least she had tried, which was more than she could say for Jackson.

"What makes you think she can help us?"

"Because she's our only connection with our future—with our own time. Look, Jackson, if TP comes looking for us—and I'd bet money they will because my father is going to be very angry—so *when* they come looking for us, they'll start with Dr. Alvarez—because they almost certainly know where she is. And when they come looking for her, they're going to have a time machine to get back in. We have to be ready to use that machine and bring Dr. Alvarez with us."

Only as she finished speaking did Suzanne look up at him. His passiveness angered her. The lack of information for them to work with frustrated her. "You do want to get back, don't you, Jackson?"

"Of course."

"Then help me."

"Help you do what? What's that damn map going to tell us?"

"I don't know. But it's the only clue we have. Bryan and your precious Mnemosyne didn't give you anything else, did they?"

He shook his head. "No. And don't call them my Mnemosyne. I'm beginning to think they're probably in league with your father to dump us back here."

"My father's not that kind of man. He doesn't deal with criminals."

"Oh, really? I don't have any proof of that. Do you? And I don't have any proof that the Mnemosyne are criminals. But I do know what's happened to me. That I have proof of, and this whole time your father has been in charge of Temporal Projects, hasn't he? So how come I keep getting stranded back in time? How come that's what's happened to me every time I've made one of these trips since joining Temporal Projects? Joining because of you, if I remember correctly."

"I don't know. I'm not sure." She hated the guilt he

laid on her because she had already felt it without his help. "It's all too complicated and confusing to me, and I just don't know what to believe."

In his heart Jackson wanted to believe her, but he found belief in anything very difficult at the moment. "What you mean is, you don't want to know what your father's doing."

Suzanne saw the frightened uncertainty in his eyes and bit back the sarcastic reply that started off her tongue. "You're right, Jackson. I don't want to know. I don't have time to cope with that right now. What I do have to do—what the moment demands of me right now—is to find us a way home . . . a way for both of us . . . together. Okay?"

He couldn't hold steady under her gaze, so he looked down at his hands, wishing he was home—wherever that was. "I'm sorry, Suzanne. It's not your fault the Russians ran over our time machine. I'm just more than a little scared, that's all."

"Me, too. Now come over here and help me look at this. Why would Bryan have given us the map if it didn't contain answers?"

Jackson crossed the room and stood by her side. The map looked like nothing more than a jumbled network of black lines to him, but he knew she was right. He had to do something. "Exactly what did he say to you before we left?"

She forced a little smile to her lips. "Don't lose the map."

"That's it?"

"Oh, before that he told me what buildings to watch out for—the central committee building, parliament building, the radio station, and the presidential palace."

"Easy enough."

"For you, maybe. Do you see any of those buildings labeled on this map?"

Jackson stared at the map trying to find someplace to focus on it. Then he saw them. The tiny hand printed letters jumped off the map at him. "There!" he said, stabbing the map with his finger.

She bent closer and stared at where he pointed. "Raphid? What's that?"

"Well, it's not Czech. At least I'm pretty sure it's not Czech. But read the letters. R-A-P-H-D could stand for Rosita Alvarez, Ph.D., couldn't they?" The rush of certainty had swept past as quickly as it had come, leaving him nothing but the fading heat of inspiration.

Suddenly Suzanne felt some little hope. "So where is that compared to where we are?"

He squinted. "There to . . . here. If we can go up this street . . . seven, eight . . . twelve, maybe thirteen or fourteen blocks. Hard to tell."

"So, let's go."

"Uh . . . well"—he shrugged—"why not? I mean, it's better than sitting still and waiting for someone in a uniform to discover us and ask who we are and why we're here."

Minutes later they walked up the sidewalk with the citizens of Prague while military vehicles dominated the traffic in the street. Armed soldiers stood on every corner, but the pedestrians flowed around them without hesitation. Jackson and Suzanne did their best to fit into the flow.

"The folks don't seem to be paying much attention to their guests," Jackson said quietly after they had walked many blocks in silence.

"I know. It's almost as though they think that ignoring the invaders will make them go away. Do you know—I mean, have you ever read what happened here?"

"The Russians won, I think, in the short run. But as I remember it, in the long run, it was the Czechs who led the old Eastern bloc out of economic disaster and provided the free trade models that Russia and everyone but the East Germans ended up using. So the Czechs finally won, but it took them a hundred years longer than they expected it to."

Suzanne grabbed his elbow. "Turn here," she said, pushing him around a corner.

"This isn't the right street to—"

"Soldiers. They were watching us, I think. Walk normally. Don't let me run."

He stared at her in surprise and suddenly saw how frightened she looked. With a forced smile he took her hand in his and said, "Don't worry, if we just keep walking like we know where we're going, we'll be all right."

"But I may have just gotten us lost. And the soldiers. What if they're following us?"

"Shhh. Don't look back. Don't. Just take it easy, one step at a time. We're not lost. There are street signs, and people to ask, and, when we get the chance, the map in my pocket. Besides, we're only a few blocks away. Just keep walking casually. When we come to the next corner, we'll cross the street. As we do, we'll check to see if your soldiers are following us, all right?"

"All right."

"Good."

"How can you be so calm?"

"By shaking in my socks."

Despite herself, she giggled.

"Not funny," he said, but the smile he gave her was real.

At the corner they crossed the street. Jackson risked a long glance back the way they had come. A pair of soldiers with rifles over their shoulders walked up the street, but their attention did not seem to be on Jackson and Suzanne. "I think we're okay. Let's keep going this way. It parallels the—"

"Check out that building."

He looked around. "What building?"

"The one at the end of this street. Isn't it like the one you described to me from the photograph. Arched windows with lots of little panes. Crenelated top. Gargoyles."

Jackson looked up and almost stopped in his tracks. "It is. It's the same building. I don't believe it."

"So the map was right—or you were right about the map."

"Whichever. But now what do we do?"

"Go find out what kind of building it is, what's in it, if anyone there's seen someone matching Dr. Alvarez's description."

He took a deep breath. "Time to test my Czech vocabulary, huh? Well, when it's time, it's time."

They were twenty meters from the front door when a blow from behind staggered Suzanne.

"Killers!" a shrill voice screamed as a second blow knocked her to her knees. "Assassins!"

Jackson recognized the woman with the crazed eyes and grabbed her by the sleeve of her heavy coat before she could hit Suzanne again. "Dr. Alvarez! Stop it. We're here to help you."

"Let go of me!" Dr. Alvarez swung a large cloth bag at Jackson.

Jackson released his grip and sidestepped the blow. "Stop, please, Dr. Alvarez. We're your friends."

"Not that Brelmer bitch." Dr. Alvarez took another swing at Suzanne. "Came to finish up your daddy's dirty work, did you? And you thought I wouldn't remember you? It takes more than displacement to make *me* forget a person's face." The woman's bag landed heavily on Suzanne's shoulders.

Jackson lunged at the woman again, grabbing her by both elbows this time. He struggled to pull her away from Suzanne as the stream of pedestrians flowed around them, apparently unnoticing. Alvarez spun around and started toward him instead. As he tried to fend her off Jackson saw something over her shoulder that frightened him much more than she did.

"Dr. Alvarez!" Suzanne shouted, scrambling to her feet. "Dr. Alvarez, stop!"

Without thinking, Jackson slapped Alvarez as hard as he could.

She collapsed to her knees with a moan.

"Get her up! Get her up. They're coming. Your father and Slye. Now. Get her up," Jackson babbled, pulling at Alvarez's elbow. "Help us, woman. We need each other."

"Where?" Suzanne asked as she helped pull the overweight woman to her feet. She tried to look around, but couldn't see anyone for the crowds. "Where are they?"

"Behind you. Come on."

"Let go of me," Alvarez growled as though seeing them for the first time. "I know who you are. You're Time Police. You're the enemy."

"They're your enemy," Jackson shouted in her face as he shook her. "They're behind us. If we don't get you out of here, we're all in big trouble."

Alvarez's eyes narrowed suspiciously, but she seemed to be listening. "All right," she said. "We'll see who is friends with whom. Follow me." She turned and began to push her way through the crowds that lined the street.

Suzanne glanced around before following her, and saw her father and Captain Slye. They were less than half a block away, walking fast. "Hurry, Dr. Alvarez, they're right behind us."

"In the building," Alvarez said in a hoarse monotone. "I have a place in there."

Chapter Twenty-nine

They ran.

A man in uniform pointed an accordion-nosed camera at them.

They ran past him.

Hand in hand, Jackson Dubchek, Suzanne Brelmer, and Dr. Rosita Alvarez, citizens of the Second Republic in 2249, ran up the steps of a grand building in Prague, Czechoslovakia, 1968, as fast as the chubby Dr. Alvarez could run. They burst through the high glass doors into a deep, warm lobby.

Even as they followed Dr. Alvarez across the marbled expanse, Jackson knew that Brelmer and Slye would be right behind them. Dr. Alvarez led them between small groups of well-dressed people who stood and sat on little islands of oriental carpet listening to portable radios or talking in hushed tones about the tanks in the streets—led them to a wide black marble staircase that curved up into the building between golden banisters. Jackson couldn't tell if they were in some kind of hotel or club or what.

Halfway up the stairs Dr. Alvarez turned on them,

forcing Jackson to take a quick step back down to the last riser. "All right, now tell me, who are you two? And don't bother trying to lie."

"The Mnemosyne sent us—sent him," Suzanne said, looking back and surprised not to see her father and Captain Slye yet. "They sent him to help find you and bring you home."

"They're crooks, subversive psychos and welfare cheats. They play bridge, for god's sake, and read poetry aloud!" Rosita laughed harsly, then turned her suspicious eyes on Suzanne. "And you? Do you expect me to believe Brelmer's daughter would be running around with a messenger of the Mnemosynes?"

"I came to find you too. I want to help you. And I want to find out why Temporal Projects thinks it's necessary to displace people like you and Lester Wu."

"Don't you know? Doesn't daddy . . . trust his little girl with any . . . real knowledge?" Rosita puffed out the words, as she resumed her climb up the stairs. "The Time Police . . . want to control history. They're behind this invasion."

"What?"

"It's true. . . . They goaded them . . . the whole Warsaw Pact. . . . Time Police have . . . agents in every . . . capital in Europe." Despite her heavy breathing, her voice conveyed total conviction.

"That's hard to believe," Suzanne said, amazed that this woman could state such an absurdity so calmly. "Why would—"

"Hard for you, maybe. . . . not for me . . . not knowing what I know." Rosita paused at the top of the stairs to smile at Jackson and Suzanne. "Who do you think set the whole network up?"

The stairs fanned out onto a wide mezzanine that had couches and chairs and more islands of nervously chattering people. Jackson looked back down into the heart of the lobby just as two men in off-green uniforms pushed through the front doors.

Brelmer and Slye.

An immediate buzz of complaint rose from the people in the lobby. "Hurry," Jackson said. "They're here."

"The lift." Dr. Alvarez pointed.

"Elevator," Suzanne said when they reached the cage-fronted box. "Antique elevator."

Dr. Alvarez said something to the uniformed operator, and much to Suzanne's surprise, the elevator went down, not up.

"Where are we going?" Jackson asked.

"You'll see." Her voice was calm, her manner, sure.

He and Suzanne exchanged looks of curiosity, neither sure where this would lead them. Then to Jackson's surprise, she took his hand and gave it a gentle squeeze. To Suzanne's relief, he returned the gesture with a brief smile.

The elevator passed the first floor, then sank below the ground floor and past an obvious basement level to stop at a brightly lit hall where an armed guard stood looking at them. "Ah, are good see you, Doctor Al'rez. You room are ready."

"Thank you, Alex. Watch out for the Russians behind us. This way, you two."

Again Suzanne and Jackson exchanged looks of curiosity, but Suzanne read concern in his face as well.

"Yes, Russe," Alex said with a grin, patting the holstered pistol on his belt.

Dr. Alvarez turned down the hall in a direction that Jackson was sure took them under the front of the building. Every twenty meters or so they passed pairs of pad-locked doors, one on each side of the hall.

"Alex won't be much help if your father and his mutant follow us," Rosita said, "but there's no help for that. Here we are." She held a key ring in her hand and, after flipping back part of the door trim, inserted a key in a hidden slot. Seconds later the door swung open backward with the padlock still in place. "Cute, huh?" With an odd gleam in her eye, Dr. Alvarez led the way into a rather large room that contained a narrow bed, two desks, and a bookcase overflowing with papers and books. As soon as they were both in, she shut the door behind them.

Several muffled shots echoed down the hall.

Jackson spun to face the door. "Oh, damn. Here they come."

"They won't find us here," Rosita said.

Two more shots sounded.

"Like hell," Jackson replied. "Her father and Captain Slye will literally sniff us out if they have to."

Suzanne had a sudden image of her father pursued by real Russian soldiers, and a shiver of fear and guilt ran through her.

"Don't worry." Dr. Alvarez waved some kind of automatic pistol at them. "Move away from the door, Ms. Brelmer."

"Suzanne. You can call me Suzanne." She stepped away from the door, but Dr. Alvarez kept the muzzle of the pistol waving directly at her.

"I'd rather call you Ms. Brelmer. Sit, please."

A distant *crack* stopped everything except their breathing for a long moment.

"Now, you two can tell me what kind of trick you and TP think you're trying to pull on me."

"What in the world are you doing?" Jackson asked. Almost immediately he found her pistol pointed at him. It no longer wavered in her hand. "Look, Dr. Alvarez," he said slowly, "we have to find a way out of here—a way to get the three of us back to 2249. We can't be playing stupid games with guns." He thought he heard footsteps in the hall outside. "Shhh."

"This is no game, young man," she said, her voice getting louder. "This is a real gun, and I know how to use it and I will. I know why your people dumped me here, but it's not going to work. I know where they're vulnerable, and I'm going to stop them and their damn Russian invasion if it's the last thing I do. At the very least I ought to be able to save President Dubcek." She smiled in a lopsided way. "One of your relatives?"

"So they say." The look he saw in her eyes and the tone he heard in her voice made Jackson wish he could convince himself she was as crazy as Lester had been, instead of dangerously sane.

"Now you know what you came to find out, Ms. Brelmer. Or is there something else you wanted to ask me? What part of Voxner's anatomy your father had to lick to get my old job, perhaps? No? What about you, young man? No questions for the Oracle of TP?"

Jackson swallowed hard, realizing suddenly that this might be his only chance to obtain the answer to the one question that had been burning in his gut since the whole thing began. "Why the displacements?" he whispered.

"Because the powers that be decided certain people posed too much of a threat to Temporal Projects. Next question."

"Why me?" Jackson looked from Rosita to Suzanne, asking the question equally of both of them.

"Because your name is on the list," Rosita answered without any hesitation. "They got a list from people out of the future. It was a list of the most dangerous rebels who would fight against the Time Police. You were at the top of the list, Mr. Dubchek."

"That's not possible." Jackson turned to Suzanne, waiting to hear her deny it, and saw the confirmation in her eyes. "I didn't know anything about the Time Police until you recruited me. Why would I fight against something I knew nothing about?"

"I begged them not to do it, Jackson. I told them they were wrong about you."   Suddenly Jackson wanted to laugh . . . or cry. He couldn't tell which. If only—

Kraback! Kwerk!

Pieces of the door crashed inward.

Jackson dived for Suzanne and dragged her to the floor. Suzanne clung to him for life.

A shadow filled the smoking doorway. Dr. Alvarez fired her pistol. The shadow fired back. Both cried out.

She fell to her knees, her free hand holding her head. The shadow tumbled to the floor.

Jackson's ears rang as he foolishly tried to keep himself between Suzanne and the firing.

A second shadow filled the space. Again Alvarez fired. Blood trickled down between her fingers and down her face.

"Daddy!" Suzanne screamed.

Brelmer collapsed through the doorway.

Dr. Alvarez steadied her aim on the fallen man.

Suzanne scrambled out of Jackson's arms toward her father.

Jackson lashed out with his foot, kicking the pistol

from Dr. Alvarez's hand. She looked at him in astonishment.

Another shot flashed up from the floor. Alvarez's hands clutched her chest.

Slye, Jackson thought as he rolled away from Alvarez. Slye shot her. She slumped to the carpet in front of him, eyes open in surprise, fingers splayed across her the front of her coat, dead, very dead.

"Help, me, Jackson! Help me. Oh, god, Daddy, please don't die. Please don't die." She cradled her father in her arms. Blood ran freely from the hole in his head.

Jackson crawled toward her, seeing Slye's hand twitch at the same time. Wrenching the pistol from Slye's grip, Jackson put it to the Time Policeman's temple just in front of his unnatural ear, and held it there, shaking, furious, afraid, uncertain, unwilling.

Slye's crystal eyes shifted as his body tensed.

Jackson pulled the trigger. The gun bucked against Slye's skull.

Suzanne shrieked.

Jackson unthinkingly tucked the pistol into his belt before turning to Suzanne. Its heat surprised him.

Blood covered the jacket. Tears rolled down her face. "Are you all right?" His voice echoed oddly in his ringing ears.

"It's Daddy. He's . . ."

"Easy. He's breathing. Let's get something around that wound. And pray that he comes to if you believe in that sort of thing."

"I'm praying."

Jackson looked around for something to make a bandage from and finally decided to use Alvarez's dress. She didn't need it anymore. "Good. Pray hard, because if he doesn't come to, we're all going to die in Prague in 1968."

Suzanne helped him tear strips from Dr. Alvarez's dress and slip, and, somehow, bandaging her father's head calmed her a great deal. Consequently, she was startled when Jackson jumped toward the door, pistol in his hand. "What?"

"Shhh," he whispered.

Brelmer opened his eyes to see Suzanne's blurry face above his. He smelled burning powder and a crushing pain throbbed in his head. When he tried to speak, only a groan escaped.

"Daddy? Daddy, oh, god, Daddy, I'm so glad you're all right. I was so—"

"Ask him where the time machine is," Jackson said, cocking his head. "There's fighting going on somewhere real close."

"Listen, Daddy, we have to leave now. You have to tell us where you left the time machine. We have to get you home."

Again Brelmer moaned. He heard words, real words, but they made no sense.

Time machine. Daddy. Fighting. Please. Close. Home.

"Suzanne, we've got to get out of here."

Brelmer understood. In the fog Suzanne needed the . . . She needed the . . . She needed the . . . She needed the time machine. The pain forced his eyes closed.

"Daddy, please. We have to get you home. Where did you leave the time machine?"

Without opening his eyes, Brelmer reached up and fumbled with the button on the breast pocket of his uniform. Her sticky fingers helped him, and he let his hand drop.

"It's an address," Suzanne said, holding the piece of paper out to Jackson. "It's got to be on your map."

"Let's hope so." He took the paper and dug the map out of his pocket. It took him several minutes to find the street and approximate location of the address. It took him several more minutes to figure out several routes just in case they ran into trouble. "All right. I think I've got it. Can he walk?"

"I don't know." Her father rested in her lap and his bleeding seemed to have stopped.

"Tell him he has to."

"Daddy? Daddy? Wake up, Daddy. We have to go now."

Brelmer opened his eyes to whirling pain. "Uh . . . can go where?"

"Home, Daddy. To the time machine, first, then home. Come on, let me help you up."

She pushed him to a sitting position, and the world twirled around the point of his pain. He swallowed hard and gritted his teeth. "Mmm."

Suzanne climbed to her knees and helped him to his. Then she stood up and steadied him as he pulled himself to his feet.

They swayed together, but he forced his body to stand still. Only then did he realize that it was the interpreter, Dubchek, leaning against the door frame. "Him."

"Yes, Daddy, him. Captain Slye is dead. So is Dr. Alvarez. Jackson is going to help get you home. Do you understand?"

"Him."

"He understands," Jackson said. "Let's go."

Together they half carried Suzanne's father down the hall, away from the direction of the elevator. Minutes later they reached stairs Jackson had suspected would be there. At the top of the stairs, daylight shone through the dirty window of a locked door.

Several kicks broke the lock and they stepped out of a building across from Rosita Alvarez's hotel. "This way," Jackson said, putting Brelmer's arm over his shoulder.

People stared at them as they walked the several blocks to the street on the paper, but no one spoke to them.

As they paused before the correct address, a harsh voice shouted something.

Jackson and Suzanne turned together to see three soldiers in off-green uniforms like her father's approaching from half a block away, rifles in their hands.

Chapter Thirty

"Ignore them," Suzanne said. "We just go in."

"It's the basement," Jackson said, helping Brelmer down the first step.

"Of course."

The soldier called again.

Brelmer grunted, trying to see where they were, trying to understand what was—

"Keep going," Jackson said when Suzanne hesitated. At the bottom of ten iron steps they reached an open door.

The voice shouted a command.

"Quickly, quickly." They squeezed through the doorway and Jackson pushed the flimsy wooden door closed. It had no lock. It had no handle. "Now where?" he asked, peering into the dimly lit foyer. A narrow hallway led into the darkness and on either side of it stood doors with chipped and peeling paint and graffiti written on them. It reminded Jackson of New York.

"There," she said. "That triangle on that door is a TP symbol. . . . Locked," she said with disgust.

Boots rang heavily on the outside stairs.

Fear rode over the top of her disgust as she realized the soldiers would find them at any moment.

Jackson snapped his head back and forth, then suddenly knew what to do. He pulled the pistol from under his coat and pointed it at the door handle, just like he'd seen them do in a hundred old holos. "Hold your ears."

Suzanne covered one ear and pressed the other against her father's shoulder. She smelled blood, fresh blood. Jackson fired several times. A swift kick from him popped the door open.

Light fell into the room and reflected off a dark, shiny object—a time machine. "All right!"

As quickly as they could, they dragged Suzanne's father into the room. Shouts echoed behind them.

"Get him in!" Jackson said, opening the door to the time machine and spinning to face the entrance at the same time.

Suzanne pushed and shoved her father into the machine. Tears flooded her vision, but she shook them off. Nothing was going to stop her from saving his life.

Brelmer moaned with a searing pain that ripped the top of his head off. For the first time in his life he wanted to die.

Jackson fired three times at the doorway. All at once he wondered how many shots the pistol had and realized he had no way of knowing. What he knew about pistols wouldn't fill a computer screen.

Bursts of flame roared through the entrance. Bullets ricocheted off the walls and ceiling. Jackson dropped behind the time machine door, in imitation of other scenes from old holos.

"We're in!" Suzanne shouted through the ringing in his ears.

Jackson crawled in the time machine, slammed the door closed, and threw the locking bolt. He knew from what had happened at Brezhnevgrad that they were safe for the moment.

"Hurry, Jackson. Get us home! Daddy's bleeding again."

Quickly Jackson set the controls, checked the settings, then altered the preset geographical location.

Sparking bullets rang off the front of the time machine. The window vibrated under a thudding hail of fire.

Brelmer groaned and thrashed in the rear seat. Something was wrong, and he knew it, something to do with the pain.

"Please! Oh, god, hurry! Hurry, Jackson."

With the flip of the switch, Jackson initiated the transmission sequence. The whine of the machine joined the ringing in his ears.

The universe tilted. Suzanne tilted with it. Her father vomited. She fought for control of herself in order to help him. Flashing lights and swirling darkness spun them through the voids of time.

Brelmer died a thousand times. He was born a thousand and one times. The black forces of terror pushed his head through the vise of birth over and over, squeezed screams of pain out of him to the mad cackling of a nightmare.

Jackson clutched his gut and squeezed his eyes shut, but forced them open again when his stomach threatened to empty itself.

Suddenly everything stopped and he stared out the window of the time machine not believing what he saw. In front of them rose a giant sign that read:

> *Future home of*
> *Nouvelle Seville Luxury Hotel*
> *and Convention Center.*
> *Your Republican Tax Dollars at Work.*

Jackson laughed. He laughed so hard it hurt. Then he couldn't stop laughing.

Suzanne realized finally that they had arrived, but when she looked up, unsure of why Jackson had become hysterical, expecting to see a transmission room at Temporal Projects, she was stunned. "Where the hell are we?"

Before Jackson answered, her father gagged.

"Where have you brought us, you idiot? My father needs help, medical help, and he needs it now!"

That snapped Jackson out of his laughter. "We can get help here. They'll send for an ambulance."

"Where are we?"

"Springfield," he said, climbing unsteadily out of the time machine. He looked up the side of the crater to the Mnemosyne headquarters and would have laughed again if . . . well, it didn't matter. Without looking back, he scrambled up the side of the crater to find help.

The next day he stood beside Suzanne in the train car. Her father lay in a private medical compartment with a nurse and a doctor in attendance and one of Senator Voxner's aides standing watch.

"This is it," Jackson said stupidly.

"You mean goodbye?" A wellspring of feelings had opened up for her since their safe return and she did not want to lose what she felt. "We'll see each other again, someday. You wait and—"

"I mean goodbye forever." On impulse he took her

hand and kissed it, then just as quickly let it go. "You're the most fascinating woman I've ever met, Suzanne Brelmer, and I hope to never see you again."

"Gee, thanks." Tears fought with each other for the chance to fill her eyes.

"You're trouble, Suzanne—you and your father—and I want no more of either of you. I can't cope." Something twisted inside him, something that made him want to add a qualifier, but he resisted. "Like I promised him, I'll stay out of the time business, and you can stay out of my business."

"Which is . . . which will be what?"

"Staying alive. Staying free. Making music. Who knows? Nothing complicated for a while, I can tell you that. I just don't want to have—"

The departure chime sounded.

"Then it is goodbye," she said. She kissed him quickly, full on the lips with her arms wrapped around him because she had to, then she released him just as quickly and turned to walk away.

"Right." He sighed as he turned the other way and left the train. "And goodbye."

Chapter Thirty-one

Jackson leaned back in the soft ultravine of his first class train seat and looked out the vista-window at the last few kilometers of Springfield slipping past.

He had read in the fiches of old newspapers at the New Nineveh Library that every path out of Springfield had once been littered with cheap hotels and fast food-emporiums. The city parents in charge of promoting tourism had complained without avail that the ugliness and squalor did not represent the proper image to people passing through, did not encourage them to stay and discover the real Springfield.

Only after the establishment of the Second Republic had the city been able to change things. As Jackson's train rolled through kilometer after kilometer of greenbelt, he thought about how pretty all the parks looked and how perfect all the people looked. He could see them jogging along the trails and working out under the trees. Some just strolled hand in hand, enjoying one of the first warm days of spring. All of them looked fit and healthy, well fed and secure.

What would they have felt if foreign powers invaded

Springfield the way the Warsaw Pact countries had invaded Prague? Those people in the parks had never felt the mindless horror of terrorist attacks, or been hungry to the point of starvation, or even smelled the stench of diesel smog. Springfield's gently rolling hills did not bear on their backs the burden of junkyards full of rusting, useless car bodies the way the hillsides of Wheeling, West Virginia, did. Even the suspicious redneck mentality that Springfield had once been known for a century earlier had been reduced to a humorous remnant in stories his Gran'pa Jack had told.

It was all better than it had been. Everyone agreed on that. No one wanted war or turmoil, sickness, or sudden death back as parts of ordinary life.

Jackson turned away from the unvarying beauty of the greenbelt and closed his eyes. He didn't want those things himself, and he didn't wonder that Lester Wu had gone mad in the face of them—or that Rosita Alvarez had been on the edge of sanity. They hadn't been bred for that sort of life. They hadn't been brought up with the skills needed to overcome that kind of adversity, to live with that kind of pain—psychological, social, physical, or personal.

Neither had Jackson.

He was a man of his time—the twenty-third century—and like his fellow citizens, all he wanted was a place to live, the necessary credits to pay his way, and the free enjoyment of his life. Branson offered him all of that. Jan and Pac Verba had agreed by phone to help him get settled and introduce him around the clubs so that he could find work. Once that happened, it would just be him and Odar'a playing along for life, and maybe, if he got lucky, some nice lady with half the sexual appetites of Chrys Calvino and half the brains of Suzanne Brelmer. What more could a man ask from life?

The train gathered speed and something about the rush of wind past the window finally coaxed Jackson into opening his eyes. Immediately he recognized the landscape—the Mark Twain Republican Forest, three hundred years a preserve for each generation to visit and see what the land had looked like before being settled and tamed and trimmed into the neatly landscaped greenbelts of the cities.

The forest showed the first touches of spring. Every year there came a magical week at the end of winter that Jackson always looked forward to—a week when the land went through its mystical transformation and awoke to new life. Every year as winter drew to a close, he would wake earlier and earlier each day to see if overnight the black branches and dull gray mud of winter had changed to the pale vibrant greens of spring. As he looked at the forest from the speeding train this year, he could see pink splashes of redbud amid the new green, and flashes of white that hinted of wild plum and dogwood blossoming among the oak and hickory.

The magic was still there in the forest. Centuries old traditions of Ozark granny doctors said that if you picked the right blooms from the right trees at the right times and boiled them down with the right herbs and roots and berries, the result would be a universal salve that would heal all wounds and cure all sickness. Jackson wondered if that universal salve would heal the sick feeling he had inside.

As Jackson's climate-controlled train car rolled through the ancient forest, he tried once again to convince himself that the world was just as good as it looked. He

certainly didn't want for anything. Even if he couldn't get
steady work and his credits ran out, the Second Republic
would take care of him, find him a place to live, find him
a job—or give him one—and provide the credits he needed
to live on. The Second Republic would even find him that
special woman—if he asked it to—or at least a reasonable
facsimile thereof.

So what was wrong? What more could he want? Why
couldn't he get rid of the gnawing in his gut that reminded
him it was all illusion? Why couldn't he accept the idea
that the government could issue him happiness the same
way it issued him a room to live in and a job?

Everyone else seemed happy. None of those people
he'd seen in the greenbelt looked tired or depressed or
lonely. They all seemed perfectly willing to put their trust
in the wisdom and care of the Second Republic. So what
was wrong with Jackson?

He felt as though he had been poisoned by Temporal
Projects. Once he had seen the mistakes the government
could make, he would never—could never—trust it again.
John Reed had died trying to escape what they had done,
and Jackson finally thought he understood what had driv-
en Reed to take the chance he had.

Jackson shook his head with a long, slow sigh. If there
had been someone to comfort him, he might have cried.
From the job he enjoyed at New Nineveh Library, he had
gone freely into the Temporal Projects program because
they told him his government needed him and his skills.
He'd even felt proud of the fact that they wanted him.

Then they'd dumped him in New York, F.D., without
warning and without reason, and without money—with
police chasing him through a past he knew little or nothing
about, and why? Because of a list—a list from Buddha

only knew where that told them someday he would be a threat to Temporal Projects.

He hadn't even known they existed! And he wouldn't have cared if they hadn't lured him into their system and then turned his ordered life into an insane potpourri of times and places. They had replaced his peaceful existence with terror, panic, death, and paradoxes so confusing that he knew that he could never sort them out. They had hounded him from one time to another, tried to kill him more than once, had dumped him from one dangerous situation into another, had lied to him repeatedly, and had proven beyond any reasonable doubt that he had little or no control over the events in his life.

And, just to make sure he stayed confused, they had pushed him into the arms of the Mnemosyne Historians who were the reverse side of the same dirty coin.

"Breathe in. Breathe out. Slow down. Breathe in. Slow down." He closed his eyes and repeated the ritual until he had calmed himself.

In the new future that had started when he said good-bye to Suzanne, he had finished with them. They were all going to leave him alone. All that business with TP and the Mnemosyne was part of the past. Slye would certainly leave him alone. Slye, the man who had given Jackson his first dose of real insanity, Slye was dead—dead in a year so far back that not even his ghost would be able to come back and disrupt Jackson's life.

Irene and the Mnemosyne had reluctantly promised to leave him alone—probably because they gave him credit for bringing them the time machine he and Suzanne and her father had returned in.

Praetor Centurion Lieutenant Colonel Friz Brelmer had promised to leave him alone—at least partially, Jackson suspected, because Suzanne had told her father that Jackson had saved his life.

And Suzanne . . . well, he and Suzanne would leave each other alone. Theirs was a promise unspoken.

"All in the past . . . in the past . . . in the past." Jackson murmured the words over and over to the rock of the train like some mantra that would wash the anger from his heart. "Soon we'll be in Branson, just Odar'a and me, and the Time Police and the Brelmers and the Mnemosyne and all the rest of them can live in the past forever."

Outside the newly green trees slid by under perfectly clear skies washed with that special shade of Ozark blue. Ahead lay a life of good music, good friends, and simple joys. His troubles lay behind him.

Jackson leaned back with a smile and forced himself to forget part of what he'd learned—that sometimes, sometimes the past came back to clamp its jaws down hard on those tender spots where the present least expected to be bitten.